T0167441

The Skeleton Woman

The Skeleton Woman

A Romance

Renée

First published in 2002 by Huia Publishers,
39 Pipitea Street, PO Box 17-335,
Wellington, Aotearoa New Zealand.
www.huia.co.nz

Published in Australia by
Spinifex Press Pty Ltd
504 Queensberry Street
North Melbourne, Vic. 3051
Australia
women@spinifexpress.com.au

ISBN: 1-876756-30-6

Copyright © Renée 2002

All rights reserved. Without limiting the rights under copyright reserved above,
no part of this publication may be reproduced, stored in or introduced into
a retrieval system, or transmitted, in any form or by any means
(electronic, mechanical, photocopying, recording or otherwise), without prior written
permission of both the copyright owner and the above publisher of the book.

National Library of Australia Cataloguing-in-Publication Data
Renée, 1929– .
The skeleton woman.

ISBN 1 876756 30 6.

1. Abandoned children - Fiction. 2. Lesbianism - Fiction.
I. Title.

NZ823.2

For Bernadette (yes, again)
With Love

Listen. The Skeleton Woman is restless. Her bony feet are tapping on the earth. Secrets are about to be revealed. The Skeleton Woman is the keeper of secrets. Some are kept for an hour or so, a couple of days perhaps, weeks, others are kept for years and years before she decides their time has come. Revelations come by which-ever means appeals to her. Tappitty tap. Out of a clear blue sky the voice of a dead woman is heard. Now we know what really happened to the man who betrayed her, the mystery of the separated children is unravelled. Tappitty tap. The little man shivers inside as he hears the sound of the Skeleton Woman tap-dancing. As it becomes louder he hears her tell the world what he did. Tappitty tap. That child, older now, says I was lying, I was lying, I can't stand it any longer, I was lying. And those who believed the woman was guilty have to face the ugliness of their own eagerness to believe the worst simply because she was different. Tappitty tap. The skeleton of a man is discovered beneath some pipes where no one thought to look. Tappitty tap. Sometimes it seems that the bigger the secret the longer the Skeleton Woman keeps it hidden. The decision about timing is always hers. And that's her biggest secret of all. She never lets on when your secret will fly. You'll never know until you hear that sound. Tappitty tap ... tappitty tap.

From a reading by Ada Anthony of Peter Paul Pearl's novel, *The Man Who Loved Rain*. Dowse Art Museum, Lower Hutt, March 1990.

ONE

It's that edgy time just before the equinoctial gales slash all the weeping cherry blossoms to smithereens and break the hearts of the early irises. Usually people in the Hutt would be moaning about those damn blackbirds fossicking in their newly weeded flower gardens and throwing soil all over their paths. They would remark how last year the strong winds sculpted the river into quite high waves and wonder if the same thing would happen this year. In supermarket aisles they would recollect other edgy springs, other blackbirds, other high tides. But not this Friday. Not this spring. This Friday there's not a lot of talk over the trolleys. The black planes cutting off the tops of the black towers have taken over people's eyes and throats. The thought of those poor people in the planes, those in the New York Disaster and those who died in a Pennsylvanian field or at the Pentagon. There doesn't seem much point in drawing attention to blackbirds or high tides when five thousand people are said to have died in the towers, when people in wheelchairs had to be left by the able-bodied because the lifts weren't working and there was no time to steer a wheelchair down the flights and flights of stairs. People in New York streets gasp and weep over small black figures falling out of windows and the sight of firemen injured and bloody, going back into the chaos. People in the Hutt Valley gasp and weep too, remembering other tragedies, other heartaches. This is too big, too much. The images play on, over and over, as though if they're repeated enough times the world might actually get a grip on it. At the fringes of their consciousness in the Hutt Valley they hear the sound of tapping. 'Oh,' they say, gratefully, 'wind's getting up.' Tap, tap go the bony feet of the Skeleton Woman, tap tap, tap tap, as everyone's life changes forever.

On that blustery Friday, early evening, Rose Anthony reaches into a cupboard in her kitchen, grabs the gin bottle and a glass, deliberately moves her thoughts away from black planes and black towers against a blue, blue sky, and focuses on her Skeleton Woman wall hanging which she has designed and which is in Auckland being judged (this process is called being juried but Rose always thinks judged) for the prestigious Stacy Wall Hanging Competition. She must hear soon.

Rose has spent most of the day – in between listening to her customers express shock, grief, outrage, what should be done to the terrorists – furtively living and reliving the row with Olga. It seems self-absorbed in the extreme, but she can't stop it any more than she can stop her concentrated, intense, addictive listening to the news full of stories about last phone calls from sons and wives trapped on the planes, speculations regarding the identity of the terrorists, President's Bush's face as he says what the people want to hear, and the mayor of New York, who inspires the television presenters to think of words like inspired, calming, heroic. Earlier, on the day before the planes, she'd canvassed all the witty, sarcastic, cutting things she could and should have said to Olga, had rehearsed her attitude (more hurt than angry), her words (I have said all I'm going to say), and her tone (distantly courteous), when Olga apologised. Which she hasn't. In fact she hasn't contacted Rose at all, not even over the tragedy in the States. Rose is sick of it. Surely Olga wants to know how Rose is feeling. About the planes, the blue skies, the people running through the debris, their faces, the priest who had a heart attack and died as he went to rescue people. Evidently not. Rose doesn't ask herself why she hasn't rung Olga. That doesn't come into it. Rose is not at fault so why should she take the first step? To be home, alone; to have the freedom or determination to think about, speculate about her wall hanging's future glory is restful, relaxing.

Especially since Sibyl's phone call.

'It's come back,' Sibyl had said.

'Oh shit,' Rose said.

'Chemo this time,' Sibyl said.

Rose knew Sibyl had this appointment with the specialist, had meant to remember to ring her this morning and wish her luck. A year ago she and Sibyl had met in the ward where they were wheeled after their respective operations for breast cancer. They each knew who the other was of course, the Hutt being a relatively small place. Sibyl was a schoolteacher (English and drama) and Rose had, until four years ago, been one too.

Rose thought Sibyl probably knew why she'd left the profession and come back to the Hutt, why she'd set up a second-hand bookshop, but if she had she'd waited until Rose broached the subject before she said anything.

'Sometimes I get really sick of life,' Rose had replied to Sibyl, thinking of a building falling and people running.

'Yeah?' Sibyl said.

I'll kill myself, Rose thought. 'What are you doing tonight?' she asked.

'Off to a work do of Kitty's. A farewell for someone on transfer. Drinks and nibbles. Hope they have better riesling than they did last time.'

'I'll be in touch tomorrow.'

Rose vows to remember this time and has written it on the small jotter pad on which she writes her grocery lists and anything else she has to do. Signs of age, she thinks, when I have to write down stuff like this, although she's actually been making lists since she was at school.

The Skeleton Woman has survived the first round of the Stacy, where the judges look at photographs and choose what they want to see in the flesh, as it were. The Skeleton Woman is dancing, top hat at a jaunty angle, cane held just so, both legs off the ground in one of those leaps you see dancers do which makes them appear to be floating. Behind her is a skyline which at first appears to be a city; a closer look reveals that it's a river with blotches of light, silver and gold and blue lights. The river merges with trees and ends on the right in a stark area with stones and a large bird. Three borders frame the work. The middle one has keys, boxes, envelopes, diaries, cupboards, letters, all the items that conceal secrets appliquéd on it. The other two are the same deep bluey purple. It's worked in hand and machine appliqué and embroidery with various flourishes of beads, sequins and buttons.

'Dramatic,' Olga said, 'beautifully dramatic but sinister.' She suggested Rose have a card printed explaining the story of the Skeleton Woman and that this is sent with the slide of the hanging when it's couriered up to Auckland for the first judging.

Rose thinks the more mystery the better. The trouble with most people is that they shy away from mental effort. Rose shies away from emotional effort, but that's a different matter.

Or so Rose thinks.

Now Rose waits for the organiser's letter telling her how her hanging has fared. It's her first big competition so she can't expect to get better than a Highly Commended, but she does want that. Not just Commended but *Highly* Commended. For a week now every time she goes to the letter box at home or takes the mail from the postie at the shop she holds her breath until she's inspected the envelopes. Rose is not sure she actually wants the letter. Perhaps it's better to still be able to dream, although indulging in dreams about the possible success of a wall hanging seems almost immoral at the moment. But the dreams will stop anyway once she's received the letter and its probable bad news, and she can stop kidding herself she's made something really special.

Rose's mother Ada, who told her about the Skeleton Woman, would be delighted if she could see Rose's version. Her mother was, no doubt about it, an oddity. A staunch socialist whose hobby was fine needlework. Every room in her house a mess of papers except the sewing room where there was neatness and order, threads, needles, pins, scissors, tailor's chalk, transfer paper, all precisely set out in drawers, all transfers labelled, all books and magazines filed alphabetically, fabric colour coded and then graded according to what Ada called value. Now that Rose is the sole occupant every room in the house is neat, clean, tidy, free of papers, while you can hardly get in the door of the sewing room for the mess of fabrics, threads, rulers, rotary cutters, cutting boards, scissors, jars of sequins, beads, buttons, drawing pads, pencils, rubbers. Rose knows where everything is though, can lay her hands instantly on that small piece of yellow fabric, that metre or so of silver thread, those fine small scissors. She will clean the room up when she hears about the hanging. If she does it now she'll interrupt progress, dam up a channel, impede a communication between the judge and the hanging. Or so she feels. Rose distrusts the notion that one should go with one's instinct except where her needlework is concerned. Her needlework is the one area of her life that is constant, can be relied upon, is not going to provoke rows or suffer a return of cancer. It can be relied upon to cause frustration, sore neck, sore arms, tender fingers, headaches and tired eyes, but also huge delight and pleasure. It provides balance. Most other things in her life, Rose finds, sooner or later end up on the debit side with absolutely no delight or pleasure at all.

'You're a pessimist,' Olga told her.

'No,' Rose argued, 'I'm a realist.'

There's probably nothing inherently strange about mixing socialism and needlework at all. Perhaps it's a class thing to think that. In Rose's head, as she is sure is in everyone's, there are stereotypes that have one kind of person getting involved in socialist politics and the other in the perhaps quieter (more genteel middle class perhaps?) craft of embroidery, cross stitch and appliqué. What would Ada have thought of those planes? Of those poor people trapped inside them, not knowing exactly when, but knowing without any equivocation at all that death was going to be the end of this journey. At least with the cancer, Rose had had hope. And so far, fingers crossed, she's OK. Although that's what Sibyl had thought. Rose has an appointment at the hospital clinic on Monday, when the specialist will examine her breasts, her glands, under her arms, and tell her what the latest mammograms reveal. She has determinedly not thought about it, will not think about it until she's walking into the hospital, but Sibyl's news has buggered that plan.

Rose has had a busy Friday. The Book Stops Here had a good day. Perhaps it's those frisky little breezes blowing dust into the gutters and snatching newly delivered copies of *Hutt News* out of the letter boxes and onto the streets so that sheets of it slap against cars and snap into shop doorways. People who felt a lift of the heart because winter has ended now feel that – in view of what's happened in New York – this was pre-cipitate. The idea of going home with a good book, pulling the curtains and settling where it's safe, still and warm, is very appealing. Books have practically walked out by themselves. Lots of general fiction, practically a shelf of Mills & Boons and Westerns, that really nice old Bible, some Auden and Spender (sold to the same man) and that big coffee-table sized book of *Life* photographs which has been in the shop since Rose first opened the doors. Eight Georgette Heyers (coming back into fashion) and at least five Goosebumps (going out of fashion), plus the only two Harry Potters she's got. Ten people had come in with cartons of books to sell, only one of which Rose bought. Some gems there. One, to Rose's astonishment and pleasure, a Margaret Atwood in very good condition, some Marge Piercy and Amy Tan. The Margaret Atwood sold thirty minutes after Rose placed it in the window. When she got back from doing the banking there were these two women, grey-haired, tracksuited, fit, both out for their daily walk. Both had decided at exactly the same moment to have a quick look in Rose's window, both wanted Margaret Atwood, both thought they were first and had a right to it. In the end Rose flipped a coin. The one who chose tails won *The Robber Bride* and went off triumphantly. 'I know I shouldn't be going on like this about a book,' she said, 'but on the way home I'm going to take a Lotto.' Rose tried to interest the other one in an Alice Munro or a Carol Shields thinking well, they're all Canadians. No luck. The woman knew Alice Munro was good, but she didn't like short stories, and she reckoned Carol Shields was actually born in the States in the same place Hemingway was born so she wasn't really Canadian was she. Then she saw one of Ian Rankin's she hadn't read and grabbed it. While she was waiting for her change she said, 'When I really want a book I feel as though there's a cat inside me snarling and lunging and I get all jangly and horrible, but once I get the one I want, the cat settles down and begins purring and I'm OK. I've always felt that. And reading a book's sort of comforting after watching television.'

Rose agreed. Rose nearly always agrees with customers.

Rose longs for a large gin and tonic to ease the ache across her neck and shoulders, dull the ache of those firemen's faces with their mixture of hopelessness and optimism, quieten the burning under the scar on her breast, comfort the pain the row with Olga has left in her chest, ease the terror induced by Sibyl's news. If it can happen to Sibyl it can happen to Rose. For one instant after Sibyl had told her, Rose felt a quick charge of relief. This time the bad news was not for her. Immediately she was bathed in guilt, hotter and sweatier than the menopausal hot sweats which began two years ago. She hoped this wasn't obvious in her voice, but was afraid it was. You got pretty sensitive to that sort of thing when you were the one with the bad news. Rose should not get cocky, she still has her own appointment to get through. They'd taken forever doing the mammogram. 'It's the staples,' the woman said, 'we need to establish clearly that what's on the screen is staples and not – ' Once, Rose had to redo the mammograms because the specialist had not been happy with those ominous blurs at the top of the breast. When he rang to say the blurs were staples Rose began breathing properly again. Then thought staples? Staples? I'm walking around held together with staples? Don't exaggerate Rose, she hears her mother say. The awful anxiety between that clinic visit and the doctor's phone call had stayed with her, although submerged, but with Sibyl's news was up above the surface, clearly visible.

While she's sipping the gin and tonic she will have a read of the morning paper – she'd only had time to read the headlines. Then she'd have another gin and tonic and something delicious to eat. She feels better already. Smiling, one hand tightening around a glass, the bottle in the other hand, Rose is stopped in her tracks by a mewing sound. It pierces the kitchen, and Rose swings round. She becomes aware her mouth has dropped and is mildly irritated. In a section of books in her shop, people's mouths are always dropping, along with their members throbbing and their breasts heaving. There was one customer, late thirties, who appeared every Wednesday lunchtime for her fix. She picked one of these books off the shelf, turned to page seventy-nine (she said there's always a steamy sex scene on page seventy-nine), and read avidly. She and her husband made love on Wednesday nights because they both played bowls on Saturday evenings. She liked to read about heaving breasts and throbbing members, to get her in the mood. Not enough to buy the books however.

Rose has ceased to be surprised at what her customers say to her, what they confide. It's like she's a priest or a minister. They have absolutely no qualms about telling her intimate details of their lives, that they have sex with their husband every Wednesday, that they think their mother is having an affaire with a real-estate agent, that their brother is very angry because his sister has got a blue vase of their dead mother's and he always wanted it. 'I said to him, "Take it then, if it means so much," and he goes, "No. Mum didn't want me to have it or why would she put your name on the bottom of it? It wouldn't be right." I said to him, "Did you tell Mum you wanted it?" And he goes all huffy and says, "No, but she knew." I mean, what can you do?' Rose doesn't know, and even if she did, she wouldn't say. Her customers don't tell her things actually seeking advice, they just want to tell her. It might be that they think that because she owns a second-hand bookshop she will listen. Only staff in independent bookshops know anything about books these days, the big chains just want people to shift product, but even the staff in independent bookshops are too busy to listen to their customers' worries. Someone in a second-hand bookshop will have read everything, will know the full extent of human passion and perfidy, and what's even better will have, or make, time to listen. It might be because she's had cancer that they think that. People, in the main, are funny about cancer. They either spill all their furtive, mysterious, sad or spiteful skeletons out of the closet, or they walk away, frightened witless at this revelation of their own mortality. If Rose and Sibyl's bodies can produce lumps, it could happen to them. Rose and Sibyl think they pour out these confidences out of a kind of compassion. To make them see they're not alone. That others are suffering too.

It might be nothing to do with either Rose being a second-hand bookshop proprietor or having had cancer, it might just be that Rose's customers sense that Rose is good with secrets, particularly her own.

That bloody cat from next door must have got itself locked in the pantry again. Serve it right. She'd only taken to shutting the door because it persisted in sneaking inside. The cat doesn't do anything in the pantry except sleep on the window sill, but Rose is not going to be blackmailed into providing shelter for every stray cat which chooses to ensconce itself in her pantry. The window sill is not even in the sun. Well, the cat can wait. Might teach it to steer clear. She walks back past the table and the mewing sounds again, though louder this time. It isn't coming from the pantry, Rose, it's coming from the box of tomatoes. Surely Wesley Neville hasn't — well accidentally of course, somehow or other, one never thinks logically in these circumstances — surely Wesley hasn't shut a kitten inside the box with the tomatoes? He's a rip, shit or bust man, is Wesley. Always busy, busy, busy, racing to work through the list of jobs in his head so he can get everything done and then rush out and save a few people from damnation. Although she dislikes almost everything else about Wesley Neville, she has to respect his ability to work. Maybe a wild kitten jumped in when he wasn't looking. Or perhaps his mind was on his wife Jo, who is acting – has been acting – strangely all winter. Jo, whom Rose has known forever, since before they were both at primary school, in fact. Jo and she, once very good friends. Best friends. In fact Jo's birthday is the day before Rose's, which means Jo turns fifty tomorrow. Once that would have been cause for celebration, now it's of only mild nostalgic interest. Lately, Jo has taken to coming over in the evenings and just sitting. Which is unnerving. 'Are you all right?' Rose asked many times. 'Fine,' Jo said. But she still turned up around this time, sat in Rose's kitchen for an hour or two, saying little. She even did it when Olga was there. 'She'll say something eventually,' Olga said, 'they always do.'

'Who?'

'People. When some people are upset they don't talk. For ages sometimes. But sooner or later they do.'

Rose puts the gin bottle and glass down on the bench and approaches the box. Definitely the source of the sound. She pulls carefully at the plastic, noting, for the first time, the holes pierced in it. She inches it back. The sound becomes louder. This is no cat. Her heart gives a sort of sick jolt. If it was an earthquake it would be about three on the Richter scale. Not strong enough to do any real damage but enough to remind her, if she needs reminding, of her body's vulnerability. Her heart hesitates, settles to a jerky flutter in her throat, she tells herself she is hallucinating. Her heart is as strong as an ox. Perhaps she's having an attack of something. Maybe she's dying? Maybe this is it, the big whammo.

Rose, not exactly whooping for joy at turning fifty in two day's time, worried about the possible return of the breast cancer, nowhere near recovered from the shock of the sudden death of her mother in a road accident two years ago, not to mention the other thing that happened four years ago that she doesn't talk about to anyone, thinks that with the addition of the row with Olga, the ongoing puzzle that is Jo, plus Sibyl's news, and over all, over all, those black planes cutting the tops off those black towers under a blue, blue sky, that maybe her heart has finally had enough. Or perhaps something in her brain is giving way. Does the Skeleton Woman make clear that final mystery with such sound effects though? Who would know? There are those who claim to have had near-death experiences, have seen tunnels, lights, have felt a huge happiness, but nobody really knows for sure, do they? Rose has always thought the huge happiness is probably relief that they're actually still here.

The noise gets louder and Rose thinks oh for fuck's sake, whoever's in charge, let me have the gin and tonic first. Rose is definitely having a problem with reality today. She knows there is no one in charge, that it is all random. Random acts of cruelty. Random arguments. That's what it's all about.

She isn't having a stroke, or a heart attack, and the cancer hasn't struck her brain. There in front of her, eyes screwed tight shut, mouth open, cries developing at the speed of light into a piercing wail, there is, definitely, no question about it, there is a baby.

Something between a shout and a scream comes out of Rose's mouth and the crying halts, then starts up again. 'Christ almighty,' Rose says. She has never invented a god either as a crutch or a comfort, but the sight of a baby in a cocoon of something soft and pale of no discernible colour, in a cardboard carton on the table in her kitchen, acts like a trigger into some sort of atavistic speech pattern lurking inside her. A baby? This is the face of an enraged apple. Tears spurt down its cheeks, saliva oozes from its open mouth. Ugly, noisy and the last thing she expects to see in her kitchen. Perhaps it's someone's idea of a joke. 'Oh shit,' Rose says, 'oh God, oh shit, oh God.' She sees a piece of white card tucked down between the rug thing the baby is wrapped in and the side of the box, sees her own name. 'For Rose Anthony', the words on the card say. For Rose Anthony? Black felt tip, the letters large and round like a child's, easy to read, no possibility of a mix-up. For Rose Anthony. That's me, thinks Rose, I'm Rose Anthony all right. Someone has given me a baby. Someone's given me a baby? Yes, Rose, she tells herself, some bloody fool has given you a baby. 'Bloody hell,' Rose says. The baby's screams turn into hysterical bawls.

What should she do? Ring the police? Social Welfare? The ambulance? She'd read – everyone's read – about babies left under bushes by young girls afraid to tell their families they'd had a baby, but she'd never read about one being left on a doorstep. Except in Fairy Tales of course. Perhaps this is why she dislikes Fairy Tales. Everyone is so bloody irresponsible in Fairy Tales. People leave babies all over the place in Fairy Tales. They abandon them in woods in the depths of winter, drop them down dark holes, shut them in secret rooms, give them to little men in exchange for gold. Rose has never been able to suspend her disbelief long enough to accept the basic tenet of Fairy Tales, that such beings as fairies exist. Rose is never comfortable with fantasy, only ever opens a science-fiction book to check there are no pages ripped out, is the only reader in the world, she believes, who does not warm to a hobbit or an elf. Rose enjoys fiction, and it is true that Fairy Tales are fiction, but even in fiction she likes stories rooted in things she knows can and do happen without any magical interference. Down-to-earth things. Hate, love, betrayal. Things like that. Her mother liked non-fiction for the same reasons.

Rose wishes she could stop thinking about Ada. It's pathetic, a woman a couple of days off fifty grieving so bitterly for her mother, who after all was nearly seventy-four when that car, driven by tourists, came round the corner on the wrong side. But seventy-four is not old, Rose thinks, not these days. She has a deep resentment, as though she's been cheated of something. She might be nearly fifty, but she needs her mother around. She needs to say out loud, 'You were right and I was wrong.' And if Ada was actually standing in this kitchen, she would deal with this baby.

Bad smells always make Rose heave. She's tried everything. Holding her breath, visualising something sweet-smelling, affirmations, deep breathing. Nothing makes any difference. She starts heaving and then she's sick. She never travels on the ferry over Cook Strait because if she smelt someone being sick she would be sick too. She avoids hospitals when at all possible, dodges away from anyone who says they feel sick. She has got better over the years, but only marginally.

She stares at this screaming apparition in front of her. Even in hospital when she'd had those ghastly nightmares, her brain had conjured up nothing as awful as this. She can see that, even with its face all red and screwed-up, this baby is not all that new. Newly born babies have a red, wrinkled, sunburned look to them, some even have peeling skin. This one looks more settled into its skin than that. And it's had lots of voice practice by the sound of it. Think, she tells herself, think. What would Ada do?

Her mother had determined ideas about what kind of a daughter she would raise. Her daughter would not be demanding, bad-mannered, illiterate, lazy, all those unattractive traits Ada saw in the daughters of neighbours and friends. Ada might not have had much say in the nature side of things, but she could definitely do something about the nurture. Ada was successful in her ambitions. Rose grew up to be good-looking, intelligent; she loved books and was as hard a worker as her mother. Rose's dark hair and olive skin were her father's, as was her care about her appearance. Ada's curly brown hair was always a mess, her strong, thick eyebrows always frowning over a government report or a piece of needlework, while Rose, once she was old enough to buy the creams and lotions herself, was always peering at her face, patting it with moisturiser, dabbing it with crème powders, brushing on eye make-up, mascara, spraying behind her ears with perfume. She went to the hairdresser regularly to have her dark hair cut and wore it in a very short stylish cap. Rose took vitamins, went on walks, drank glasses of low-fat milk, ate yoghurt, tossed up delicious salads, looked after her body. This is why she got so angry with it when it produced the lump. Here was she who has practically made a career of looking after herself, and here are these other people, eating takeaway foods dripping with saturated fats, whose main exercise is flipping through the channels on their television, who wouldn't reach for an apple if there was a chippie in sight, here they are with not a sign of a lump. There is something seriously wrong somewhere. Rose reaches out and touches the carton, looks closer.

This baby is no changeling, no fairy prince, no princess stolen away by elves as revenge for some malicious slight or broken vow. This is a human baby. And this human baby is actually addressed to her. For Rose Anthony. In black and white. Why do we say that? In black and white. If it was written down in red and yellow, would it be less true? Although, given a choice, Rose goes for black and white every time. She loves black. She loves the look of herself in black. Wears it a lot. 'Like my aunties,' Olga reckoned, 'they live in black.'

That her daughter actually cared about clothes, make-up, liked nothing better than a wallow in *Vogue* or *Vanity Fair* to see what the latest trends were, Rose knew, was always a puzzle to Ada, whose recreational reading was *The Socialist Worker*. Rose has never had a lot of money but she dresses well because Ada taught her to sew and she buys at sales. Rose is prone to quick irritations and angers, inclined to hasty judgements, remembers hurts and injustices forever, is a worrier, but when she sews is creative, patient, takes great care.

Rose also turned out to be a lesbian, but you couldn't have everything, Ada decided, after her first denial: 'You can't be a lesbian, you wear mascara and shave your legs.' Ada hadn't much time for Rose's tendency to be sick at the drop of a hat either and at first was sure that if Rose just pulled herself together – bad smells are part of life after all – she would grow out of it. Rose never has, but Ada thought perhaps she would grow out of being a lesbian. Rose didn't and Ada got used to it. It's the way Rose is made and that's the end of it.

Ada would have liked a grandchild and Rose didn't want children, but it could be worse. Like Ada, Rose could have married someone who had a heart attack in her neighbour's bed. Ada never said so to Rose, but she hoped intensely that Rose would find someone who appreciated her. Someone who saw that under that stylish exterior, the sharp intelligence, hidden carefully beneath the stoicism, under that surface worry-wart, there was someone vulnerable and sensitive who needed looking after. Ada knew this was foolishly protective, that most mothers had dreams of this sort, that most mothers thought there'd never be anyone who would understand their offspring as well as they did, so she was not too surprised when her hopes were not realised. Her daughter had a few short-lived love affairs and two longer-term relationships framing these. The first transformed itself into a long and affectionate friendship which saw Rose and Erica enjoy an occasional shared holiday. They kept in touch by letter, now emails, and were interested in each other's love lives. The last, with Marcy, ended in absolute disaster four years ago. The trouble is, Rose has always acted impulsively in affairs of the heart. Her excuse is she doesn't intend to wait around for the knife to fall. She sees it coming, gets in first.

She draws her arm back from the carton. She cannot physically touch this shitty mess and that's that. She'll ring someone. Olga? She instantly dismisses the idea. She will not ring Olga. Although Olga is much more experienced with babies than Rose. She's only had one of her own, but she has numerous sisters and cousins who all have babies and who all come to stay with Olga for holidays, usually all at the same time. It would drive Rose mad, it's a wonder to her that Olga survives as she does. 'They do everything themselves,' Olga said, 'I provide the accommodation, the beds, and they do the rest. And it means they get to know each other.'

The row has shown very clearly that Olga is totally blind to Rose's needs. Their arrangement had suited Olga when it suited her. If it doesn't suit her any longer that's no reason for Rose to change it. It was a shock to discover Olga was far from happy with the one night a week they'd agreed to. 'The one night a week *you* decided was the way *you* wanted it, Rose,' Olga said, when Rose reminded her about it. Leave it, she tells herself, leave it, deal with this damn baby.

The world has slipped a cog, nothing is the same, planes crash into towers, lovers leave, cancer comes back, babies turn up in tomato cartons. It started tipping a year ago, Rose sees that. 'I'm sorry Rose, the results have come back. The lump's cancerous all right.'

You dealt with that, thinks Rose, a baby's nothing compared to that.

'I can't say no chance,' the surgeon said at the first clinic after the operation, the lab report open on the desk in front of him, 'but I can say there's a very low chance of a recurrence. We'll need to monitor things of course,' he said. 'I don't expect any changes, but we'll keep an eye on you for five years.'

Just so Olga and Rose didn't get too carried away, as they were walking out of the hospital they met a woman who said, 'My mother had breast cancer and she had an operation and it was thirteen years before it came back.'

Olga always came with her to the clinic. 'You can't go on your own,' Olga said, 'you don't know what they might say. In any case, two lots of ears are better than one.' Which was true. Rose quite often missed or forgot something the surgeon or radiographer said, but Olga was there, Olga remembered. 'I'm Rose's partner,' Olga would say, holding out a hand to these white-gowned men and women who would take it and smile. They couldn't help it. Who could help smiling back at Olga when she smiled at you?

Rose feels a wrench, as though somewhere in those deep waters inside her a large creature is waking, lumbering painfully to the surface. Tears scorch her eyes but don't fall. Olga will just have to understand she likes her life to herself, her house to herself. It's different for Olga. She's used to people around. It's the way she and her family operate – open homes, particularly for family. Any birthdays, weddings, christenings in the area, Olga's immediately making up beds, getting out sleeping bags, checking the cupboards. The last tangi there'd been ten staying and they had to hire a minibus. Of course everyone contributed, but even so. Now Olga had accused Rose of not liking her family and even hinted at something worse. 'Lucky I know you're anti *all* people,' she said. Rose was so offended she got up and walked out of Olga's café where they were supposed to be having dinner. How dare Olga. How dare she. Practically accusing her. Rose walked home and Olga didn't follow her to apologise and has not contacted her since.

The reason she's not been touch with Rose probably has nothing to do with the row at all. She's probably been landed with yet another desperate woman to accommodate in one of her spare rooms. Rose just could not do what Olga does for Safe and Secure. She's sorry for those unfortunate women and children and she will help in other ways – a donation, clothes – but she won't have them in her house. 'Anything could happen,' she said to Olga, 'I could get a visit from an irate husband, possibly a gang member, they could wreck the place. I'm not taking the risk.'

'Believe me, they're not all gang members,' Olga said, 'but that's all right.' Although it obviously wasn't.

Rose sees herself through Olga's eyes. Mean, selfish, hard. As far away from being her mother's daughter as it is possible to get. Why couldn't Olga leave things as they were? Why ruin everything? Hasn't Rose made compromises too? Don't go there Rose.

'There, there,' Rose says to the baby. Weak, but anything's better than delving into that stinking carton. The baby takes absolutely no notice. It probably thinks she's speaking another language. It isn't alone in that. Rose often thinks she's speaking another language. Probably no one says 'there, there' these days. Perhaps they say something like 'Cool it, kid.'

'Cool it, kid,' says Rose, but the baby continues to ignore her. Food, she supposes. Food? She can feel panic rising. She looks at the gin bottle, Sairey Gamp popping into her head for obvious reasons. Don't even think about it Rose. Now come on. Pull yourself together. You're a grown woman, time you got over this nonsense. You are not going to be defeated by this absolutely unbearable stench. She takes a deep breath, holds it, gingerly puts both arms into the carton and scoops the baby out. An even stronger smell of shit comes with it. 'Oh shit,' says Rose, heaving violently. She grabs the towel hanging by the bench and tucks it under the little body. No sense in her being covered in shit as well. Too late, something yellow and wet has stained her red cotton shirt. Rose grabs another towel and holds it to her mouth. Her entire body is shaking with the effort not to actually be sick. Bugger, fuck, shit. The pillow in the carton is soaked. The baby's been lying in this mess a while. It's heavier than she expected. Like a lump of warm clay with damp wadding around it. Rose holds it slightly away from her and jiggles it awkwardly. It continues crying. She sees another, smaller box at the end where the baby's feet had been and (thank God!) a wad of what looked like throwaway nappies at its head. Rose doesn't approve of throwaway nappies, but one's principles are as straw in the wind when fragrant theory meets stinking reality.

Noisily dragging air into her nostrils, head averted, she scrabbles with one hand. A couple of bottles, some teats, a packet of formula and a dummy. That seems to be it. Rage stirs. If she could get hold of whoever left this child on her doorstep she would strangle them. Slowly. What to do first? Her nose wrinkles, her mouth curls, she holds the towel tightly to her lips with her free hand. Keep breathing Rose. Surely there's something more than shit to smell like this.

She will have to ring someone, she can't deal with this. Who? Plunket? Are there Plunket nurses still on tap? No, of course not. She distinctly remembers one on the radio complaining about no funding. Maybe Olga put the baby on her back porch. One of her deserving cases. No. Olga wouldn't do that. Olga thinks Rose is a selfish, egocentric, emotionally stingy obsessive-compulsive because she refuses to share her house with Olga, share Olga's house with her, or consider selling this house and buying one in tandem with Olga. Olga would prefer to run naked through an electrical storm rather than leave a baby in Rose's care.

'Never mind,' she says, patting the towel pressed against the baby's back, 'never mind.' This is addressed more to herself than the baby. Get rid of the stink Rose, wash and change the baby Rose, do something, anything to stop the noise. I can't, she thinks. I just can't. Sweat trickles down her face. It's not a hot sweat, it's the humidity. The rain hasn't cooled the atmosphere one little bit. It's been like this for weeks. It won't get better until after the gales. Here in the Hutt Valley it's always warmer than the rest of the region anyway. Yesterday the radio weatherman said there would be another six weeks of the same. All la Niña's fault of course, he ended cheerfully. Maybe this baby is la Niña's doing as well. Its crying makes the clamminess worse. A north-westerly of course. It's all too much. Rose's head is bursting.

'Shut up,' she yells at the baby, then is immediately guilty. For God's sake Rose, pull yourself together, you don't yell at a baby! 'Please,' she begs. The cries are deafening and so physically intrusive her brain is being stabbed by them. The walls are closing in. 'Right,' she says encouragingly, 'right.' She can't stand in her kitchen jiggling a screaming, stinky baby all night because she's scared of being sick. She has to do something. She walks up and down agitatedly. She really does not want to unpeel this malodorous bundle.

Ringing Olga is out so who else? Certainly it has been a horrible time, and yes, she got tired, but she is over it. No need to take it easy any more. No need to sell the shop. No need to sell this house, no need to do anything. She's felt well all the way, not sick, no pain to speak of. Under her arm, where they've taken the lymph nodes, is numb in parts, the operation scar stings sometimes. Her right breast looks as though someone's pointed it sideways. So what? The radiation staff had been wonderful. Which was great because lying under that big dome – completely alone, invisible rays piercing the skin, bang on the little tattoo they'd done to mark the spot, burning the area where the lump was, hopefully putting a stop to any further betrayal her body might have in mind – was absolutely horrible. She trained herself to think of the wall hanging. She planned the design, the fabrics, the colours, the appliqué, the embroidery stitches, even the wooden rod she would use to hang it from. She got some odd looks from staff and patients when they saw her reading a book about the skeletal system. The cover had a large skeleton grinning out at the world. That would be why.

She got through the radiation in good shape. Well, she has a breast that looks to the side. There are worse things. Olga said it was a matter of time. The incision under the arms has pulled it a bit, but it will settle down. 'You mean I'll get used to it,' Rose said.

'You have lovely breasts,' Olga said, 'I love them, but I love you more.'

There were a nasty few days after the operation wondering what the lymph nodes would reveal. The whole experience was disturbing, yes she'd never be the same again, yes at times the anxiety is unbearable. Does that mean she has to stop doing everything she likes? She's built The Book Stops Here up from nothing, it's starting to pay its way with something left over, why would she sell up now? It's true there are times when she moans. Whose job is perfect?

'Shush, shush, there now, shush, shush.' Look on the bright side Rose. Olga has done you a favour. You will now have lots more time to think about another needlework project. You will now not have to feel like an immigrant in a strange country every time you're in the middle of her relations, especially her sisters, especially Puti. Puti is Olga's oldest sister, taller and larger than Olga, authoritative and direct like a sergeant-major. Puti was often in charge of her baby sister when they were young and she's forgotten (or ignores) the fact that Olga is now well old enough to run her own life. Rose knows Puti doesn't like her. Which is OK because she's not that struck on Puti either. Her eyes, Rose thinks, weighing, judging, finding Rose wanting. Too bad, thinks Rose, if she doesn't approve of make-up, too bad, although she knows it's not really the make-up, it's because Rose is Pākehā. 'Puti's not as conservative as she seems,' Olga, who loves her oldest sister, said. It's a mystery. Well, no more of that, thank goodness. Rose might, at last, go through Ada's room, sort through her clothes, the dressing-table drawers, that big old trunk she kept underneath her bed. She has dusted and vacuumed, washed and ironed the curtains, brushed the blinds, but that's as far as it goes. She knows she should have done the job of clearing the room out before, but there's been the cancer operation, the radiation, then the wall hanging. Soon she's going to run out of excuses.

Rose opens the linen cupboard and pulls out some towels and the softest facecloth she can find. With the baby clamped to one side and the towels to the other, dry-retching, she leans against the wall for a few moments, then goes back to the kitchen. Soap can wait. Everything she has is perfumed. She doesn't know much about babies, but she knows they have delicate skins.

While she shushes, rocks, spreads the towels over the table, unpacks the carton, quivers inside from the battering sound which (God alone knows where it gets the strength) goes on and on and on, she remembers Miss Graham who, centuries ago, told her Sunday school class of attentive seven year olds the story of how Moses was found in a basket beside the river. Or was it in the bulrushes? As far as Rose recalls the baby was found by Pharaoh's daughter. Maybe it was Pharaoh's sister? Whatever. The baby was placed there by its mother because the current pharaoh had passed a law decreeing all male babies be killed, or was it all male Jewish babies? Yes it was. Or so Rose remembers. Well now she knows how Pharaoh's sister (or daughter) felt. 'Bloody cheek,' she mutters, 'bloody cheek.' Then she thinks, oh Olga.

Sibyl said Rose was not being fair to Olga. 'Just because Marcy was part of the whole sorry mess doesn't mean you have to turn into a control freak,' she said. Sibyl had a thing about control, about power. She agreed that teachers have power, but she said they should exercise it as little as possible. They should lead by example. Every teacher should start from where the child is, not from where the teacher thinks they should be. Sibyl had her own strong ideas about the way we all learn. 'Show me a lifetime learner and I'll show you a good teacher,' she said. As her students got more School C passes than anyone else in the Hutt the principal was not going to argue, even though Sibyl's paperwork was always well behind. Sibyl pretended not to care about the fierce competition there was to be in her English class. Sibyl was not perfect however. She said she didn't believe in too much control, but in her class non-appearance of assignments was only allowed twice. After the first non-arrival Sibyl would say there seemed to be a personality clash and the student was told to shape up or ship out. After the second, Sibyl showed she meant what she said. She was not persuaded by abject apologies or promises of future diligence, was unmoved by parental grovelling. 'You get two chances and then you're out,' she would tell the student in front of its parents at the beginning of each fifth-form year, 'so you know the score. Between us, we make up your learning plan. You don't have to be an Einstein but you do have to show me you're working. I do my best. If you work I'll stick with you, however long it takes but,' and Sibyl would shrug, 'my personality can't accept lazy students, it affects my teaching of the other ones, so that's the way it is.'

'You're talking about being a control freak?' Rose asked.

Something in Rose's voice made Sibyl laugh. 'OK,' she said, 'OK.'

The baby cries on, drearily, messily. It knows it's unwanted, a nuisance, a piece of flotsam washed up on an unwelcoming shore. Up until this moment Rose would have said the boom box from next door was the most intrusive sound she'd ever heard. Now she knows differently. How do mothers put up with it? How did Ada put up with it? She probably didn't have to. Rose is certain she never bawled like this. Now, where will she bathe this horrible baby. No good unpeeling it without having the water ready.

So much for wanting her luck to change. Well now it has. It's got worse.

Rose runs the water into the sink. Lukewarm. She pads the taps with a tea towel, dips her free elbow in the water twice just to be sure. When the noise from next door started some weeks ago late one afternoon just after the new tenants moved in, she went over and asked them to turn the noise down. 'I can't hear my own radio,' she said. She smiled, was pleasant.

'Turn yours off then,' said the smart-arse who answered her banging on the open front. Knock-Knock was the name he went by, Rose discovered later. He looked like a giant foetus. Horrible. She wouldn't mind betting there were times after he shoved his bug head out of her womb that his mother wished she'd got rid of him when he was just a twinkle. There are people only a mother could love, but in Knock-Knock's case she'd have to be deaf, dumb and blind.

Not satisfied with mere rudeness, Knock-Knock walked down the front steps and over to the tap on the house to the left of the steps. He turned it on, picked up the hose and played it on the steps so that her shoes were splattered. 'Better move honky,' he looked at her as though she was someone from a plague-infested planet, 'or you're likely to get wet.'

Rose was so shocked that that was what she did. Moved very quickly off the steps and away. 'It's the treatment,' she told Olga later, 'must be. I'm still feeling the effects. I'm fragile. He senses that. I'd never have done that before.'

'I'll speak to Puti.'

'No,' Rose said, 'don't. I've got a plan.'

Now. The table is covered with towels, the sink ready. The formula and bottles are on the bench. She's managed to tip the pegs out of the washbasket and line it with towels. She has folded a hand towel and wrapped it in a tea towel for a pillow. When the baby is clean she will lie it in the basket, find something to cover it with and then have a go at making the formula. Then and only then will she decide whether to ring Olga and see if there's anything that organisation of hers can do.

She can't put it off any longer. She must now unwrap this stinking heap, and that's that.

TWO

'What on earth's going on?'

'Aaah!' Rose jumps. It's Jo making her nightly visitation. Bugger.

Rose's shout makes the baby jump and its crying now enters a new and, as far as Rose is concerned thinking of her eardrums, uncharted realm.

'I knocked twice,' says Jo as though this excuses the fright she's given Rose. She carries a carton of tomatoes. 'These were still on the porch.' She sounds as though she thinks her husband's tomatoes deserve better treatment. 'What's that baby doing here?'

'I thought it was the tomatoes I ordered.' Rose raises her voice.

'It's not one of our boxes.'

'I didn't see that. The rain. I was in a hurry.'

'Do you mean it was just left on your porch? Abandoned? When do you think they did it?' Jo raises her voice as well.

Rose's irritation levels kick into action. That's Jo all over. A poor grasp of essentials.

Since Jo married Wesley Neville, a lifetime ago, Rose and Jo's association has been based on the bare bones of their former friendship – that is to say, habit. A smile, a greeting, a disinterested question or two about Jo's son or daughter, Jo's garden. *Rigid, the skeleton of habit alone upholds the human frame.* So Virginia Woolf's Mrs Dalloway thinks, and Rose believes Mrs Dalloway is right. But there's something definitely wrong when someone with whom you've only had the most superficial contact for thirty years starts visiting, uninvited, unannounced, unwanted, every night.

Olga said when Rose asked her, 'You'll just have to wait until she decides to tell you or when she can't hold it in any longer.'

Rose looked at Olga as though this was no help at all.

'You could ask her,' said Olga.

'I have asked her.'

'Well,' Olga said, and Rose thought there was an un-sympathetic tone in her voice, 'you'll just have to wait then, won't you.'

When do you think they did it? The old Jo had this propensity to ask silly questions. So that's a good sign. Although who cares *when* someone placed a baby in a cardboard carton on her back porch? It's the *who* that worries Rose. It's the *what* she's having to do about it that riles her. It's the *why*, as in why me?

Jo says, 'How is it you didn't see them? What were you doing? You look terrible.' More words than Jo's used in months. This should make Rose feel better but it doesn't.

'Of course I look terrible. I need a drink and some food. I don't need a screaming baby.'

Jo asks, 'What time did you find the box then?'

'For God's sake Jo, will you stop with the interrogation? It wasn't you, was it?'

'What?' She isn't outraged – Jo doesn't do outrage – but she's really surprised. 'Are you mad?'

This is no answer, but it's effective in stopping Rose's questions.

The rain falls steadily, the room darkens. It is hotter. Outside the window the silver birch shakes and shivers. The wind is starting up in earnest. Rose puts the light on.

'Why would someone leave a baby on your doorstep I wonder.' Jo fixes Rose with her intent stare. Her thick greying hair is caught into a twist at the back, her blue eyes are large and forceful, some fine wrinkles yes, but you don't notice them. Jo wears a silk shirt, the same colour as her eyes, and a blue patterned skirt. For the zillionth time Rose wonders why Jo married Wesley. What must it be like to be married to someone who goes up town at the drop of a hat and hands out leaflets urging people to come to the Church of the Golden Light and find out what true happiness is. Wesley was a Methodist when they married, but he's been a leading member of the Church of the Golden Light since its inception, must be fifteen years ago now. The Jo Rose had once known would not have put up with it. Or the rituals. The Church of the Golden Light is very keen on rituals. They have rituals for housewarmings, the first frost in winter, births, deaths, divorces, accidents, illnesses. Rose knows, none better, how we all change, but surely people don't change that much. Much as they would like to, Rose and other critics cannot entirely dismiss members of the Church of the Golden Light as a bunch of crazy new-age Christians who like singing on hilltops in the pouring rain. On joining, members vow to be their brother's (or sister's) keeper, to be socially responsible human beings whatever the personal cost to themselves, to help until it hurts and to be silent about it. To do them justice, Wesley included, they live these vows. Members keep to the vow of silence, but it's impossible to silence those they help. So word gets around and the Church of the Golden Light is more respected than jeered at. Rose doesn't doubt Wesley's sincerity or commitment, more his sanity.

'Why would anyone leave a child on anyone's doorstep?' Rose demands.

'Well,' Jo prepares to take charge. She undoes her sleeve buttons and rolls up her sleeves. She's always been a very practical and efficient woman. It's thanks to her that their Good Samaritan Bed and Breakfast is as sought after as it is. Certainly there's a kind of captive catchment among church members who travel to the fortnightly Golden Light Unconditional Compassion weekends, but those who do use the Good Samaritan in preference to local motels, which are cheaper, always return. So it provides, thanks to Jo, the icing on the cake of their basic income from Wesley's tomatoes and garden tours. 'What this child needs is a bath. Now.'

Rose says, 'I've got water ready in the sink.'

'The sink?' Jo does a Lady Bracknell.

'The tub in the laundry is full of shop dusters soaking and the bath is too big. The sink can be sterilised afterwards.'

The shuddering sobs have become quieter. The relief from the screeching is immense. Rose can feel her eardrums calming.

'What is it?'

Rose rolls her eyes. Trust Jo.

Jo takes the baby from Rose, who is so surprised she lets her, sets it down carefully, makes sure the towels are between it and the table, and undoes the outer rug. The stink is now overpowering. Rose feels herself beginning to heave again. 'Oh hell,' she says and grabs for a towel.

'No wonder it's upset,' Jo says, 'lying in this mess.' Why does everything Jo says sound so accusatory tonight? Never mind Rose, Jo's actually said more words tonight than she has in the previous six months. Rose wipes her lips and concentrates on deep breathing. The trouble is *she* smells now. That first stain has been joined by others. Jo removes the nappy. It's a boy.

'Oh,' Jo gasps as she removes its top, 'oh, no.' They stare at the flaring purple weal on the baby's left arm. It runs from shoulder to elbow. A steelier blue with dirty yellow smudges extends on to the shoulder and pales out towards the chest. Rose is sick into the towel. 'Oh no,' Jo says, 'oh no. I can't bear it.'

A clammy, sweaty sickness pervades Rose's whole body. That little stick arm is so small, so thin, the chest so defenceless. The small eyes lock on Rose and it waves its blue arm vaguely in the air. Oh go away, thinks Rose, go away. I'm not equipped to cope with this. Cancer yes, black planes, yes, all in a day's work, a beaten baby, no, please, go away.

'Obviously not broken,' Jo says. She is deathly pale. 'I'd better ring Alice Hudson. And for goodness' sake Rose, control yourself. Shall I get you a bucket?'

Rose shakes her head angrily. She takes an extra deep breath, undoes the towel on the tap and runs a glass of water. She makes herself drink it slowly, every damn drop.

Ring Alice? Jo is ringing Alice Hudson? Why is she ringing Doctor Alice Hudson?

'She's on the committee of that group that has something to do with this sort of thing,' Jo says, as if Rose has asked her question out loud, 'what's it called? Safe and Secure.' Jo's tone says exactly what she thinks of such a name. Rose wonders why, if Jo thinks Safe and Secure is such an awful name, she's a member of a church called Golden Light.

The baby begins to cry again. Rose sighs, rewinds the towel around the tap, straightens her shoulders, picks up the baby, and delicately and very carefully lowers him into the warm water. He gives a shocked screech and a stream of piss hits Rose in the face. 'Bloody hell.' She is momentarily blinded. Fortunately she doesn't relax her grip. The baby, now immersed in water and piss, but who cares, he's quiet, lies supine against her supporting arm. The arm looks even bluer through the water and the little heart is beating fast. As Rose watches, it slows and steadies. Surely the injury must have been an accident. People didn't hit babies on purpose. Don't be stupid Rose. People did and do anything. You should know that. Remember that little girl? Bianca something, Porterus, something like that, Bianca was sexually molested, doused in petrol, set alight, and then given two hard blows to the head. The father, or was it uncle? One or the other. Their treatment of this child had only come to light because the child had died. Was this child in danger of being a Bianca? Was that why he'd been left with her? She recalls an item on the radio just this morning. A child, eighteen-month-old Anthony Waiouru, taken to Auckland's Starship Hospital the previous day, badly beaten, unconscious, has died. Police are investigating. There's that ship with two hundred and fifty so-called slave children on board which is missing. The radio says authorities are worried that the captain will cast his hostages overboard to get rid of the evidence. It appears that there is a thriving market in child slaves in some parts of the world. The children's parents sell them because they are starving. For God's sake, Rose tells her brain, if you can't come up with something more cheerful, for Christ's sake shut down.

'Alice Hudson's coming straight away,' Jo reports.

'I was thinking of that poor little devil, Bianca.'

'And the one in England, eight I think, killed and left in a paddock.' Jo, who has a little colour back but still looks ill, picks up the packet of formula. 'Ugh,' she shivers, 'there's far too much of this sort of thing. I'm sure it never used to happen so much. The media just blows things up.'

Rose, dabbing and patting, sweating profusely, doesn't reply. Bathing a baby is a slippery business. She mustn't hurt him any more than he is already. Responding to Jo's stupidities will have to wait. Should she even have bathed him? Maybe she should have waited until Alice came? Too late now. He does seem happier. The water is a pale mud colour but still warm. Rose doesn't like the feel of the small body, like a chicken without fluff. The bones inside the wet flesh have sharp edges on them although there is healthy flesh around the hips. And no more bruises, thank God. 'That's going to have to do,' Rose tells the baby, 'we'll get some proper soap tomorrow.' What am I saying? By tomorrow, whoever he belongs to will have turned up, and he'll be gone.

There was a little girl in Palmerston North who went missing and was found some hours later by her uncle. She'd been taken to a local cemetery then sexually assaulted and raped.

It must be true, your brain files everything you read and when the right stimulus comes along there it is. Or is it just that once you are alerted to something, your eyes suddenly open to that world where these things happen. After Rose knew she had cancer, she was amazed at how often this disease was mentioned on the radio, in the papers, on television. Even in the supermarket. She remembers overhearing two women talking as she eased her trolley past their two on her first trip after she got the news, when there seemed to be something deeply ironic about shopping for food when you might be dying. 'It's gone to the kidneys,' one said. 'My dad's went to the liver,' said the other one. Rose has no doubt that these news items, these conversations, were going on before she knew about her own condition, and it's she who's become more noticing, not the other way round.

'I attract people with cancer, or people who've had cancer, or those who know someone who has cancer,' she told Sibyl after they met in the hospital ward and compared notes.

'Tell me about it,' Sibyl said dryly.

Right at this moment Rose wishes her brain was arranged differently. She'd often pondered on the fact that she remembers every bad thing that ever happened to her with great clarity and instant recall while the few good things are always vague, veiled in sunshine, making details hard to conjure up, just a sad feeling of remembered happiness with no particular focus. She has accepted that her brain attracts evidence of similar happenings to the one she is currently experiencing as if wanting to make her entry into any new (to Rose) world of say heartache, rejection, injustice, a mother dying, cancer, less isolated although still scary. Now it seems as if her brain is actually ahead of the game. That it retains horrible news items so they'll come into her head as a confirmation when she faces something outside her experience, like here, like now. Memory, memory, thinks Rose. When we've got it we grizzle about it, yet we feel so wary of anyone who's lost it.

The baby cries, a wailing heartbroken sound holding a world of loss, tragedy, pain. And no wonder, Rose thinks, hesitantly drying the hurt arm. Jo holds out a nappy and Rose fixes it around the baby's bum, realises she has nothing for his top. 'Watch him,' she orders Jo and gets a piece of the soft muslin she uses to strain apple jelly. Jo bends over the baby, frowning, staring at his face, at the bruising. Rose wraps the muslin round his chest and very carefully bundles the little body in a large towel. She holds her hand out for the bottle and Jo hands it to her. Rose sits in the old Morris chair and feeds the baby. And joy and rapture. A magic wand has been waved. Peace falls.

After the lumpectomy, after the lab report said the lymph nodes had no cancer in them, after the six weeks of radiation therapy and after another lab report said the cancerous lump had not been estrogen driven and therefore they couldn't say what had set it off and that if the lymph nodes hadn't been clear she would have had to have chemotherapy, Rose discovered that her appreciation of a beautiful woman, a handsome man, a lovely child, a setting, was ten times more intense. Rose knew this increased awareness had to do with mortality. She had always liked looking at people, gardens, interiors, always got a great deal of pleasure from seeing furniture well-placed, ornaments just so on shelves, pictures, banners on walls. Now she almost purrs every time she enters her house, sees her kitchen. She decides she's a late learner. It seems everyone in the world except her knew about the fragile line between the health of flesh and blood and muscles and the disasters which lurked in the dark ready to pounce. She has had to wait until she was nearly fifty to realise that between one breath and the next is all there is and that heartache, rejection, injustice, her mother's death, are only spurs on that road to realisation. Now she's alive to it. It's not easy to break habits though. 'We should take time to enjoy the sight of a tree, a piece of fabric, a particularly well-designed book cover, because we might not get another chance,' Sybil said, 'all this rushing about we do.' Rose agreed, but they both continue to rush about.

On the wooden bench the blue bowl, in which are green salad leaves, thinly sliced red onions and slivers of bright yellow peppers, stands by the glass bottle with the glass stopper. Beside them the bottle of olive oil, the bottle of malt vinegar – which Rose prefers over other vinegars or lemon juice because she likes richer sharper dressings – the pot of mustard, bowl of sugar and smaller one of salt wait for her to do something creative with them. The smell, the dirty sink, the noise, this weight in her arms sucking steadily on a teat, haven't altered a thing.

She recovered this large old Morris chair in a fabric designed with vines and leaves a la William Morris during that first winter four years ago after she came back home to live. 'I've been meaning to do it,' Ada said, 'just haven't had the time.' The chair stands opposite the black fake-leather high-backed chair with its own footstool in the same pretend leather which Rose bought because she couldn't afford real leather and because she likes touches of black. Olga used the black chair and footstool on Sunday nights. Rose would not give up the Morris chair which would have suited Olga better. Olga was a large woman. The wide wooden arms are exactly the right width to hold a glass of wine or a cup of coffee, a book, a mug, glasses, or in Rose's case, embroidery materials, threads, needles, scissors, thimble patches. Rose's bum was half the size of Olga's, but she likes a bit of space around it when she sits. 'You could use one of those little black trolleys for your embroidery bits and pieces,' Olga hinted, because she really coveted that chair. Rose has made a wonderful job of covering it. But it is Rose's house, her chair. Rose is very possessive about things she's made and is amazed when someone spends six, eight months on a piece of embroidery, appliqué, quilting, and then gives it away. Or sells it. She can't do that. She allowed Olga to show some of Ada's works on the walls of the café for the opening when the paintings she'd bought didn't turn up on time, but that was different. Even though she loves Olga, who knows all about the whole sorry mess four years ago and who believed Rose instantly, without question, Rose couldn't give up her chair. 'Why didn't you go to the police, have the girl questioned, at least get a lawyer, an advocate on your behalf?' Olga asked, but only once. Not like Ada who kept on and on asking.

In the centre of the room stands the ordinary old oak table, the only thing of Ada's, except for the chair, remaining in this kitchen. The rest of the house is still as Ada left it because Rose is not made of money, has to do things gradually. On the table, the unstained macrocarpa bowl with yellow lemons looks as lively and lovely as it did when she arranged the lemons this morning. The presence of the cardboard carton – which should have contained tomatoes to make into relish the next day – has not changed a thing. Rose has changed though. She will never approach a carton of tomatoes with the same kind of innocent expectation as she did earlier that evening. Rose read about a woman who'd opened up a carton of bananas and found a tarantula staring up at her. The woman said she would never feel the same about bananas ever again. Now Rose knows how she feels. Never, ever, again. In fact she wouldn't care if she never saw a tomato ever again. She wants to ask Jo to take the real carton of tomatoes away, but knows she won't.

Rose loves this kitchen. It's the biggest room in the house and it's the first one she made hers. She likes the way it accommodates a table and dining chairs, and the two big chairs. She doesn't know why this room is so large except that large kitchens were a feature of bungalows built by Elmore Hipp in the twenties and thirties. It was a rarity then and it's not common now, perhaps because most people like to hide the messy detritus of cooking, like to pretend it all happens smoothly, without fuss, all done by a genie in the kitchen. Rose rarely entertains, enjoys cooking, is adept at cleaning up as she goes; so she loves the big room. In any case, if people don't like seeing a mess on the bench they can stay away.

She likes to look around and tick off the treasures she's made. The scarlet cushions on Olga's black chair. Or bought, like the blue bowl she fell in love with and paid off. Or exchanged, like the macrocarpa bowl which she'd seen in a car-boot sale where she'd gone looking for books. The seller was happy to swap the bowl for some Wilbur Smiths. She loves to look at the mauve biscuit barrel with the thin black lines on the lid and the ring of flowers painted on a wider black line on the body, which Olga gave her, and which is either placed on the table or, as it is at the moment, on the alcove shelf beside the pantry. Every piece has served its time and is allowed to stay because it fits into the picture. Olga says Rose loves setting scenes, that it's the drama teacher in her.

Rose loves this room, loves this house. It has outlived its location, bungalows have gone out of fashion in favour of townhouses, it badly needs a paint, all sorts of maintenance really, but she loves it. And in spite of the cancer, in spite of noisy neighbours, in spite of Wesley breathing down her neck about selling to the church because Elmore Hipp's descendants are among the founding members, in spite of Jo's bizarre behaviour and, above all, in spite of Olga's ultimatum, she will stay here. People in New York are staying, they're not going to leave their homes and they have more of an excuse than she, Rose thinks. It's human nature. It's the reason you make a house your home. Rose knows very well that New Zealanders, the majority of them, move house at the drop of a hat, but she ignores this. It's a rare weekend when she doesn't observe furniture balanced precariously on a hire trailer, or stowed in backs of station wagons. It's a common sight to see moving vans in drives disgorging their loads into a house while the new owners yell at their kids and dogs to stay inside the fences.

Jo offers to hold the baby, but when Rose shakes her head, she gets busy and cleans the sink, finds a plastic bucket from the laundry, shoves the clothes in, rolls up the shitty nappy in a section of the *Dominion*. 'What?' she asks defensively as Rose takes a sharp inward breath.

'I haven't read it yet,' Rose says, and yes, she sounds annoyed. 'I was saving it. You should have used some from the cupboard under the tub in the laundry. That's where I keep old newspapers.'

'Sorry.' Jo doesn't sound sorry at all. In the circumstances, she intimates, Rose being deprived of a read of the morning paper is hardly a major worry.

Rose sighs and turns back to the baby. Jo's always been difficult, she thinks.

THREE

Alice's jacket is rain spattered and tiny drops sparkle in her fair hair. Until Doctor Alice Hudson was in her forties she had a square body; now, approaching fifty, she's slimmed down (ageing, she says) and it's more oblong. Alice was once Alice Moore who was in the same class as Jo and Rose. Different times, different lives. Alice removes her jacket and hangs it over the back of a chair. 'Is this OK?' she asks, 'it might drip.' Rose nods and then wonders if Alice is being sarcastic. Jo looks at Alice and Alice looks at Jo. 'Hello Jo,' says Alice.

'Hello Alice,' says Jo.

Rose wonders how long it is since Jo and Alice met as adults. Probably Ada's funeral. Alice Hudson is Rose's doctor and they get on well. She's been great all through the cancer business. Alice has a husband, recently retired. From whizzing around in some high-powered job in the city he now happily spends most of his time making furniture. They have four grown-up children, a couple of them with spouses and young children, who come home at Christmas and school holidays. Alice's books at the surgery are closed as far as new patients are concerned, but she still finds time to be involved in Safe and Secure. Astonishing.

Rose puts the baby on yet another clean towel – at this rate she'll be washing towels for days – and Alice bends over him. Her touch on his body is sure and kind. Jo and Rose watch intently. 'Nothing broken,' Alice says, while the baby, who has not enjoyed being unwrapped from his warm coverings, gives fretful little cries. 'How did he hurt his arm?'

'I don't know,' Rose says. Then immediately sees, or thinks she sees, what Alice is meaning. She rushes into speech. 'It wasn't me,' Rose says, 'it isn't anything I did, if that's what you're thinking. We just discovered his arm like that. Ask Jo. He was left on my porch. Someone,' she insists as though Alice is arguing the opposite, 'someone left him on my back porch. I thought he was a box of tomatoes. There was a card. He's addressed to me.' Rose reaches for the card and shows it to Alice who regards it in silence. Rose dashes into more explanation, hears herself babble, is unable to stop. 'I just thought you might think – silly – of course you don't – must be the shock I suppose. You don't usually expect to find a baby on your doorstep, unless you're Pharaoh's daughter of course.' Rose runs out of breath.

'Take it easy Rose,' Alice frowns, 'of course I don't think you did it.' The lines deepen in her forehead.

'I should think not.' Jo sounds affronted on Rose's behalf, then spoils it by adding, 'but the strangest people, people you'd never suspect – ' catching Rose's eye, 'not that I'm suggesting – oh for goodness' sake Rose, you know what I mean.'

'You'll need to report it,' Alice says, 'someone's hurt the baby, or there's been an accident or something.'

Alice reaches for a clean nappy from the packet and changes the baby. Her hands are brown and the nails cut short and neatly filed. 'Circumcised,' she says, 'that might be a clue, not as popular as it used to be except, of course, for religious or cultural reasons.' She folds the large, soft towel around his body and gives the boy back to Rose. 'Someone knows you,' she says, 'and that someone trusts you.'

'I can't look after a baby.' Rose sounds aggressive and means to. 'I really can't.' She offers the baby the bottle, which still has a little liquid in it. 'I don't have time. I've got the shop, the garden, my sewing, the house. I think leaving him on my door-step without asking my permission is a bloody cheek.' The baby stops sucking and moves uneasily. 'And don't you start,' Rose glares at him but lowers her voice.

'Will you ring the police?' Jo asks.

This is exactly what Rose wants to do but she says, her voice rising, 'Don't stir the pot, Jo.' The lines on Alice's forehead carve deeper runnels. 'I've had enough for the moment. Besides it's Friday night, the police'll have enough on their plate. Alice says there's nothing broken. Anything else can wait until tomorrow.' What the hell did I say that for, she thinks.

'What about your shop?' asks Alice, 'aren't you open on Saturdays?'

'I'll have to take him with me.'

'I'll look after him,' Jo says decisively.

'No,' Rose is equally firm, 'he wasn't left with you, he was left with me. I'll take him with me.' We're like two kids arguing over a doll or a teddy, she thinks. 'He'll be OK.'

'Well I for one can't go on calling this baby "him",' Jo recovers. 'He has to have a name. Charles. That will do.'

'Charles? Like hell. We're not all royalists Jo.'

'Well what then?'

Rose clicks her tongue irritably. 'George,' she says, remembering Byron for some reason. Probably because she's reading a book about Ada Lovelace, née Byron.

'Weeell,' Jo says, then stops whatever it is she is going to say about royal names not being confined to Charles.

'George.' Anything less like George Noel Gordon, Lord Byron, than this baby in her arms, Rose has yet to see. George Byron, sometimes called Geordie, a beautiful baby, born with a crippled foot and a leg shorter than the other, had suffered tortures as various doctors subjected him to racking, stretching, straightening that leg. Poor, beautiful Geordie who became a poet and political agitator, given to excesses of all kinds, especially sex and drugs; a man who made his wife very unhappy during their short married life and whom she suspected, along with the rest of the world, of having sex with his sister. A short man who worried about his weight and who, it is speculated, was manic-depressive, now called bipolar, a disease that the daughter he disdained allegedly inherited. Maybe this isn't such a good name. George the Fourth. George Formby. There is an actor though. George. Curney? Oh well, never mind. George will do until the parent or parents come to claim him. Clooney, that's it.

'George? Why George?'

'Does it matter?'

It is Jo's turn to breathe deeply.

The baby's sucking slows down, stops altogether every now and then until he remembers the teat in its mouth and gives a casual pull on it.

Alice's light, quick voice sounds tired. 'The child is between three or four months I'd say. Pākehā. Someone will have to find out who he is and why he was left with you. It's not fair on him otherwise. We need to know how he was injured. There may be other children needing protection. You've read the papers. The statistics are deplorable. Every day, every hour it seems sometimes, another child is hurt. Some of them badly enough to kill them. I think you must tell the police.'

'Oh please,' Jo says. She shakes her head, not denying the truth of what Alice is saying, more to ward it off.

Alice looks at her as she puts her stethoscope back in her bag. 'Just in this region there are thirty-five women in hiding Jo. They have fifty-two children with them. Not all of them at the refuge itself of course, a few are in Safe and Secure homes because of their circumstances.'

'Circumstances?' Jo sounds as though the word offends her.

'Their partner or husband might be a policeman, a social worker, or someone with a lot of money. Someone who knows the location of the refuge or who can find out. Those women need somewhere totally secret. Until their safety can be ensured.'

'And you think this baby's mother could be one of those?' Jo is incredulous and horrified at the same time.

'Perhaps. Many women are too frightened to do anything about it because of what their partner might do if he found out. This baby's mother might be one who decided there was something she could do.'

'Yes, but who is she?' Rose sighs. 'Why leave him with me? I don't know anyone who's had a baby. Well not recently. Some of my customers have babies, but I'm sure they're older than this one.'

Like Jo, Rose is a coward. She wishes Alice hadn't told them those numbers. Out of sight, out of mind. There was another case where a man pinched a baby all over to stop it crying. She hadn't been able to read any further so she doesn't know what else happened to make it a newspaper item.

'There'll be someone,' Alice says, 'there'll be someone. Quite likely someone who comes into the shop. Think, Rose.'

Rose shakes her head. 'I'm too tired. You're right, I should contact the police tonight.' The three of them stare at George who, snug in Rose's arms, closes his eyes. He really is an ugly baby, thin of face, small eyes, prominent chin. Maybe it's the effect of Jo putting royals into Rose's mind, but she thinks this baby is very like photographs she's seen of paintings of that ancient Spanish royal family who all had long, jutting, prominent chins. The males were lucky. They could grow beards. Hapsburgs. Does she know anyone called Hapsburg?

'Damn,' Rose says, but softly, 'I've got to find his mother. Perhaps she'll turn up tomorrow.'

'Needle in the haystack stuff probably,' Alice says, relenting. 'OK then, I'll ring the after-hours number for Child, Youth and Family and tell the duty officer. Establish that you're a respectable member of society. So they'll be quite happy for you to look after him for the time being. They'll visit of course, look you over for themselves.'

'You don't want them poking and prying, do you?' Jo sounds horrified, as though a social worker from CYFS is on a par with the KGB.

'No,' Rose nods. Jo is right. Rose doesn't want to be looked over by anyone, even if it means she gets rid of this child. 'No. I don't want you to contact the police or the social services. I'll leave it for tonight. Someone left this child in my care. For Rose Anthony.' She holds the card out to Alice. 'That's what it says. For Rose Anthony. For some reason, someone decided to leave George with me. So he's not really abandoned or anything. I'll give it till tomorrow. But just wait till I see them. I think it's bloody disgraceful plonking a baby on my porch as though he's a carton of tomatoes or a box of vegetables.'

'How will you manage? At the shop.'

'I'll manage,' Rose says, then spoils it. 'Have to, won't I?'

Alice is unconvinced, but she decides to go along with Rose for the moment. 'Call me if you need me. And if the mother hasn't turned up by Monday morning I want you to clearly understand, either you ring the police or I will.'

Rose nods.

'Good,' Alice says. 'Ring me if you need me, otherwise I'll see you Sunday.'

'Sunday?' Rose's mind is blank.

'Your birthday dinner.' Alice smiles faintly at Rose, 'Olga invited me. It's not a surprise is it?'

'No,' says Rose, 'no. I'd just forgotten for the moment.'

Bloody Olga and her bloody 'I know you hate surprise parties so I'm telling you. Potluck dinner at your place.'

'Like hell,' Rose had replied, 'if there's one thing I hate it's potluck dinners. Everyone brings salads and they're not really filling so they all get pissed. If I'm going to have a dinner here on my birthday, I'll cook a proper meal.'

'We could have it at the café,' Olga offered.

'Here,' Rose said.

'You're so – so hard on yourself,' Olga said but she smiled. 'What will you cook?'

'That's mine to know and yours to wonder,' Rose said, and heard Ada in her voice.

How could she forget her own birthday? More to the point, how could she forget she was cooking a three-course dinner for – how many? Olga (if Olga's still coming), Alice, Uncle Claude and his wife, Elena, who will be there under protest. Elena is not keen on Rose. Not because Rose is a lesbian, she just doesn't like her. The feeling is mutual. Sibyl and Kitty. Then, aghast, Rose remembers she hasn't asked Jo. Partly because if she asks Jo she'll bring Wesley, but mainly because Jo is so off-hand lately, so angry and just so odd. Now she'll have to ask her.

Alice looks amused, as if she realises Rose's dilemma. She hesitates, then says, 'Your birthday tomorrow, Jo, I remember. Have a lovely day.'

Jo sniffs. 'I haven't got time to worry about birthdays.'

That seems to be that. But Alice persists. 'How's everyone Jo?'

'Fine, we're all fine.'

'Lizzie and the baby doing well?'

'Blooming,' Jo smiles as she lies. Rose knows this is a lie because she knows Jo hasn't seen her daughter for months, doubts if she's even had more than a passing glimpse of her grandchild. Rose doesn't know what the trouble is and doesn't want to. She'd had little to do with Lizzie who, when young – it seemed to Ada, who reported it to Rose – was either over-indulged (Wesley) or over-disciplined (Jo). Thelma Millet, dark and shiningly beautiful even when she was in her sixties, Jo's mother, the woman in whose bed Rose's father died, and who, months later became, to everyone's pleasurable amazement, Ada's good friend, told Ada and Rose that Jo was far too strict with the girl and Thelma wasn't surprised when Lizzie hit puberty and rebelled. 'Jo says Lizzie over-dramatises things, but who doesn't at fifteen?' Thelma asked. Or at fifty for that matter, Rose now thinks.

There'd been some trouble, a party which got out of hand, police called, some of the adolescents, of whom Lizzie, beautiful as her grandmother, was one, arrested for drunkenness and throwing bottles. All smoothed over because Lizzie was under sixteen at the time. As soon as Lizzie turned eighteen she got herself a job (receptionist in a real-estate firm) and took herself off to a room in a mixed flat. Nothing Jo said would stop her. When she was twenty, there was some sort of reconciliation. Probably brought about by Wesley. Or perhaps by Royston Hipp, with whom Lizzie became involved, God knows why. Royston was of average height, average looks, good teeth though, and was, Rose thought, as dull as he looked. He must have hidden charms. The Hipps Senior, like Wesley and Jo, were stalwarts of the Church of the Golden Light. Royston and Lizzie had attended the same Sunday school, endured or enjoyed the same rituals on birthdays, and now, meeting again after a few years' independence, apparently discovered they liked each other in spite of this. After a year they got engaged, and a year later, they married.

Rose was surprised to be invited to the wedding, but she enjoyed it. It involved a combination of wacky rituals amongst which was a ritual called the Entering a New Life ceremony, which consisted of Golden Light members and adherents, plus a number of rather surprised wedding guests, gathering together on a hill with lanterns and flowers and singing songs, despite the pouring rain. No whisky served of course, only weak tea in a thermos, while cheerful and hearty voices sang something about the morning of life and new beginnings. All of which was permeated, Rose has to admit, by genuine goodwill, except perhaps from where she was standing.

'Heard from Claude?' Alice asks Rose. Rose's uncle – with his wife Elena's blessing and the district nurse and Alice's approval – had taken off for a week saying that if they were going to nag about it, he might as well see something of the South Island before he got too old. Alice had arranged the home help to give Claude this break. Elena is crippled by terrible arthritis.

At the mention of his name Rose sees Claude. Grey hair, thin face, big nose, pale-blue eyes always narrowed against something in the distance, wearing his usual loose corduroy pants and checked shirts, an old brown sheepskin jacket when it's very cold, his old red swannie when it's not. Sixty-nine and looking every year of it.

Good old Claude. Reliable, honest, funny, staunch, always ready to get on his soapbox. Her favourite uncle. Well, her only uncle. But he would have been her favourite even if she'd had ten uncles.

'Just a postcard from Reefton,' Rose says.

'I'll see you Sunday,' Alice says. She turns to go. 'Spoken to Sibyl?'

'Yes,' says Rose.

'About Sunday. It's not really a party,' Rose says to Jo, after Alice leaves, 'just a dinner, and I didn't really want it, but Olga insisted, so if you and Wesley are free, six o'clock, here.' Hardly the most enthusiastic of invitations, she thinks.

'Thanks,' says Jo, 'I'll see.'

Hardly the most enthusiastic of acceptances. So we're even, thinks Rose. Now all I have to do is decide what we're going to eat. Bugger Olga.

FOUR

Three years ago Olga Irihapeti Porohiwi wandered in to a Retail Association meeting thinking it was a meeting of the Hutt Tramping Club. Brown boots, socks, trousers, checked shirt, dark-green jersey, swandri jacket, tall, spiky scrubbing brush haircut, large brown eyes. She looked slightly surprised as she took in the suits, the fairly formal clothes, not realising they'd all come straight from work. It took an hour of the wrangling, arguing and heated discussion before she realised she was in the wrong place. She was just about to leave when Rose got up and spoke. (Olga told Rose later she was so struck by Rose's cool common sense, her marshalling of facts, her clarity and, after all the once-round-the-pig's-arse that had gone on since she walked into the room, her succinctness, not to mention the stylish aubergine jersey and pants and dark-wine fluffy vest, that she decided to stay and see if Rose would come and have a drink with her.)

It wasn't until Rose's name was mentioned that Olga clicked that this was the same Rose Anthony who was in the same class as her at Wai-iti Primary all those centuries ago. If she'd heard a whisper about what really drove Rose back home, she didn't say so.

Rose knew Olga immediately. No mistaking that walk. Olga's mother walked with that same ease and assurance, as did her three older sisters. It had been the first thing Rose noticed about them all those years ago although she couldn't have put words to it then. Rose believed it came both from an enviable quiet confidence that they are who they are and are proud of that and because somehow Mere and Sam Porohiwi and their daughters didn't see, or perhaps choose not to see that, for some of the parishioners, this locum minister and his wife were a hell of a shock.

Now, however, Rose struggled with an unwelcome feeling. She knew who Olga was all right, but there seemed more to it than that. She felt as though she'd been holding her breath all her life and now she could let it go. This Olga was a stranger, but Rose knew instantly what it would be like to touch that spiky hair, hug that tall strong body, kiss those full lips, laugh at the absurdity of such a meeting place. She knew all this and yet she hadn't seen Olga for forty years. Rose pushed these delicious images away. She had never believed in the phenomenon of love at first, or even second, sight and she didn't intend to start now.

What on earth was Olga doing back in the Hutt? Olga was setting up a café. To be called Olga's. 'Not very original,' grinned Olga. Rose listened to Olga's plans to use walls and shelves to showcase Māori art, her search for really good staff, her running battles with the designer.

Rose didn't accept Olga's invitation because she didn't like pubs but did say — as a test or to put her off or more likely because she saw in sharp focus, ridiculous as it was she decided a second later, a flash of herself and Olga lying entwined on Rose's bed — 'I've got some gin at home if you'd like a drink.' Rose didn't make a habit of asking strange women home for a drink, but Olga was so funny about thinking it was the tramping club, about the trials and frustrations she'd endured with her interior designer who wanted old bricks and mellow wood while Olga wanted primary colours and lots of glass, steel and black granite, that the invitation was out before Rose knew it and there was another damned flash of Rose and Olga in the shower together. For God's sake Rose Anthony, she scolded herself, what are you? A perv or something? But Olga smiled and Rose had to smile back. A drink would be all right, Rose decided, just one drink.

After a couple of gins Olga discovered Rose had no interest in tramping, had never liked the bush. 'Not like the bush? Next thing you'll tell me you hate rugby.' Olga grinned, admitted to her secret addiction. She was a rugby fan. 'You are a New Zealander,' she said, 'you must at least have some glimmerings about the national game. It's a very old game you know, started well before that Rugby schoolboy, Webb Ellis, ran with the ball.'

'Webb who?' Rose asked.

Olga smiled, refusing to be provoked. 'It began with whole villages pitted one against the other. Went on for days at a time. Brutal, savage affairs with blunt instruments.' Olga rolled the words out with great enjoyment. 'Wasn't just in England either, the games were played in Europe and in Ireland. A sort of ritual bloodletting by the sound of it.'

'Well that hasn't changed from what I've heard,' Rose said. She refilled Olga's glass. 'I remember your mother,' Rose said, 'how is she?'

'Tramping. Somewhere in Peru at the moment,' Olga said. 'Leo, my son, takes after her. Mum and Leo are into the real thing. The more Spartan the better. I'm a fraud really. Too lazy to organise my own tramps, I leave it to the club to do that. You should try it. There are guided tramps you know, where someone else carries the gear.'

'Are you allowed to take mascara?'

Olga laughed.

Mere and Sam Porohiwi were not just a new experience for Methodists. Sam, apart from being Māori, had a history as well as a theology degree, was an ardent socialist and member of the Friends of China Association. His attendance at the local history-group meeting caused a flurry, but it was nothing compared to the surprise when he got up at the Hutt Socialist AGM and began an impassioned speech about the links between class and race. The Friends of China were already regarded as a bunch of loonies so his presence at their gatherings caused no concern because hardly anyone knew about it. When the old minister decided, while he was on his year's sabbatical and had time to think, that it was time he resigned, everyone went into a tizzy. They wanted Sam and they didn't want him. Those who were uncomfortable with Sam being Māori were won over by his lucid and witty sermons and by the weekly get-togethers at the minister's house to which all parishioners were invited and where the most delicious cakes, baked by Mere herself, were served. Those who were at odds with Sam's socialist leanings discovered his love of tradition and were calmed, and those who were not going to be won over by anything were by then in a minority. There were second thoughts by all these parties when they learned that Sam and Mere would consult with their whānau before making the decision to go or to stay. Perhaps the parishioners didn't like the feeling they too were being evaluated. What say Sam and Mere's family advised them not to accept? What would that mean? What would they do? Some recalled failures at school and at work, times when they were made to feel they didn't measure up, and felt that tightening in the stomach that always preceded the call into the headmaster's office, the performance review with the boss. This didn't do them any harm. The tiny minority who really wanted Sam *because* he was Māori were surprised but delighted when he accepted the invitation. Most felt a huge sense of relief. Few of them worked out why.

Sam, as well as being a minister who enjoyed the cooperation and approval of most of his flock, which is the most he or any minister or priest can ever hope for, developed a new enthusiasm. He became an avid collector of ordinary people's stories on tape. Long before recording oral history on tape became a serious profession somehow he persuaded old Māori to talk into his machine so their as yet unborn great-great-great-grandchildren could hear their voices telling their own stories. Somehow he persuaded old Pākehā that he was trustworthy and wasn't interested in telling anyone anything he heard during their sessions. If they felt uncomfortable with his presence they just had to say, and he would set up his big cumbersome tape recorder, show them where the stop recording button was, and leave them to it. Somehow they knew he could be trusted not to listen to their tape if they'd placed an embargo on it. And they were right, Sam was trustworthy in that way, but the reason he persuaded, coaxed, jollied old people into putting their lives on tape went a lot deeper than they realised. Sam knew how many of his people's stories had been lost and how skewed this made written history. It must be the same with Pākehā history. It became crucial to him that all so-called ordinary people's stories should be told. History was really just a patchwork cloak of life stories and events with an overall summary written from a particular historian's point of view. If some or most of the patches were missing that cloak would never be a shield for the generations to come because there would be holes in it.

By the time he set up his tape recorder for Ada to record her story, just before he retired and moved to Hawke's Bay, it was a neat little machine that was smaller, lighter and ten times easier than the old one, and he was much loved by everyone, even non-Methodists. Ada said that after Sam left her alone with this little black box and after she got over the strangeness of talking into a machine, she forgot all about the little black tape recording her words. 'I just rambled on until it ran out,' she told Rose. She'd placed them in the Oral History Archives in the Alexander Turnbull Library. 'You listen to them first,' she instructed Rose but, just to be on the safe side, put an embargo on them so they couldn't be listened to until after she died, and then only with Rose's permission. 'You listen to them first,' Ada repeated, 'then you'll know what you'll know.'

Rose hadn't listened to the tapes yet. One of these days she would. Rose didn't get into Wellington much during the working week. She could if she wanted to, but she doesn't. There's something vaguely repellent about the thought of listening to her dead mother's voice coming out of a machine.

Rose was always slightly uneasy in Sam Porohiwi's company, as though she'd farted in church or something. It was Ada, not Rose, who had scorned his proffered sympathy and refused to see him when Rose's father died in Thelma Millett's bed, but it was Rose who relayed her mother's words through their closed back door, who always felt those words standing between them. Her mother had been listening so Rose had no option but to repeat the message as instructed.

'Mum says she doesn't want to see you and that you should spread the word. She says she is not fodder for you or those backbiting busybodies. She says to say they'll soon find someone else to drool their poison over.'

Ada either forgot or decided to ignore these words when she agreed to tape her life story. Of course by then, all those years later, Ada knew Sam much better. 'Water under the bridge.' She dismissed Rose's discomfort. 'Sam's not a worry, he's really staunch, not really like a minister.' They'd been on various committees together, marched for various causes, knew each other as comrades if not as close friends.

Rose asked Olga, 'What about your father?'

'He's in Peru as well,' Olga said, 'but if I know Dad, he'll be sitting somewhere talking to someone.'

'And your sisters?'

Olga rolled her eyes. 'Still around here. They live in Wellington, which is a bit close. They still boss me around. Remind me if I ever come back as a girl baby to come back as the oldest. Being the youngest means it doesn't matter how old you get, everyone still thinks they can tell you what to do.'

Olga remembered Ada. Mentioned the accident and expressed sympathy. She hadn't known Peter Paul Pearl who became Ada's lover, although she knew who he was. Knew he died in the early nineties.

'He just died in his sleep. Far too young. Mum was devastated. They fell in love almost as soon as Peter came to board with us, and they were lucky. They stayed that way.' Rose didn't sound as though this pleased her.

'You didn't like him?'

Rose sighed. 'It wasn't up to me. Ada did. She liked that he wrote and read books, that he could talk about books, that he had a subscription to *Landfall* and one, until it carked, to *John O'London's Weekly*. After that he got the *Literary Review*. And he had the same ideas about unions and social welfare. She thought he was wonderful, she *deferred* to him. He liked that. I didn't. I thought he was using her. Took me a while to see I was mistaken. I was so sure he was out for what he could get. Understandable perhaps. He sort of came out of nowhere, a shadowy wife and two daughters in the background, as well as two not-very-successful novels. Ada made him really comfortable and I thought, yes Mr Pearl, you know when you're on to a good thing. I thought he'd decided that if he made her believe he loved her, he had a cushy number for life. I couldn't have been more wrong. He did love her. Better than that he was good for her, made her very happy. She was a truly happy woman.' Rose's voice sounded desolate.

'He wasn't a bad writer,' Olga said, 'some good stuff in his novels about the bush. And he didn't go in for beautiful Māori maidens eager to go to bed at the drop of a hat either, which is a bit different to his contemporaries.'

Rose was surprised Olga even knew Peter's name. His three novels were well out of print. Occasionally *The Man Who Loved Rain* turned up in a batch of books from an estate sale, but the other two had completely disappeared. Rose always gave a good price for it, for old times' sake, and it sat on the shelf in the shop until sooner or later Rose, feeling a sense of sadness and pity, took it home. She had a full set of his novels on the bookshelf at home plus six copies of *The Man Who Loved Rain*. She inherited the set from Ada and kept it and the extra copies because of that.

Olga has heard about The Book Stops Here. She'd heard, she said, about Rose throwing out most of the stock: not just throwing it out either. Ripping it up so no one would bother to steal any of it from the dump.

'It was pornographic,' Rose sniffed, 'stuff I'd never seen before, didn't even know existed. I felt dirty even touching the things.'

'You believe in censorship?'

'I believe in hygiene.'

They talked so much they both felt hungry. A ham sandwich for Rose, a plate of grilled ham, a couple of fried eggs and a piece of fried bread for Olga.

After another couple of drinks Rose and Olga ended up in bed where, contrary to her appearance of phlegmatic large tranquility, Olga turned out to be a thoughtful, considerate, enthusiastic lover. Somehow Rose was not surprised she enjoyed not just the sex, but Olga herself. Her body was large but didn't crowd the bed, and to lie cuddled in her arms was the most comforting feeling Rose had had for a long time. It was then she told Olga the real reason she left her teaching job.

'Bitch,' Olga said, and Rose didn't know whether she meant the girl, or Rose's lover at the time, Marcy. Then Olga smiled and said, 'You're lovely Rose, do you know that? You're lovely.' She sounded faintly astonished at herself. 'Really lovely,' she repeated and chuckled. 'I'm a woman of few words,' she said, 'but I make good use of the few I do have.'

'You're a bit of a surprise,' Rose said.

'What about you?'

'Always. Don't tell me no one told you. About me.'

'As a matter of fact,' Olga's arms tightened around Rose, 'when I was asking about various people I used to know, there was, now I come to think of it, a slight pause when I mentioned you. I thought it was tied up with your shop, and throwing out the books, and having the feminist section in the shop. They always told me about that.'

'Surely they mentioned the lesbian/gay section?'

'Oh,' said Olga, 'no they didn't. Now that's really interesting.'

They both thought about that for a minute. It was interesting.

'They didn't mention a Māori section either.' There was just the faintest question in Olga's words.

Rose smiled then Olga smiled and Rose knew she was somewhere near what she thought must be contentment. She was not really sure what to call it because she hadn't felt like that before. Was this how Ada had felt about Peter Paul Pearl?

Olga noticed the hanging on the wall. Naked, she got out of bed and stood staring at it, her fingers tracing the minute, beautifully worked stitches. 'Mmm,' she said, 'I knew your mother was a good needlewoman, I didn't know how good.'

'That's mine,' said Rose.

Olga turned, her face one huge smile. 'Why didn't you say?' she demanded, 'why didn't you say? Here I've wasted time raving about tramping and rugby, and all the time you kept this secret. Why?'

Rose laughed. 'Didn't think you'd be interested.'

Olga shrugged. 'I don't do much now, but my sisters are guns. They were brought up on tukutuku and they still do that and some weaving. They also do the Baltimore, and crazy patchwork and,' she rolled her eyes, 'the doubling wedding ring, the nine-patch number. They're real competitive. And very good. I suppose that's why I opted out. I only go for things I can win.'

Rose showed her Ada's precise and elegantly stitched Baltimore patterned quilt in what had been Ada's bedroom, and the wall hanging Ada called *Hutt Valley* which hung in the sitting room. Its blocks of finely appliquéd images represented what the area meant to Ada.

'Wow,' Olga said when she saw the block with the small feathered maro on it, 'kei te pai, kei te pai.'

'Mum had help with that,' Rose said, 'two women she'd been on some protests with, they helped her. And these two are Ada's family, see that's Africa and those little dots are the islands her grandfather emigrated from and that small skeleton is the Skeleton Woman. And this is my block.' Olga looked carefully at the sunflower sewn with its head turned away so the large deep brown centre couldn't be seen. The border was a series of books piled one on top of the other. 'Āe,' she nodded to the block, 'āe.' She grinned at Rose. 'What's this about a Skeleton Woman?'

So Rose made some tea and they sat at the kitchen table, and Rose told Olga the story of the Skeleton Woman.

FIVE

'Once upon a time in a distant country there lived a race of people made solely of bones. They had no skin, no hair, eyes or flesh. They saw their world, heard the sounds of that world and felt the touch of that world through their bones. They were called Skeleton People. The women of the Skeleton People were the Keepers of Secrets. All Skeleton People loved secrets, but only women were chosen to be Keepers of Secrets. Right from an early age girls were taught all kinds of dancing. The tango, the waltz, the slow foxtrot were primer stuff. After them, the Irish jig, the Scottish reels, the English morris dance, the Spanish flamenco, the subtle complexities of the hula. They practised, practised, practised and when they were very, very tired they practised some more. They became very dexterous with the Māori poi and worked and worked at the small, precise movements required for the dance of the emu and the more ponderous steps for the dance of the platypus.

'Yes, they loved all those different dances, but the one that really, really thrilled them, the one they yearned for with every bone in their bodies, was the tap-dance. That was the ultimate, their number-one dance, unattainable until the day of their thirteenth birthday when they joined all other girls celebrating their coming of age in the Great Hall. There they were initiated into the intricacies, the differing beats, the mind-boggling routines, the ecstasy of the tap.

'At the same time as they were introduced to tap-dancing, the skeleton girls learned that, if chosen, they must leave their island and travel to the land of the flesh-covered ones to be keepers of secrets there. Skeleton women kept safe every secret they were told or learned. They kept them safe until the time was right to let them fly. The women were chosen for this task because the men, although good at keeping secrets too, were needed at home to care for the children and old people.

'The skeleton girls went home and continued to practise. They worked and slaved and tapped until it was time for them to compete for the next stage. Once every five years on the Saturday night of the full moon, in the depths of their snow-white winter, competitions were held to see which young woman could tap the fastest, who had the most inventive routine, who could keep going the longest. These tap trials were famous all through their land. Only the very best dancers from these trials were chosen to continue, only twenty would be entrusted with studying towards the final test, and from that only one of them would be successful.

'Skeleton girls and their families travelled from towns, villages, mountains for their daughters, sisters, granddaughters to audition. Skeleton People came in their hundreds and filled the Great Hall. Eventually the twenty were chosen. For the next twelve months they worked under special coaches and teachers, all aspiring for the top prize, that of the coveted honour of Top Tap and Assistant Keeper of Secrets. They spent hours with Grand Keepers who taught them listening, reflection, patience. One of the most important aspects, one that worried every one of those twenty students, was how did they know when the time was right to let the secrets go. Some secrets seemed easy, surely only good came of their finally being set free, but it appeared that releasing or keeping secrets was always harmful to someone. Even secrets kept for decades before they were unleashed could end in tears for some quite innocent people. There were times when keeping a secret seemed to do more harm than good, when innocent people would be hurt. No matter, advised the Grand Keepers, until the time was right the secret had to be sealed up. There was intense self-doubt, there was guilt, there was indecision. Only experience brought the resolution required, only experience would equip them with the skills to support their colleagues through that most formidable of tasks, and only experience would give them the fortitude to accept that while they were learning each and every one of them would make mistakes. Take that biggest secret of all, death. How were they to know when that must be set loose? How did they weigh up the cost? This core accomplishment was debated, discussed and deliberated upon by all aspirants to the title of Assistant Grand Keeper. All knew that their entry into Assistant Grand Keeperdom would hinge not only on their proven ability to keep secrets, but very largely on their demonstration of sound judgement on the right time to break them. Examples would be put to them by their examiners. It was whispered that some of the cases presented would be trick ones and that examinees would be expected to see the difference. Each girl trembled as she waited her turn. Only one of their number would triumph. Results would not be known until after the Great Tap-Dancing Competition. When the big night came all the Skeleton People, old and young, those in perfect condition, those with bone diseases, those suffering from broken bones, all made their way to the Great Hall. They came on foot, on stretchers, in wheelchairs, using crutches or walking sticks. They came to do honour to the competitors and to be part of their most famous and deeply revered ritual.

'They sat in silence until the tap-dancing started. All twenty aspirants danced in turn in the middle of the Great Hall. The tap-tap-tapping was felt in every part of every bone in every body in the audience. Every bone, big or small, long or short, rattled with pleasure. One by one, as the hours went by and the various rounds came and went, it became apparent who would be chosen. At a certain time, and none knew when this would be, a particular dancer would receive the longest and loudest rattle the audience could summon up. It was the most chilling, the most exhilarating, the most inspiring sound everyone present would ever hear. That dancer was now declared the winner. And, as always happened, that dancer was also the one who, in the Grand Keepers' judgement, had passed with honour in the examinations. So the people's choice and the teachers' choice was the same.

'For the next five years the winner travelled around the land of the Skeleton People and demonstrated the skills which had made her the winner. Once a dancer won that tap-dancing marathon she became teacher and mentor to aspiring Keepers of Secrets as well as serving her time as Assistant Grand Keeper. She would not be invited to be one of the Grand Examiners until she'd had at least thirty years' experience at keeping secrets and in that time broken at least two very difficult and complex secrets.

'The hardest thing of all lay ahead. Leaving her island and living among the flesh-covered ones. She was advised that she must prepare themselves for the shock she would experience when she first saw the ugliness of those who have flesh covering their beautiful bones. Of course flesh gives protection to the bones, that had to be admitted, but a Keeper of Secrets never lost her preference for the clarity, the simplicity, the openness of her boniness compared to that strange soft mass of veins and arteries, muscle and ligaments, called flesh. Nevertheless she had made her choice and when the day came she sipped the potion which made her invisible and she travelled to the land of the flesh-covered ones.

'When she was living in the land of the flesh-covered ones, every now and then when the time was right, the Skeleton

Woman began to dance. Nothing could stop her. It didn't matter how much the flesh and brains and eyes and hair begged, pleaded, commanded, the Skeleton Woman danced her wild dance, arms and legs clapping, tapping, days and nights merging into days and days, nights and nights, weeks, months, until the secret took wing and flew out. This was her destiny. And theirs. Every time a secret was ready to fly, dance the Skeleton Woman must until the secret was out. She would do this over and over and over until the day it was time for her to go home, time to return to the land of the Skeleton People, time for another Skeleton Woman to take her place.

'So,' Rose smiled at Olga, 'when you hear that tappitty tap, tappitty tap, you'll know somewhere someone's secret is being freed. And you'll know that one day, one day it will be yours.' She drummed her fingers on the table. 'Tappitty tap, tappitty tap.'

SIX

'Wow,' Olga said, 'wow. So that's why that mayor in the States finally got hauled off to jail for shooting a black woman twenty years ago and why all that stuff about the Lost Generation in Australia is coming out. The Skeleton Woman. Brilliant. I must tell my sisters about this. They'll want to hear you tell the story too.'

Rose was not absolutely certain Olga was serious and it really didn't matter one way or the other. It was true that most long-held secrets did come to light in very strange ways. Look at the way that man, now forty, who killed his fifteen-year-old girlfriend because she smiled at someone else all those years ago, has just been arrested; and that woman who killed her children, three of them, buried the bodies in the vegetable garden and said her ex-husband had got custody and taken them to Australia. The skeletons were dug up twenty years later after the woman went into the local police station and confessed – prodded, Ada reckoned, by the Skeleton Woman.

'It's morning,' Olga said, 'I'd better get to work. What are you doing tonight?'

And that was the start of it. Rose doesn't really know now why she stipulated the one night a week. Self-preservation? Fear? She only knows that, at the time, having Olga to stay over one night a week was the most she could manage. This – thing – she felt was too much; she needed time, time to think about it, time to get to grips with the strangeness of it. She doesn't know why Olga accepted her dictum. Perhaps she thought

Rose would change her mind? They saw each other most days or spoke on the phone, and sometimes there was a longing to forget caution and say, see you tonight, but Rose didn't. She knew she was walking very carefully across an abyss and she was buggered if she was going to fall in. Not then, not ever again, was she going to abandon her independence, her home, her separate existence. If she did, she'd be lost.

'Before you,' Rose told Olga once, 'I hardly knew any Māori more than to say hello.'

Olga smiled. 'Maybe it was safer that way. For you.'

She had a point. 'But,' Rose said, 'whether you're Māori or lesbian or heterosexual, in some company the margins are where you live.'

Olga scoffed. 'Margins? That's a head thing Rose. Of course people try,' she said, 'my sisters got a bit turtly when I said I had realised I was a lesbian, but Leo and Mum and Dad were OK. Some of the whānau look sideways, but they just have to get over it. You can't let the majority call the shots. They will if you let them.'

'What about your family and me?'

'They'll get used to it.'

'I don't think your sisters like me.'

'It's not you. It's us. It's what we represent. They tend to forget, or not want to remember more like it, that it's all happened before, plenty of times, just not in their family. And it's usually heterosexual. So they've not only got the Māori–Pākehā thing, they've also got us. They don't like it. Not in *their* whānau.'

'Is that what they say?'

'That's what they say.'

'How do you stay so – so calm?'

'Me? Calm?' Olga laughed. 'You know what they call me?

Rocket. That's my nickname.' She hugged Rose. 'You're the one Rose, you're the one. With you I'm calm.'

'I don't know what to do.'

'You don't have to *do* anything.'

'Sometimes I feel as though I'm drowning in guilt.'

'No guilt,' Olga said, and now she sounded angry, 'no guilt. OK? For Christ's sake Rose, it's guilt that writes those bloody pathetic letters to the paper every time there's a settlement, guilt that moans when someone talks about closing the gaps and they think it means just Māori, guilt when someone jumps up and down when a council suggests having seats sets aside for Māori. Guilt sucks.'

Rose, who'd marched during the Springbok Tour, been part of groups since that discussed domestic racism, had done the Project Waitangi course on the Treaty of Waitangi, had attended classes in te reo Māori which hadn't taken, felt that if she wasn't allowed guilt and she couldn't plead ignorance, what was left? She was adrift and it was too hard.

'Just live with it,' Olga insisted, 'live with it. It'll get easier.'

Olga took whānau responsibilities seriously. 'Depends a lot on how you've been brought up. Mum and Dad were very serious about keeping in touch,' she told Rose, 'particularly as they mixed, because of Dad's job, mainly among Pākehā. I think my father's family saw him as something of a John the Baptist, the forerunner, the spreader of words among strangers. But they knew he could do something for the young Māori who were coming from the country to the city who didn't know a soul. He made contact with the Ngāti Pōneke Young Māori Club and took lots of youngsters there when they turned up on his door homesick to the core. Ngāti Pōneke was the place where they started to feel that maybe, if they could just come to the club every week, they might be able to hack life in the factory where they were working, might somehow be able to survive living in the city. Nanny and Koro had known Temuera Tokoaitua who was the pastor at Rangiatea in Otaki in the thirties. Great man. He used to bike to the railway station in Otaki, catch the train into Wellington and bike to St Thomas's in Newtown to take the service, then hop on his bike, ride back to Wellington Railway Station and travel home to Otaki. Dad knew Kingi Tahiwi who organised the choir as well. So Nanny and Koro insisted Dad take the job in the Hutt, but they said he must come home every third week. They said it only takes a couple of generations and with the third you're in trouble, and they were right. Do that and you've got once were warriors all over the place.'

Olga called the book and the film *Once Were Warriors* brilliant documentaries. She added, 'Puti could take you to some houses where *Once Were Warriors* happens every night.' Olga had three sisters. The oldest, Puti, the one who scared Rose the most, worked for Child, Youth and Family; the next one, Marama, was a case manager for Work and Income; and Makere, the one next to Olga, was a theatre administrator for Patu Whero Productions. Rose didn't know why she's so certain they don't like her – they're all pleasant, Puti especially, which is probably why Rose was scared of her. She was the one closest to Olga, the one Olga loved and argued with the most. Sure she was friendly, but when she looked at Rose, there was a reserve, a coldness. Rose was certain she was not imagining it. Puti didn't think that Rose is good enough for her baby sister.

'How did you get your name?' Rose asked Olga.

'I'm named after Mum's best friend who was on the train at Tangiwai.'

Rose remembered that tragic rail accident on Christmas

Eve, 1953. There'd been a sudden discharge of water from the crater lake on Mt Ruapehu and a huge lahar smashed down and took the Whangaehu Bridge with it. The passengers didn't have a chance. The train came charging along to the bridge and just fell into the air and down to the torrent below. A few of the passengers managed, with the help of two who'd got out, to escape, but only a few. Many of the passengers had been travelling home for Christmas, a Christmas that was now, and forever after, marred for their relatives and loved ones, and for those who survived the horror.

'Mum's friend Olga was on her way to be with Mum who was due with me. They were young nurse probationers together and they'd both been at the births of each other's children. It was a promise they made after seeing the way some nurses treated Māori patients. Olga wasn't Māori, but she wasn't going to have my mother given anything but the very best. I was born three days after Tangiwai. There was never any question what I'd be called. Olga Irihapeti – Olga, after Mum's friend, and Elizabeth, because the queen was here on her first state visit as queen. Mum's a bit of a royalist I'm afraid.'

Puti, Marama and Makere were all, as was Olga, as much constrained by habit, protocol, family pressures, as anyone else. Olga and her sisters took seriously their attendance at tangi and made huge efforts to be there at least long enough to pay their respects. Olga worried for days if she had to miss a tangi she thought she should have attended. Olga and her sisters lived and worked in the day but the past, family events, history, was a living presence. They looked into the eyes of the past, the future was behind them, touching them on the shoulder every now and then just to keep them on track. You had Olga and you had the woman in *Once Were Warriors* and you had Knock-Knock, thought Rose.

When Rose complained to Olga about Knock–Knock it was the first question she asked. 'Māori?' she said and Rose nodded.

Olga rubbed her forehead as though tired. 'Never ending,' she said, 'never ending.'

SEVEN

'When is child abuse, child abuse? That's a question police in child protection units face all the time.' So said a visiting British detective inspector from Scotland Yard quoted in the *Dominion* a day or so ago. 'But,' he added, 'the first priority must always be the safety of the child.'

Rose's eyes had gone straight to the paragraph about a teacher wrongly accused. 'What if the teacher leaves the profession as the result of a wrong accusation?' was the next question from the reporter. The detective inspector shrugged. The article didn't say this, but Rose imagined him shrugging. 'That's the price of vigilance. I'm not happy about it. I just don't know the answer.'

The price of vigilance. Rose sees the point. She agrees with it. In principle. She just didn't like it in practice. She knows, oh yes Rose knows, there've been dozens of cases where a child tells a parent or a teacher and is not believed because the man – it's usually a man – is so good at sports coaching, or works so hard for the school, it couldn't possibly be true. Or the child is from what is called a special class, so no one believes them anyway. Then a few years down the track the Skeleton Woman gets tapping and out it all comes. The guy is charged, convicted, and the child, now an adult, says lock him up forever.

I was just unlucky, thinks Rose. Occasionally she wonders what happened to that girl, what other lives she has damaged. Apart from Rose's. Apart from her own. 'I can't believe you just walked away,' Ada said. Over and over. Rose knows Olga can't believe it either. They've never really discussed Rose's actions, or lack of them, once Rose made it clear it was a no-go area. Rose knows why. That old two-faced scoundrel, Fear, masquerading as Realistic Anxiety. Pathetic really. She'd disappointed Ada, Claude and now Olga. All right for them, she thinks, it wouldn't have been them hounded by the media, filmed, hassled, investigated, every foible, every action, held up to be chewed over and spat out by the voracious mouths of television, radio and daily papers. Found guilty before she even opened her mouth. She feels a brief surge of anger then feels it dissipate. They were right. In theory anyway.

George sleeps until midnight. Jo offered, seemed to take for granted Rose would want her to do a shift while Rose has a sleep. Why should Jo suppose that because she's had two children and Rose has had none that Rose will not be able to cope? Or that because Rose doesn't want the child she won't look after him? Jo left reluctantly, and Rose could hardly wait to see her out the door.

She makes up more formula, fills the two bottles and puts the rest in a jug. She fills the kettle ready to turn on when George wakes. All through this he sleeps peacefully in Rose's washbasket. He has a lot to sleep away. Rose wonders if his little brain will retain all that's happened to him over the last couple of days or whether, with continued security, kindness, it will forget. Brains forget nothing though, she knows that.

She assembles a sandwich from the salad makings and a slab of cheese, puts everything away, washes her hands, rubs on some hand cream, sets the gas heater on medium, grabs paper and a pen and settles down at the table to work out who George's mother might be. She listens to George's breathing and wonders if his mother is missing the sound. It's not loud, but it is louder than one would expect from such a small chest. Now she's used to it this room would be empty without it. The rain has lessened but there have been heavy falls in country areas according to the radio. Rain is urgently needed, but this heavy downpour on brittle ground is causing flooding problems. Sibyl and Kitty's basement was underwater last time the river flooded.

When Sibyl, early fifties, grey-haired, infectious laugh, got her first lot of bad news, she'd gone straight from the talk with the surgeon, bought a packet of cigarettes and two bottles of chardonnay, gone home, lain down on her bed, had smoked the whole packet and drunk all the wine, all the while saying to her body, 'I'll teach you, I'll teach you.' Sibyl told Rose this while they were sitting up in bed in the hospital ward, and laughed. Rose nearly cried.

'I was as drunk as a skunk when Kitty came home, and she could hardly see me through the smoke. She thought the house was on fire!' She laughed again, so Rose laughed too.

Today though, Sibyl told her that after she left the surgeon, she drove to the river, parked the car and walked along the bank. 'I used to walk there when I was a kid,' Sibyl said. 'We had a dog. I thought of that little girl throwing the ball and the dog jumping to catch it. And then I came home.'

Rose was resentful. 'The surgeon said he was pretty sure he got it all. And the lab reports confirmed that. What happened?'

'This is the left one,' Sibyl said. 'It's either a mastectomy and no chemo, or they'll take out the lump and I'll have chemo and then radiation. Hobson's choice. Especially as I'll probably end up having the lot.'

Sibyl's news was as much of a shock, as bad a blow as that first mammogram result of her own. Rose hadn't known that kind of shock could be so undermining. If her body could grow a lump without her even realising it, anything could happen. She would never forget that first clinic. All the way home from the hospital, her breast throbbing, the pain almost unbearable from the fine needle aspiration, she thought maybe she should just have the breast cut off and be done with it. Why had she never realised how bloody delicate her body was? Instead of going straight back to the shop she'd gone home. In the kitchen she cried angrily and pounded the bench. 'Fuck, fuck, fuck!' she yelled every time her fist hit the bench. Over and over. Stupid. Didn't make her feel any better, and when she saw the red swelling on her hand, she felt worse.

Louise, the third patient in that ward, had also been anxious to know what the lab had to say about her. She thought the surgeon was not quite so sanguine about what was found in her body. She volunteered that after she first got her bad news she went home, and when her husband came home from work she told him exactly what she thought of him. He spent up large on antique furniture but was niggly about her housekeeping allowance and checked every purchase. Rose felt Sibyl stare at the words "housekeeping allowance". 'And he wouldn't let me go out to work.'

'What do you mean, he wouldn't let you?' Sibyl looked at Louise as though she was from another planet.

'He has ways,' Louise said, 'if I do anything he doesn't like he has ways. Well, it sounds so silly, he just doesn't talk. Keeps it up for weeks. I hate it. When I knew I had breast cancer I thought what the hell, I might be dead next year, I'll give him something to remember me by.'

'Why don't you leave?' asked Sibyl.

'I don't know,' marvelled Louise, seemingly unsurprised by her own passivity, 'I don't know. You get used to it. The devil you know and all that. The kids I suppose.'

'I thought your kids were grown up, left home.'

'Yes,' said Louise, 'I suppose it just doesn't seem worth rocking the boat.'

Rose thought of Claude and was grateful, which was absurd, but there you were.

Rose hadn't seen Louise for some months. Not since that awful twenty-fifth wedding anniversary party she'd invited them to. Why did they go? 'Solidarity,' Sibyl said.

The husband spoke and said how happy they'd been, what a fortunate man he was and how Louise was 'an inspiration to us all'. Everyone said how great and what a treat to see such a wonderful marriage when so many were falling by the wayside. Rose and Sibyl and Kitty sat and smiled, and sang for they are good fellows, and clapped, good-mannered witnesses, observant ghosts.

'Bastard,' Kitty said over and over, in the car on the way home to Rose's for a cup of tea, 'bastard. I'd give him antique furniture. Right where it hurts.'

Sibyl and Kitty had a house and a little bit of land in Upper Hutt where they kept chooks and bees, and grew vegetables. They'd lived in the area for thirty years. Kitty worked for a garden centre further up the valley and Sibyl taught at Wai-iti College. They bought their house and its two acres because Kitty loved the area, liked the work, and all their friends were in the district. 'No one stays in jobs for life these days,' Sibyl said, 'but it suited us. I like teaching and Kitty likes working with plants. It just suits us.'

Kitty drove Sibyl and Rose into Wellington every weekday for six weeks when they were having radiotherapy treatments. 'Do you think she's worked too hard?' Kitty asked Rose one day. 'Teaching is so demanding, and all these forms and things. Some nights she works till midnight.'

Rose said, 'If hard work caused cancer, lazy people wouldn't get it would they?'

'I wish Sibyl was a bit lazier,' Kitty said, 'wish I could get her to slow down.' She shook her head, but indulgently. She knew Sibyl. 'I used to smoke,' said Kitty, 'you can get it from inhaling other people's smoke can't you.'

There's nothing to be said to this or any of the other speculations Kitty threw up in an effort to find an answer to an unanswerable question. Poor Kitty. Sibyl told her once that she and Kitty had been girlfriend and girlfriend from when they were eighteen.

'We probably got together too young,' she said, 'because we did a lot of growing up together which was not easy, but I've never regretted it. We've both wanted to murder the other at times, but we've never wanted to leave.'

Wondering if Sibyl and Kitty are all right, hoping they haven't had the flooding the radio talks about, hoping they've got home safely through this downpour, Rose's mind shifts to her mother, Ada. Ada always seems closer in the kitchen even though it's now totally unlike the untidy, dark, hot kitchen with its crackling-under-your-feet lino Rose knew as a child.

The last time they'd spoken, Ada told Rose for at least the millionth time that she'd made a huge mistake. 'You'll regret it,' she said, 'I know you will. It's not too late. It's always best to have these things out.'

'You're repeating yourself,' Rose said.

'And I'll go on repeating myself until you do something about it,' Ada said.

There was another time Ada said that. Claude was there.

'And I'll go on repeating myself Claude until you put a stop to asking that stupid question. Just leave it. Thelma and I are friends now and that's the end of it.'

'How can you forget that Sim died in her bed?'

Rose saw her mother's face set the way it did whenever Sim's name was mentioned. Before Ada could tell Claude off any more, Rose said, 'Harry Oliver said, "Sim Anthony's let it out once too often." That's what Harry Oliver said.' Rose didn't like Harry. She had to be polite to him because he was Ada's boss, but his hands gave her the creeps. They seemed to have a life of their own. Rose made sure she was never on her own with Harry.

'For Christ's sake girl, you shouldn't be repeating things like that,' Claude said, 'and how long have you been there? You've been sneaking around listening to grown-ups again. I've told you about that. How long have you been there?'

Rose didn't answer. Claude stared at her then gave up. 'And that's a funny thing,' Claude said, off on another track, 'no one's ever seen hair nor hide of that bugger Oliver. Wonder where he went?'

'Mrs Millett reckons he went to Auckland so he could lose himself,' Rose said.

'Did she.' Claude was dying to say something else, but catching Ada's eye he decided to resist the challenge. There would be other days.

'This is all beside the point,' Ada said after a pause, 'what I want to know is what am I going to do about a job. Harry's buggered off, the pub's been taken over by a married couple and the wife will do the cleaning, and I'm out of a job. I need another one quickly.'

'I've got an idea,' said Claude, 'why don't you take in boarders? Do up the two rooms at the side of the wash-house and put in a bathroom.'

Ada looked amazed, as well she might. 'And what am I going to use for money?' she demanded.

'You've got a bit from Sim's insurance,' Claude said.

'I can't spend that, what if I get sick? And Rose is off to high school now, she'll want things, some training – if she ever drags her eyes out of a book long enough to do something practical that is.' This was a longstanding complaint of Ada's.

'Why don't you put it to music and we could have a sing-song?' suggested Claude, eyeing his sister-in-law warily. Ada burst out laughing and Claude grinned, satisfied – relieved too, probably.

'All right,' she said, 'but she does read too much, her head's always in a book, God knows what good she thinks that's going to do her.'

'Whose fault is that? She doesn't get it from Sim or me, that's for sure.'

'All right, all right,' Ada said, good humour completely restored, 'what's all this about doing up the two rooms?'

While Claude and Ada talked about the pros and cons of this idea and how Ada would pay for it – because even if Claude did the carpentery in his spare time and got a mate to do the plumbing, there were still the new baths (they decided to do up the bathroom inside at the same time) and the shower attachments ('Showers?' Ada said. 'You can charge another bob or two a week if you've got a shower,' said Claude) – Rose could only think of Ada's cooking and what a stranger would think of it. It was OK for Rose and Claude. They were used to it. Often Rose did the cooking on Sundays anyway, but what would strangers think of grey mince, watery scrambled eggs, lumpy porridge? If they were paying, they'd expect better, wouldn't they?

There was a pause and Rose got in quickly with what she'd been wanting to say all morning. 'It's a year since my father died and I haven't missed him. Not once. Now he's in my head all the time. Why have I started remembering my father after all this time? Why is he hanging around me? It's a whole year, why now?'

Ada frowned. 'Sometimes it happens,' she said after a moment, 'with grief.'

'Grief?' Rose was incredulous. She didn't feel one little bit of sadness about her father. How could she? And it was obvious he'd never cared much about his daughter. If he'd cared about his daughter he wouldn't have been in Thelma Millett's bed would he. He'd have had his heart attack at home in his own bed.

'Now, now Rose,' Claude said, 'Sim wasn't that bad. He was always good to Mum. And to me.'

It was all right for Claude. Sim was his brother. Rose didn't say this out loud.

'You'll have to live with it,' Ada said, 'that's the only way. You have to live with it.'

'For how long?' Rose demanded, 'how long?'

'If I knew that,' Ada said wearily, 'if I knew that.'

'Ada,' Claude said, 'listen to the way you talk to her. It's not right. That girl is too bloody old for her age, she's just a child really. Now she's got this bee in her bonnet about Sim.'

'I didn't *get* it,' Rose insisted, 'it just happened. It's not my fault!'

'Don't speak to your uncle like that,' said Ada.

'Well I didn't ask my father to come into my head. And I'm not a child, I'm nearly thirteen.'

Claude shook his head from side to side as if defeated. 'I hope you're satisfied Ada,' he said, sounding very doubtful, 'I hope you're satisfied.'

'I'm all right,' Rose said, firing up as she did whenever Claude criticised Ada, 'I'm all right. If people don't like the way I am they can do the other thing.'

'You even sound like your mother,' Claude grumbled then he saw her face, relented and grinned at Rose. 'Don't suppose you're too bad Rosie. Pass with a push.'

Rose grinned back at Claude, relieved. She didn't like being at odds with Claude.

'Where's Maisy?' He changed the subject. Not that he worried when Maisy was not there. She made Claude feel uncomfortable when she laughed loudly or talked over everyone. Or even when she was completely silent. ('I know she's harmless,' Rose heard him say to Ada once, 'I know that, it's just people like that give me the willies.')

'Over at Thelma's,' Ada said.

'Doesn't she get on your nerves?'

Ada shrugged. 'Everyone gets on my nerves,' she said.

'It's a lot, taking on someone like Maisy.'

'Someone has to.'

'Mrs Millett's teaching Maisy to sew,' said Rose.

'And good luck to her,' Ada said.

'You can duck the issue as long as you like Ada.' Claude decided to have another try. 'I'll never understand how you can be so pally with Thelma Millett when it was her bed Sim died in.'

Ada breathed heavily but didn't answer.

Rose nearly laughed at the expression on Claude's face.

'Now Claude,' Ada got in fast before he could say anything else, 'you remember the party? Tuesday night. Early. Don't want these two up too late on a school day. I wanted to have the party at the weekend, but no.' Ada frowned at Rose.

'Well Jo's is Monday and mine is Tuesday, and seeing this is the first year we've celebrated it together, we tossed for whose night to have it on and I won.'

'What's that got to do with making it easy on everyone and having it on Saturday? And you're not having the music too loud. Too loud and the party's over.'

Rose didn't answer. She knew they would have the party on the Tuesday night because Ada had promised, just as she knew that if the music got too loud Ada would turn it off.

'Maybe,' Olga suggested, when Rose told her how Ada met Peter Paul Pearl, 'your father suddenly imposed himself on your consciousness because he knew that Peter Pearl was coming into your life. Maybe he was warning you.'

It began when Peter Paul Pearl saw there were two rooms and said he'd take both and use one for a study if Ada didn't mind moving the bedroom furniture out. A study. That was the word that did it for Ada. Study. A study denoted scholarly contemplation, deep discussion, maybe even the actual writing of books. In her rooms. In what used to be her wash-house. She was half-fascinated, half in awe, from the word go. Ada had always been mad about books which was one reason people thought she got infected with socialism. I mean look at her, they said. Brought up in a household that didn't know the meaning of hunger, someone who didn't know what it was to be cold, who always had a room to herself and new clothes and shoes whenever she needed them. Ada Jones didn't have to wait till her father's pay day to buy the exercise book the teacher said she needed. Must have been all those books.

This was not how it happened though. Like most people, Ada became interested in changing a particular social system for personal reasons. If the 1951 Lockout was the springboard for her involvement with workers and conditions of work, if this began because of Sim and Claude, and was rapidly strengthened during the one hundred and fifty-one days the lockout lasted, it was the job she got cleaning in a pub after Sim's death which put the iron in her spine and made her start asking questions about pay and conditions.

After that you could guarantee Ada Anthony would be poking her nose in where it wasn't wanted. In the seventies and eighties she'd have been called strident. In the early sixties she was called 'lippy'. A lippy woman. Far too much to say for herself.

'One good thing,' Rose smiled reminiscently, 'I got the new bed from the other room and Mum put Maisy in the sleeping porch on my old one. No more sharing my bed, no more drifting off to sleep with the faint tang of Maisy's feet in my nostrils. She washed them, but I could always smell sweaty socks and dusty sandals. And she snored. Ada asked the doctor, and he said people like Maisy couldn't help it.'

'You disliked Peter Pearl,' Olga said. 'Why didn't you dislike Maisy?'

Rose tried to remember. 'I don't know,' she said, 'perhaps it was because the other kids were horrible to her, or because her father was so hopeless. Mum said he'd lost it when his wife died, but I think he was ashamed of Maisy and just wanted her out of his sight. Anyway Mum was right, someone had to. Maybe I just felt sorry for her and I didn't feel sorry for Peter.'

'Did he live up to your mother's expectations?'

'Oh yes. Oh yes. Very well set-up in no time. A desk, a couple of chairs; he had a blotter in a leather frame on his desk and a bottle of ink placed just so, some pens and pencils, a paperweight, and a ream of plain white paper. Oh, and a type-writer, a high-standing old thing.'

'You should have hung on to it. Fetch a fortune in an auction nowadays.'

'After he died his daughters came and took everything.'

EIGHT

Enough. Enough. Who does Rose know who's the right age to be George's mother? Anyone up to forty-five she supposes. Has to be someone who comes into the shop. But why would a customer, someone who only knows her from buying or exchanging second-hand books from her shop, leave a baby with her? Doesn't make sense. For all anyone who comes into the shop knows about her, she could be a complete psycho. She knows a bit about books, can talk about them or keep her mouth shut, whatever the customer wants. She can keep her temper, even with smart mouths. 'I see you've got a feminist section,' he says, obviously thinking he's very clever, very original, 'so I wondered where the menist section was.' And he pauses, waiting for applause from the other two male customers in the shop. They are Carlos Stubbs, who loves The Book Stops Here and is always keen to work when Rose needs someone, and Leo Phillips, Olga's son, on holiday from medical school. The joker doesn't get much change from them. Carlos and Leo smile at each other behind his back. Rose will deal with this idiot.

'There,' Rose says, smiling full-on at the bugger, 'there are the sections you want. Sir.' She points to the sports, westerns, and poetry sections. The man snorts but decides not to persist.

Ninety percent of the poetry Rose sells is bought by men, just as ninety percent of the fiction she sells is bought by women. Which says something about gender differences. Rose doesn't know exactly what. That men like poetry? Enjoy density? Like a cut-to-the-chase read? Want to impress someone? That women like stories? Can't handle reality? Enjoy escapism? See there are more truths in fiction than in non-fiction? But you could say the same thing about poetry, couldn't you.

Occasionally she is lucky enough to find something someone has asked her to keep an eye out for and she might talk to this customer for a few minutes, but what does that prove? The shop is open six days a week. Rose keeps it clean and inviting. Every Thursday afternoon she rearranges the front window. The week before last she had a window full of books on parenting your own kids, other people's kids, both non-fiction and fiction. It was a lively and colourful window display because she borrowed some children's clothes from the department store in the mall and pegged them to a line across the back of the window. She received lots of approving comments about that window but really, was that enough for someone to feel she was trustworthy enough to look after their baby? This Thursday for instance it had been a window of books on pets. Didn't mean Rose was any good with animals. Thinking of the black stray cat which she chases away every time she catches it sleeping on the pantry window sill, just the reverse actually, she thinks.

No, it must be someone she knows from somewhere else. Who does she know who has a baby? Doesn't matter whether you know them well or not Rose, whoever's done this is obviously not in their right mind so put their names down.

Lizzie. Thin Lizzie, Claude calls her. His idea of a joke. As out of date as 'there, there'.

'She's not thin,' Rose said, 'well maybe a little bit, it's the fashion Claude, she's got Thelma's looks anyway, lucky thing.'

Jo and Wesley's Lizzie. Rose hasn't seen Lizzie since she visited her after the baby was born. And she'd only done that because of Thelma. The baby was Thelma's great-grandchild after all. Ada would have wanted her to visit. Took Lizzie the obligatory card and some miniscule bootees. She still looked beautiful, but her large dark eyes were tired and there were blue shadows under them. That was to be expected. She'd just had a baby. Now Rose thinks of it, she's not absolutely sure whether it was a boy or a girl. The small red wrinkled face was deeply asleep when she peered into the cot.

Lizzie, when young, occasionally accompanied Thelma when she popped over to see Rose, home on holiday. A bright little face if it hadn't been for the discontented expression. Thelma had shaken her head over Jo's handling of Lizzie's refusal to go to church when the girl was fourteen, maybe fifteen. A storm in a teacup anyway because, as it turned out, Lizzie was married from the Church of the Golden Light, and married into one of its founding families, what's more. Very suitable, everyone said. Lizzie looked lovely and Royston seemed a pleasant enough young man. He might look dull, but he had a nice smile. Rose is prepared to like Royston because his great-grandfather Elmore built her house. A bit tenuous, but that's how likes and dislikes happen. Rose met Royston's grandfather – Harvey, Ada's contemporary – once, but she won't think about that at the moment. She can't remember Royston's father's name. Yes, she can. He's called Elmore, after his grandfather. Shortened to Ellie. Ellie Hipp. To the right of Genghis apparently. Come on Rose. Get on with it. Farting about with who's related to whom is a sure sign you're getting old.

Betty Home's daughter. Anne. Big girl. Shy. Wore braces for years. Betty owns Calico and Cottons, next door to The Book Stops Here, and Anne used to help out after school and on

Saturdays. Anne had a baby about three months ago. Didn't seem to be a father in evidence and Rose hadn't asked. Rose has seen Anne and the baby, smiled, said what a lovely baby, now she can't even remember whether it's a boy or a girl either. She doesn't really know Anne anyway. Pleasant enough in the shop, but her shyness and her unwillingness to smile because of the braces she wore made being served by her anything but a pleasure. Rose's association with Betty is different. It stems partly from them both having shops in the same area, but mainly because Betty has such a great shop. It is fatal for anyone keen on quilting, patchwork, appliqué, embroidery (any craft really) to enter Calico and Cottons, absolutely fatal. Rose has never gone into that shop without buying something. 'I bet I'm Betty's best customer,' she told Olga once. 'That's what Puti says,' Olga said, 'she says Betty doesn't sell fabric and sequins, she sells dreams.'

Surely Betty would say if Anne was in any trouble? But would she? Rose doesn't talk about her personal life to customers or other shop owners. Why would Betty?

There's Millie. Yes, Millie. Now Millie's a distinct possibility. Perhaps a bit obvious? Millie with the blue and red spikes of hair, the nose ring, and the long, long legs. Rose knows Millie from a series of encounters when Millie was squatting in the old house across the road. About a year ago. Must have been a little while after Ada's accident. After a screaming and shouting match with her boyfriend, Millie had stormed out of the flat they shared. She'd taken no money, no clothes, not even a sleeping bag. She was at odds with her parents who don't like the boyfriend so she couldn't, or wouldn't, go home. She remembered the empty houses in Little Salamander. She'd been to a party in one once. Perhaps, Rose asked tentatively, it was the same one Lizzie went to, they were about the same age. But Millie didn't think Lizzie was there. 'She was a year ahead of me,' Millie said, as though that decided it. Rose thinks she's wrong. There couldn't have been two teenage parties in the empty houses which both got out of hand and ended with police being called, could there? Olga had looked at Rose pityingly when she'd passed this thought on to her.

'We'd all just finished School C exams,' Millie said, 'thought it'd be good to have our party in an empty house. Someone called the police. But anyway I remembered. So that's why I'm here. I've just missed a period,' Millie told her, 'Mum'll kill me.' Rose found the girl's frankness astonishing, but engaging.

Millie didn't seem too worried. She asked if she could use Rose's shower and Rose felt she couldn't say no. She also gave Millie breakfast when Millie felt like eating and lent her a sleeping bag. Rose was awed by Millie's apparent unconcern about her situation. If it had been Rose, she'd have been climbing the wall.

'What's the use of worrying?' asked Millie. 'If I am pregnant it's no use, and if I'm not, there's no point.'

Rose thinks there is definitely something scary about this philosophical viewpoint but she can't, at the moment, see what it is. Now she wonders if it's because it leaves out worrying. Rose thinks she's probably addicted to worrying, that it's habitual, second nature. To leave it out of the loop is unnerving somehow. She thinks of the slaves her great-grandfather may have been involved in transporting to America. When they were told that they were now free men and women some stood rock still, unable to move, aghast as they stared into space at this unknown thing called Freedom. Slavery, being treated as less than human, was what they knew, was familiar, comforting. Freedom was too frightening, too strange. Sometimes it took two generations to change this. Even that was lightning quick compared to lots of white southern homes where new generations were imprinted from birth, it seemed to Rose, with their parents' entrenched beliefs on racial superiority.

She has heard news reports and seen the evidence of how quickly those kind of emotions can rise in the firing and desecrating of some Islamic churches in the United States and in the assaults on people thought to be Muslims, one death even. As though their outrage and panic over the terrorist attacks could be quietened by the use of fists, pipes, torches on innocent individuals, all of whom were citizens of the same country. These acts of aggression made an ugly contrast to the courage and resilience and yes, kindness, now flowing through New York City itself which she'd seen and heard about in those same news reports. Maybe you scratch some people and find courage and kindness where in others you find hatred and cowardice. All too deeply entwined ever to be separated.

That's how you and worry are, she thinks irritably, firmly entwined, you can't bloody live without it. If we're talking scary, Rose tells herself, you don't need to look any further than right here. She decides to leave it. She's got enough on her plate. Where was she. Millie.

Millie said, 'Anyway, he'll be back. He's crazy about kids. Always fooling around with his brothers, playing rugby and that. Actually he needs to grow up himself.' Millie was right. Her boyfriend turned up a couple of days later, distraught and penitent, having looked all over town for her, and she gave him another chance. Must be the sex, thinks Rose, what else can it be?

Rose saw Millie some months later, with her smiling mother, when she came into the shop to show Rose the baby. She can't remember that baby's face either, thinks it was a girl, but she's not sure. Millie had left her boyfriend again – for good this time, so she said. 'He wants me to marry him,' she said, 'can you imagine?' Millie's mother raised her eyebrows at Rose and her lips tightened, but then she relaxed them as she smiled besottedly at the baby. So Millie, minus the nose ring, plus her baby, is living with her parents, God help them. And I'm getting nowhere, thinks Rose.

Maybe she's going down the wrong path. Maybe it's not the mother who left the child on Rose's back porch disguised as a carton of tomatoes. Maybe it's the mother who has problems and someone has removed the baby from her care? And left him with Rose? Well, it could be. Stranger things have happened. In that case it could be someone older. Maybe it is someone older. Or maybe some fool wanted to leave a baby with the last person in the world a baby should be left with. To put the mother off the track. Obviously *someone* connected with this baby has problems. The bruises on George's arm are evidence of that. Rose feels her head buzzing unpleasantly. She is tired.

Something's up with Jo, that's for sure. It could be Lizzie. It could be anything. Maybe Wesley's having an affair. Maybe Jo is. It's true Jo and Lizzie have been at odds since the girl was fourteen – before, probably – but plenty of mothers and daughters are like that. It's not exactly new. Whichever way you look at it, for any of these women to leave their babies with Rose was too absurd to be taken seriously. Yes Rose, but it is serious because someone has. She sees the little blue arm waving. Who else does she know who could have babies?

There's Leo, Olga's son. He's safely in Dunedin isn't he? Studying to be a doctor. In his last year at med school. As far as Rose knows, he doesn't even have a steady (dated word, Rose!) girlfriend. An image of Leo, a screaming baby under his arm, struggling on and off planes from Dunedin to Wellington and then getting the shuttle to Lower Hutt, not to mention finding a tomato carton, before he drops the baby off at Rose's, makes her smile. Even supposing Leo has fathered a baby with a woman no one's ever heard of, he'd surely head straight to Olga, he wouldn't dump a baby on Rose. The whole thing is ridiculous.

She likes Leo. Last holidays he had to do some sort of survey. He dropped in for a cup of coffee and started talking about the camping weekend Olga and Rose had just had which had ended in disaster. Like Olga, Leo can't really understand why Rose hated the experience so much.

'Look Leo,' Rose said, 'just take my word for it. And that word is disaster. An absolute disaster. OK, it was my fault. Olga was so enthusiastic about the joys of sleeping in the open, the fresh air, the delights of walking through bush. Against my better judgement, I agreed. That was my big mistake. I made one condition. There must be a tent. Modern, waterproof, all the trimmings. Well there was a tent. Bright yellow and blue. It was waterproof, which was just as well because it pissed down all weekend. It was very nice sharing a sleeping bag with Olga but she trod on my mascara, my back muscles were in agony after carrying the backpack and there was no Panadol, and the dehydrated potatoes made me heave. And the rain –'

'You can't blame camping for the weather,' Leo said, trying not to laugh.

'Then,' Rose's voice was charged with indignation, 'in the middle of the second night, in the pouring rain, we were woken by a bull! The bloody thing nudged me in the back. Well I didn't know what it was at first. Then we heard this slobbery sniffle, Olga said it must be a bull, and I screamed. What did she expect? She said they must have heard me in Auckland. Anyway, it frightened the bull and it took off – quickly followed by me. I'm just not suited to any kind of lifestyle which doesn't include showers and heated towels, Leo. Pathetic I know, but that's the way it is.'

Leo grinned, he'd heard the story of the ill-fated trip from his mother and wanted to get Rose's version. He picked up the clipboard. 'What have you done with your life,' he asked, 'in twenty-five words.' He had to do twenty of these idiotic interviews to get paid.

Rose repeated the words as a question. 'What have I done with my life?'

He nodded. 'Crazy eh?'

'Not as crazy as camping. What have I done with my life. Well, I've lived it I suppose,' Rose said finally and shrugged, 'what else is there to do?'

'I like that,' Leo said, 'I like that. Now. What do you do when there are bad times?'

'I tie a knot and move on,' Rose said after some more thought. 'Or,' she added, 'I run away.'

'What do you do when there are good times?'

'The same,' Rose said promptly, and they both laughed.

What about Malcolm? Malcolm, Lizzie's brother. A sort of carbon copy of his father minus the devotion to the Church of the Golden Light and the walk shorts. Ten years older than Lizzie (Jo had had some miscarriages in between those two), formerly the head of English at Wai-iti College, now an adviser on education working at Parliament. He lives with a woman who makes cushions. Beautiful, lush creations which cost a fortune. And good luck to her, thinks Rose. There's a lot more to a good cushion than people think. What was her name? Something Irish. Finola. A little older than Malcolm, family on the West Coast. Into permaculture and organic gardening apparently. Must have to wear gloves if she wants to keep her hands smooth for the cushions. Odd partnership really, but you never know about other people. Finola. Always reminds Rose of that man. Fintan Tuohy. Changed his name to Fintan Patrick Walsh. The Black Prince, people called him. He worked from the shadows, a bit like Iago. Ada hated him. Rose never quite knew why. She had an idea he'd made a pass at Ada.

Maybe Malcolm and Finola had had a baby. And kept it secret? Getting ludicrous, Rose. She's hardly said hello to Malcolm in a year, but has met Finola once during that time because she arrived to visit Lizzie as Rose was saying goodbye. There's no way Malcolm or Finola would leave a baby with her, even if they had one. They're practically strangers. It had been funny though, the way Finola stared at her as if she was some new plant or insect in which she was interested but wary. Maybe Finola always looks at people like that.

'Those papers Malcolm did on public policy have stood him in good stead,' Leo said to Rose. He didn't say it sarcastically but his voice was not pleasant either.

'What exactly is public policy?' Rose asked, thinking of George Orwell.

Leo said, 'Theoretically it's the process of research and the analysis that goes into formulating government policy. Practically most of it gets binned, a large part is a complete waste of time and money, and a fraction, if you're lucky, might prove to be useful.'

Rose frowned so Leo added, 'I suppose it has some merit, this advice these experts hand out. Very *Yes Minister* though. What Finola sees in Malcolm I'll never know.' Oh ho, thought Rose, like that is it?

'Look,' Leo said, reaching into the New Zealand non-fiction, 'this is good. This woman was a political advisor for a number of years. Read it.'

'*Looking For Honey*. Linnie Duggan.' Rose nodded. 'OK.'

'It's good,' repeated Leo, 'but depressing.'

The life of a political advisor sounded much like her mother's life. Always beating your head against the proverbial brick wall, lots of telephone conversations, meetings, interruptions, disappointments, and even when there was a success it was always partial. Nobody ever told the truth although they didn't tell outright lies either. They couldn't afford to tell the entire truth because it would be manipulated by a journalist or an opposition politician, couldn't just say we're just having a look at this, because 'this' would then be presented as an established fact, and all hell would break loose. And if you wrote a memo about it, and it got 'leaked' to the media, all hell did break loose. You had to keep in sweet with all sections. Linnie Duggan reckoned everyone, of whatever political hue, was united in their dislike of unionists. Tory politicians think they're devils incarnate and socialist politicians see them as loose cannons who will lose them votes.

Rose liked Leo. He was easy to have around. Content to sit on a chair and read. Another serendipitous browser who said he got no time for this in Dunedin. 'This is my holiday,' he said. Although he and Olga didn't agree on everything they had an easygoing relationship which Rose thinks reflected well on Olga. Although there were always undercurrents. Just as there were between herself and Ada. We were too much alike, thought Rose, my mother and I. Both one-eyed, dogmatic, argumentative. Rose had long ago forgiven Ada the months of hard drinking after Sim died, but not the legacy of uncontrollable anxiety when she was in the company of anyone who'd had more than three drinks, her fear of their unpredictable behaviour. And she was not sure she'd ever lost the shock she got, the incredulity she felt, when she discovered that her mother was sleeping with Peter Pearl. Claude said he'd seen it coming a mile away and Rose should have too. 'You go round with your eyes shut?' grumped Claude.

Olga's theory was that Rose was, naturally enough, jealous of Peter's place in her mother's life. 'You were thirteen. Your father had died in, well, strange circumstances; you and your mother were very close, then this odd little man comes along and pushes you out of your place in the nest,' Olga postulated. 'Only human nature that you resented it, and him. Just like you've never liked Elena. Simply because Claude married her, not because there's anything inherently unlikeable about the woman.'

Rose laughed. 'Thank you Sigmund,' she said. 'You may well be right. Peter was certainly different to my father. You couldn't have got more opposite personalities. Sim was so outgoing and Peter Paul Pearl has to be the shyest adult man I've ever met. For a stranger to get a word out of him was like pulling a tooth.'

'Perhaps Ada had had enough of gregariousness.'

'As for Elena, I know she's going through hell, but in a way it's her own call. She could take more pain relief.'

'She hates the effects of them. Says she only feels half-alive.'

Rose knew that feeling only too well. They'd prescribed Tamoxifen for her after the operation but she'd hated it. Other women, she knew, either had no choice or felt no effects, but she did, so she stopped taking the tablets. She knew how Elena felt. She remembered Claude announcing he and Elena were getting married and her angry disappointment that it wasn't Ada and Claude, her panic when a few weeks later Elena asked her to be a bridesmaid. She'd said yes, of course, what else could she say? She wouldn't have hurt Claude's feelings for the world, let alone risked Ada's indignation and annoyance. Rose would never have heard the end of it. Fortunately Elena was as difficult as it was possible for any bride to be. She changed her mind on colours about six times, then when she'd settled on pink, which had been her first choice anyway, she took another week to choose between chiffon or taffeta. Rose had fancied something plain and stylish, but Elena wanted and got gathers, flounces, rosebuds and large droopy picture hats as they were called. 'I only intend to be married once,' she said, 'might as well make the most of it.' She loved Claude, there was no doubt about that and even Rose had to admit, but only to herself, that he looked happy enough. Elena wore white and had a long flowing veil. She looked like Margaret Lockwood in a B-grade movie. Totally unsuitable, Rose thought, for an older woman.

'God, I was such a judgemental little bitch,' Rose reminisced to Olga.

'Most of us are,' Olga said, 'at that age. It's all so simple and straightforward then. If everyone behaved and thought just like us then everything in the world would be all right.'

In all the wedding photos Rose was frowning or blinking. 'It was those shoes,' she told Ada when she asked crossly if it would have hurt Rose to smile. 'Elena insisted on those awful high-heeled sandals which were not only impossible to walk in but dangerous. I felt like an idiot child dressed up for a costume drama.'

Rose's injured tone made Ada's face clear and a slight grin appeared. 'Elena's not the only drama queen round here,' she said, 'and for God's sake don't add to it by whining.'

Rose must have looked mutinous because Ada said, 'Well I think Elena looked wonderful,' then she added, 'get over it Rose. You can't have things happen just because you want them to.'

'I don't know what you mean.'

'Oh for God's sake grow up,' snapped Ada, then she sighed and tried again. 'There are some things you can't change. The sooner you see that and accept it, the happier you'll be.'

Rose didn't stalk away, you didn't do that to Ada, she had to satisfy herself with maintaining a cold silence. It was all her mother's fault anyway. Anyone could see Claude was worth a million Peter Paul Pearls. You only had to look at their names for a start. What sort of a man was called Peter Paul Pearl?

Elena's condition was very hard on Claude. To see someone you love being tortured by that horrible disease must be awful. Even so the uneasiness still between her and Elena was not all Rose's doing. Elena was often cool when they met, was given to snide remarks about Rose's clothes. '*Another* new outfit?' she marvelled, or, 'wish I could afford that fabric.'

'She's probably just nervous,' Olga said.

'Nervous!' scoffed Rose, 'what's she got to be nervous about? Oh no, I know what it is. From the first time we met she thought I was a spoilt little madam, and she still does. She and Claude have been married for yonks, twenty-eight years, something like that, and I never go to Claude and Elena's without an invitation. So it's not just me.'

'What about Claude?'

'He wants to keep on side with the both of us so he ignores it.'

'I tried that,' Olga told her. 'Doesn't work. Apart from Leo my marriage was a mistake. A big one. Not just for me. We knew it and I think we'd have done something about it when Leo was older. We were meant to be friends, nothing else. ' She laughed. 'No mistaking whose son he is though.' Leo, named after his father, had inherited his dad's dark copper hair. 'Tūhoe,' Olga said.

Go away, Rose tells Olga in her head. She puts her hand to her mouth, remembers kissing Olga, feels her really close. 'Go away,' she says out loud, 'go away.'

She has to go to bed. Some sleep might do it. If she starts thinking every woman who comes into the shop is George's mother she'll be here all night. She gets up and peers at George. Should he be sleeping this long? Don't be silly Rose, apart from shitting and crying this is what babies do. She shakes her head. When you think about it, the responsibility is huge. Who could have put him on her porch?

Well she knows one regular it couldn't be. Too old for one thing. Mrs Connor, at least eighty, was a Mills & Boon fan. She exchanged fourteen Mills & Boons every week. Her memory was failing a bit so as long as she didn't do it too close to the last time she read them, she happily accepted books she'd read at least six times before. Her husband read Westerns, non-stop by the look of things because he exchanged twenty every time they came in. There was nothing wrong with his memory. He just enjoyed reading the same books. 'Doesn't like surprises,' his wife said, indulgently. They lived in what was once a state house and still found time to grow their own vegetables and keep a couple of chooks for the eggs. For a treat they would listen to the National Radio *Listeners' Requests* on a Saturday night. They enjoyed hearing the old songs. 'And it's not unknown for us to get up and have a dance,' Mrs Connor confided. Rose imagines them sitting one each side of their fireplace, both reading and listening to the radio, one occasionally catching a glance from the other, smiling and saying, 'Shall we?' Both of them rode bicycles still, their only concession to modernity, crash helmets. They rode in single file – he went first of course. 'Likes to think he's the boss,'

Mrs Connor said, in the same indulgent tone, 'and I think, well, he's getting on, why not?'

Go to bed. Go to bed Rose. Leave it to the Skeleton Woman. The only trouble with that, Rose thinks, is that she takes her time. I don't want to be greeting George's mother when I'm in the middle of hosting his twenty-first. Shit, thinks Rose, I'll be over seventy. If the cancer doesn't come back. Come on, she says to the Skeleton Woman, come on, get a move on.

NINE

The night her father had a heart attack and died in Thelma Millett's bed was the night Ada told Rose the story of the Skeleton Woman and the night she also told Rose about Manny. The two are linked because it was Manny, Ada's grandfather, who told Ada's mother who told Ada about the Skeleton Woman who kept secrets secure until she decided to set them free. The one who appeared when you were dying to take you safely to the heart of that last big secret. Ada and Rose stayed awake all night and talked about Manny and the Skeleton Woman so they wouldn't have to talk about Sim. At the time Rose was twelve and Ada, thirty-seven. Jo Millett was Rose's best friend but Thelma, Jo's mother, and Ada didn't ever speak. Rose didn't know why.

Manny was from São Tiago, one of the Cape Verde group of islands that lie spattered like grains of freshly ground black pepper off the West Coast of Africa. He came to New Zealand in the late 1860s, after jumping ship in New England and made his way via California to the gully they named after Gabriel. He ended up in the Catlins, in the South Island, and stayed in the area because he loved it. Not surprisingly, coming from islands that had terrible killing droughts, he loved the wetness, the green of it. Rose saw him, a short (Ada said he was short) stocky man, lifting his arms towards the thick grey rain, revelling in the wet, unable to believe his good fortune, standing in it until he was drenched. 'His islands,' Ada explained, 'suffered terrible year-long droughts. That's why the name is such a paradox. It suggests greenness, lush growth, abundance. Verde means verdant.'

'So why?'

'Because when it was discovered by Portuguese mariners the islands were all covered with lush vegetation. They all rushed home and raved, and their enthusiasm enticed the authorities into sending men to colonise the Cape Verde islands. They brought in slaves from the African coast to do the hard labour and the islands became a base for ships transporting slaves to Europe and America.'

'Do you mean my great-grandfather was a slave trader?'

'We'll never know,' Ada said.

'Gee,' Rose was more fascinated than horrified, 'a slave trader. That's a secret though, eh?'

'I don't think he was. Maybe I don't want to think he was. He could have worked on one of the slave-trading vessels. Another thing I discovered was that the Cape Verde islands were once sacked by your hero, the great Sir Francis Drake, in the late 1500s.'

'Oh.' Rose was disappointed. She enjoyed reading about Sir Francis Drake's exploits in the *Golden Hind*, but if he had wrecked her relation's houses and stolen things from them, he wasn't such a hero after all.

'A couple of centuries later the islands were hit by these really severe droughts. The settlers had deforested like hell and overgrazed so that made things a lot worse. One hundred thousand people starved to death. The Portuguese government did sweet nothing. So by the time Charles Darwin called in he found only dry and barren islands. You can read about Cape Verde in the first chapter of *The Voyage of the Beagle*. Bound to be a copy in the library.'

'What was his name? My great-grandfather. Manny.'

'Emanuel I suppose. Manny for short. By the time I knew

him he was very deaf and he had a really thick accent so talking to him was a struggle. His surname was Jonis, but the postmaster, who was the local justice of the peace, changed the i to e and made it Jones on his naturalisation papers. Must have thought it looked better. My father agreed with him. When he did find out what his true name was he didn't want to know. I don't know where he thought his father got his accent from. I suppose Jones was more English-sounding, more respectable.

'Manny lived in a little crib in our backyard. He never came inside the house. When it rained he sat outside, in a chair by the door, just sat there silent for hours, in the rain. He didn't let anyone inside his place, even Mum. She washed his sheets and his clothes but he always met her at the door. She said as far as she could tell from the quick glance, which was all she got, the place was spotless. He cooked for himself, had a beaut veggie garden which we shared, and bought his meat from the butcher when he called, occasionally caught some fish or killed a chook. He trusted no one. I used to think that maybe he had a bag of gold nuggets in there, or a trunk of jewels from the shipwreck. But of course he didn't. According to Mum he ended up in this country because of a shipwreck. He was one of a few survivors who landed up on a beach in the Catlins. Well, that's what she told me. I can see him now, sitting there in the rain, just staring in front of him. I used to watch him out of the kitchen window. Wonder what he was looking at. Now I think what he actually saw was inside him. Mainly though, when I think of my grandfather, I see him sitting in the rain and loving it. He loved it and he died in it. One day he left his little crib and walked into the bush. There,' Ada's voice deepened into her storyteller's voice, 'there in the lush, enveloping, verdant green that'd held him in its thrall since he first saw it fifty years before; there, the Skeleton Woman beckoned and Manny, his arms lifted in one final embrace to the rain he adored, took one last step and fell smiling on the tender drenched spread of it.'

Ada's voice changed, became hard and unforgiving. 'He walked into the bush because my father told him he would have to go into a home. My father had got this flash job with Essex and Sons, and he didn't want his father tagging along, especially not when he couldn't speak good English and re-fused to live inside his son's house. A man who deliberately stayed outside when it was raining instead of running inside like all normal people. My mother tried to persuade my father differently, but it was useless. I think Manny had been a thorn in my father's side for years. His mother died when my father was quite young, so Mum told me, and Manny and my father never got on. He only had him living on the section because he owed the old man money and it was a good way to get out of paying it back.

'When I announced I was going to marry Sim, Dad hit the roof. I can see why now. At the time I realised that for his daughter to marry someone he didn't like meant she was escaping his control, but I didn't realise till later that he had other marriage plans for me. I was going to be his entrée into the Essex family and their social standing. As it happened I did like Donald Essex. If I hadn't got that puncture and if Sim hadn't come along and fixed the tyre I might have married Donald.'

'And there would have been no me,' said Rose.

'Oh I think you'd have turned up somewhere in my life. In any case, once I met Sim, that was it. Too young,' Ada said, 'I was too young and too stupid.'

This memory's pretty suspect as memories often are. It's a while since she read it, but Rose is pretty sure the stuff about Manny's death is from Peter Paul Pearl's novel. And some of the details have surely come from later conversation, reading and some searching on the internet she did herself. But, thinks Rose, we all make our own memories, this one's got accretions that are just a bit more obvious than most. But only to me.

She remembered a customer once telling her about her mother who'd got it into her head that her daughter was featuring in a particular television commercial she liked. An ad for an airline. The customer said, 'Mum, the hair's all wrong and the eyes are a different colour. As for the singing, that's actually Kiri Te Kanawa. It's definitely not me.' Her mother listened, pursed her lips in disbelief and said, 'Well I'm going to believe what I believe.'

Ada had very strong ideas too. She didn't see why Rose or she should go to Sim's funeral service. 'Your father's dead,' Ada said to Rose, 'all the sermons, hymns, flowers, all those trimmings are not worth a tinker's curse beside the fact that he died in that woman's bed. If you want to go though Rose, you go. When all's said and done he's the only father you'll ever have.'

Ada didn't speak to her daughter as though she was another grown woman because she had any particular philosophy on bringing up children. It was her nature to be direct, to say what she thought, and it never occurred to her to modify this trait because Rose was twenty-five years younger and lots of times didn't really grasp what Ada was on about. How could she? Ada's critics said this was what made Rose different. They said they were not surprised she turned out to be a lesbian. These people also thought their little darlings never said fuck in the playground and that if there was any trouble their sons or daughters couldn't possibly be the instigators.

Rose learned, painfully at times, that she was not older than her age, that she didn't really know much more than her contemporaries. She might be ahead of the game in some areas, that was all. She knew a lot of basic things like how not to cook (watching Ada had taught her that for sure); she knew how to make a penny go further, how to grow vegetables, how to do cross stitch, and, like all her peers, how to be stoic. She also knew about sex, reproduction, knew that her father was the first man her mother fell in love with. While Ada and Rose often discussed past emotions, they never talked about the present ones, about Ada's love for Peter Paul Pearl, Claude's love for Ada, his marriage to Elena. Or about poor Maisy's death. All anyone, including Ada, said about Maisy was that people like that were prone to chest infections and that they always got them worse than anyone else. Ada and Rose never discussed the way hate and grief never quite let go. How years and years later you could be caught by a surge of rage or tears over something you'd swear you'd forgotten, become reconciled with, adjusted to. The way those matters lie, a great river underneath talk and action, disturbed by sometimes quite minor, seemingly un-related occurrences, is something Rose found hard to tolerate. Like a cancer of the emotions, Rose thought, hidden, dan-gerous, unpredictable.

Rose didn't ask questions. She wasn't an asking-questions child. So as well as Ada making assumptions about her daughter's understanding of the things she said or implied, Rose made her own assumptions about other people. She thought that when they behaved differently they were being wilfully obtuse or deliberately hurtful. Rose never quite accepted that she felt some things deeply and other people felt other things deeply and that was the way life was arranged. So there were clashes. As with Olga, as with Olga. There had never been a clash like that with Jo, just a slow diminution of what was once called friendship. She didn't really know this present Jo at all. She was a stranger. Why did that happen? When? Might as well ask why hadn't scientists found a cure for cancer? Or arthritis? Elena suffered so cruelly, it was torture.

Come on Rose, you might as well ask why isn't it summer all the time? Things happen. Jo has changed. You've changed. She hopes Olga hasn't changed. She wants to think of Olga suffering, mourning the loss of Rose, wishing she'd never opened her mouth. Quite a nice comforting image, but unlikely. Olga too is convinced she is in the right. She fell in with Rose's wishes, has done so for three years, now she's made up her mind that it's time for her to call the shots.

'I'm sick of being, in effect, your mistress,' she said, 'if you don't want to live with me, that's your choice, but I'm not going to continue like this. Fitted in between a bloody wall hanging and your bloody fucking second-hand bookshop!' Even Olga's hair looked angry. Olga has never lost her temper with Rose before. Rose sees now why her sisters call her Rocket. Olga, Rose willingly admits, is usually a much more tolerant woman than she is. Much easier to get along with. But, like the volcano Ruapehu, when she blows, she blows. In actual fact, Rose thinks, Olga should be grateful, not angry. Rose has done her a favour. Better to stop now while they've still got their own places than sell up and put everything into one place and then go through the painfully chaotic roller coaster of halving everything when they split up. Been there done that, thinks Rose, didn't like it.

Rose never complained about the way Ada reared her, it would be useless anyway. Although it was tempting to blame our parents for our mistakes, our mistakes were our mistakes, she thought. We made them ignorantly, determinedly, obsessively, but they were ours and no one but us could stop us making them.

At the front of *The Man Who Loved Rain*, Peter Paul Pearl acknowledged Ada's help and dedicated the book to her. As well he might seeing she'd given him the guts of it. But Ada saw it as a huge compliment and loved him the more for it.

TEN

The telephone is ringing, George is wailing, and there's something else. Knocking. Someone's knocking at the door. She looks at her bedside clock. 8 a.m. 'Shit,' says Rose, and grabs the phone.

'Morning Rose,' says Olga. Rose's heart lurches. Involuntarily, she smiles. Stop that, she orders herself. 'Alice told me about the baby and I wondered if you needed a hand in the shop. While you get the morning sorted. Or have you rung Carlos?' Carlos Stubbs, a local signwriter and avid book reader, looked after The Book Stops Here while Rose was in hospital and when she had to be away for treatment. Carlos is a little bit crazy. He insists on taking his wages in books.

Rose forces herself to breathe quietly. She is not going to pant into the phone. 'He's away today,' she says, perhaps a little breathlessly but not too obviously, 'if you can manage it I'd be really grateful. But what about the café?' For God's sake, she thinks, I sound like Marilyn Monroe. She takes another deep breath.

'Leo's home, he'll do it. He would rather do your shop, but there's a big order of meat coming and his back is younger than mine.'

They arrange that Olga will get the key from Betty next door. All the shop owners keep a spare key for the shops either side and it's proved a very useful practice.

'See you about midday then,' Olga says.

'Thanks,' Rose manages. She replaces the receiver, sits up in bed smiling like an idiot, then with a gasp remembers the knocking at the door.

Wesley and Jo are disappearing down the drive. She calls them. Jo has the morning paper and some mail in her hand. Rose checks, no, nothing from the wall hanging committee. One has handwriting that seems sickly familiar, but Rose can't open it now. What the hell can Marcy be writing to her about? Everything they wanted to say to each other had surely been said four years ago.

Miraculously George has gone back to sleep. In the kitchen she puts the kettle on and gestures to Wesley and Jo to take a seat while she makes a cup of tea. Her head aches yet she feels excited. Olga rang, Olga rang. Something to thank the baby for. Her voice was friendly, nothing more. That's all it was Rose. Olga doing a friend a good turn. Rose thinks of Erica. Tries to remember how she felt when they decided, by mutual consent, that they would stop being lovers and would be just good friends. Erica had taken up with Stephanie soon after so there was more to it, but Rose didn't feel rejected or unhappy. Just the opposite. She felt free, independent, in charge. The seventies were good for that. An image of herself and Erica standing on a corner shouting about something. A woman's right to choose perhaps. Something. What a terrible thing to forget such conviction, such determination. Just the details, she thinks, that's all, you've just forgotten the details, but they'll be there somewhere. Marcy suddenly, or perhaps not so suddenly given the letter, appears in her head and she's standing in the doorway of their bedroom watching Rose pack. She's saying, 'You have to understand Rose, there is no option. I must keep my job. Mum relies on me.' Of course she had an option, Rose thinks angrily, everyone has options, Marcy's mother could have gone somewhere a bit cheaper instead of that pretentious, ridiculously expensive place which she only liked because she reckoned all the best people went there. Rose's mind quickly skitters thankfully away to Olga, Olga who would have, Rose would bet her life on it, remained staunch. Still would. She thinks of that card given out to watersiders who'd maintained solidarity right through those 151 days in 1951. Each one of them was presented with a special card. Claude still has his proudly displayed on his sitting-room mantelpiece. Stood Loyal Right Through. That would be Olga. Absolutely. This morning though Olga was definitely just being friendly, definitely. However the bubbles are still racing around Rose's veins. Who cares what Marcy's letter says? Olga rang, Olga rang.

Jo spreads the morning paper on the table. 'Two Children Die in Home Alone Case,' she reads aloud; 'No Survivors Found in Towers Yet,' she adds, obviously intending to alert them to all the sorry headlines. Rose averts her eyes from the front page. Not quickly enough. Halfway down on the right her eyes spot an item about this man who has been jailed for life for the murder of his stepson, aged six. The boy had more than sixty bruises and other internal injuries. A subdural haemorrhage caused the brain to shut down. The man didn't like the boy because he was slow and because he'd soiled his pants. Rose remembers Maisy. 'Boom, boom,' Maisy is saying.

'Remember Maisy?' she says. Jo doesn't answer.

'Those firemen must be exhausted,' Wesley says, 'we'd better call another prayer meeting tonight Jo.'

Jo doesn't answer her husband. 'The postie came ages ago,' she says. Her voice implies Rose is a careless, irresponsible woman, too lazy to get out of bed and collect her mail from the box.

'They're always early on Saturdays,' Rose says. She gets cups, milk, tea, biscuits. The rain has stopped and sunshine is lapping the window sill over the sink. She peers through the glass, yes, that damned black cat is asleep on the pantry window sill. Oh for God's sake, she thinks, stay there then. Don't suppose you're doing any harm. Olga has rung, there is no boom box, the baby is quiet, looks like a good day. And in New York, thinks Rose, thousands of people are crying, have been crying for days. Stop it, she tells herself, that sort of thought does nothing for anyone. Wesley's prayers are probably more use. She thinks of the millions of prayers sent out for all the people in the towers and the planes, their relatives, loved ones. And still, not one survivor. Someone once said to Rose that if there was a God, he must be absolutely ruthless. Of course Wesley would say He gave us all free will and it's not His fault if we abuse that, while Buddhists would say we make our own karma. Rose thinks it's all too difficult for a Saturday morning. She pours the tea and indicates the biscuits. Wesley, she notices, takes two teaspoons of sugar.

Jo inherited the house Knock-Knock rents when Thelma Millett died, and sold, or donated it, Rose wasn't sure which, to the church. It was rented out on the understanding that as it was going to be pulled down tenants should not ask for any maintenance to be done. Naturally, with these conditions, most tenancies were of a temporary nature and there was a lot of coming and going. When Rose expressed concern Wesley told her not to worry. 'Some of them look a bit odd,' he conceded, 'but if we can help them a bit and they pay the rent on time that's all that concerns us. Only a nominal rent. People only appreciate something if they pay for it. We've found that out the hard way.'

Rose wondered if perhaps Wesley was using these means to get her to sell. The church would like to own her house because it was designed and built by Elmore Hipp. Although you have to be reasonable, it was impossible for Wesley to keep his eye on the neighbouring house twenty-four hours a day. She trains herself to ignore the old cars, the loud music, the occasional party that goes on all night, but it isn't so easy to overlook those poor souls who have been diverted out into the community to fend for themselves. The silence when these tenants are in occupation is somehow worse than the noise. But they will not drive her out. Rose is determined. The boom box is something else, but it will not drive her out. She has her Plan.

The other houses in this small street are too far gone to rent out, even to Wesley's down and outs. They attract squatters like Millie, others looking for a doss down for a night or two, occasional teenagers looking for somewhere to party. Wesley never moves them on. Perhaps he hopes to convert them. They're mostly alkies anyway whose squabbling and fighting over their various patches around town has erupted into vicious or violent confrontations, and who have been told to take time out by the police. So they come to Little Salamander to recuperate. Time out. Once they've had a good sleep in one of the old shells and drunk all the alcohol they've carried there, they're off. Until the next time. Some make nuisances of themselves, most are just poor, miserable, booze-sodden wrecks who become happy when the booze reaches a certain level. Below or above that they're either crying or fighting. It just occurs to Rose, something really obvious, but she's never given it a thought before. All those alkies were little babies once like George. What bruises do they have, she wonders.

'We just thought – perhaps the church can help,' Wesley says. At least he's not handing her a piece of paper with a homily on it. She has no intention of accepting any help from either Wesley or his church. Give these people an inch and they take a mile. Probably got a ritual for lost babies they want to try out. Rose looks out of the window at the sky. A wash of greys signalling more rain on the way. Some day someone is going to do a quilt or a wall hanging in greys. You'd have to have one dot or square of one of the rich primaries, yellow maybe, no, no, a shiny red splodge streaked with electric purple. It could work beautifully. Call it *Electric Grey*. No, too obvious. She thinks of Etta James. *Love's Been Rough On Me*. A great CD. Her best. And a great title for a wall hanging built up of differing greys with a red block splintered with electric purple. Too bad. That title's taken. She'll have to think of something else.

The weather looks like it could clear now. The north-westerly has lessened – Sibyl and Kitty will be pleased. Rose wonders why the hell Marcy has written to her.

She thinks about the social worker who, according to a detective, lost her objectivity when dealing with a case of alleged sexual abuse by a police officer of his teenage daughter, five years before. The social worker, described as tenaciously committed to the welfare of the young people in her care, allowed matters to go too far. The father left the police force after suffering humiliation, anxiety and distress resulting from the prosecution, which was dismissed four weeks after it was brought. It was never relaid and no criminal prosecution resulted from the subsequent police investigation. The man's daughter recently admitted the allegations she made were untrue. So the man was asking for $200,000 in damages from the social worker and the department. The price of vigilance?

What about little Bianca, what about the others she and Jo remembered last night, the ones in the paper this morning? What about those children, hundreds of them, after the Second World War, taken from their parents who were told they were dead, and moved to Canada, Australia, New Zealand, where large numbers were neglected, beaten, abused. There's a copy of the book about this disgusting event, in the non-fiction section. Rose has watched customers pick it up, open it, read a couple of paragraphs, and with a shudder of the shoulders put it back on the shelf, move away. The Skeleton Woman sure took her time over that secret.

Yes, but what about you Rose? What about that ex-police officer? Or those crèche workers? What about that little three year old locked in a room with no food, no bedding, nothing, while her mother goes out to party. Vigilance, like life, is evidently a random state. What is the answer? Gertrude Stein is alleged to have asked, as she was dying. What is the question then, she said, when no one replied. Then she died.

Wesley purses his lips. He wears his usual T-shirt and shorts. Wesley has good legs. His hair is thinning, but what's left is the same fair colour it always was. Maybe he won't go grey. His eyes are a true vivid blue, his skin ruddy. Perhaps he should wear a hat more often. Rose is much more conscious about hats and covering up than she used to be.

'Sorry?'

'Clothes for the baby, anything you need. We could ring around the church members.'

'Thanks, but –'

'I thought a pram and a cot, we could probably borrow those, if they'd be any help.'

'They're not called prams now,' Rose says unkindly, 'they're called strollers.'

'Bless you Rose,' Wesley smiles. 'I'm afraid my vocab is determinedly behind the times. If you need anything let me know. The church is not just there for us to pray and preach on Sundays, we pride ourselves on being socially responsible.'

And bloody annoying and pompous with it, thinks Rose. 'There must be a pay-off,' she says, 'human beings only do things, good or bad, if there's a pay-off.'

Jo's face tightens, but Wesley smiles. He's heard it all before.

Rose hasn't thought of a stroller though, so he has a point. Unless whoever left George turns up with these necessities soon she'll need to acquire them somehow. She's not made of money. Whoever left George should have left a note. Not just a piece of white card with For Rose Anthony written on it. 'A stroller would be great,' she adds.

'Are you sure you don't know whose baby this is?' asks Jo.

'I've told you I don't,' says Rose, 'I asked you if you knew. I wouldn't have done that if I'd known, would I?'

'You might, if you wanted to throw me off the track,' says Jo. She sounds angry.

Wesley says, 'I'm sure Rose is telling the truth.'

'Maybe we should contact someone who'll take him out of your hair,' Jo says, still with that tone in her voice, 'or, I'm happy to take him.'

'You're forgetting the card,' Rose says, perhaps a bit louder than she would have if Jo hadn't sounded the way she did: 'For Rose Anthony. George was addressed to me. Someone wants me to have their baby until they can come and collect him.' She hears the surprise and resentment in her voice, and adds, 'Can't say I'm not pissed off about it, but I have to keep him because he was addressed to me. If I do as you say and ring someone in authority the authorities might want to take him away. Then what would I say when whoever left him on my porch comes back to claim him?'

'What if he gets sick?' says Jo. 'You haven't got a birth cer-tificate, don't even know how old the baby is. Doctors have to fill in forms. They have to be given facts. What about the cost?'

'Yes,' agrees Wesley, 'you'll have to buy all sorts of stuff. You're entitled to ask Social Welfare or whatever they call themselves this week for some help. You have to remember you're just recovering from a serious illness. Are you sure you're up to it?'

Wesley's voice has a deep, caring note in it which riles Rose enormously. 'You mean,' she says, 'the cancer might come back and go to my brain and I'll forget to feed him.'

Wesley's smile falters then returns. 'Perhaps you *should* ring the police,' he says.

'Oh for God's sake, what do you want? George taken off in handcuffs?'

'We're only thinking of you,' Wesley says.

'The police have got too much to do on a Saturday to worry about an uninvited baby.'

'An abandoned baby,' corrects Jo.

'He's not abandoned. He was addressed to me.'

'You shouldn't let it slide.'

'I won't let it slide.'

'You are letting it slide Rose.' Wesley keeps on smiling.

'It's funny you didn't ring the police last night.' Jo is not smiling.

'When you two grow up,' Rose snaps, 'you're going to be real nags.' She looks straight at Jo. 'Which reminds me. Happy birthday, Jo.'

There is a silence. Then Jo says, as though it hurts her, 'Thank you.'

Wesley smiles at Jo. 'We're just having a quiet day. No guests in the B. & B. Just us. That's the way Jo wanted it.'

Jo says nothing.

Wesley says, 'We're concerned, that's all. You're just recovering from cancer, it's our duty to be concerned.'

Rose resists the temptation to pick up the rolled-up newspaper with the soiled nappy in it and stuff it down his throat.

'If you want to be of some help,' she says, 'find me a car-seat for the baby. I'm stuck until I get that.'

George cries and Jo stands up. Rose looks at her and she sits down again. Rose goes and gets George, and the first thing she notices when she carries him through to the kitchen is that he looks different. Settled? Yes, in some way settled. Perhaps it's the eyes, yes, she decides, the eyes. They look bigger. The blue looks deeper. Surely babies' eyes don't change as abruptly as this? Overnight? Newborn babies have eyes which are a kind of vague grey colour which changes over time to brown or blue or green, but that's much earlier isn't it? This morning George looks familiar, as though she knows him from somewhere. You do Rose, he spent the night in your bedroom.

'I'll hold him while you heat the bottle.' Jo picks George out of the washbasket without waiting for Rose to answer. Rose bites back her irritation. What Jo says is true. She does need to heat the bottle. She thinks that if all the people Wesley and Jo help feel like she does there must be a lot of bad vibes zooming around them.

'What did you come over for last night?' she asks Jo.

Jo shrugs. 'Just thought I'd pop over and see how you were.'

That is odd. Jo never 'popped' over. You could hardly call the recent marching in and sitting in stony silence for hours 'popping in'. When she was twelve, definitely, but from about eighteen, no. Round about the time Rose told her she was sure she was a lesbian. 'You're lying,' Jo had said, 'you've got boyfriends, you like boys.'

'Not like that.'

'You've just got all caught up in this ridiculous feminist crap,' Jo said. 'I know you. I *know* you.'

Rose thinks Jo is jealous. Not because she wants Rose sexually but because up till now, she came first with Rose. They've lived next door to each other as long as they can remember.

Celebrated their birthdays together. Like sisters, really. Although they don't look alike. Jo's skin is so fair although her hair is almost as dark as Rose's. They are best friends. Now some other woman will matter more. Jo was angry about that. But she recovered. Or so Rose thought. Now she wonders.

Rose takes George from Jo and for a moment Jo looks as though she's not going to hand the boy over. She stares at the baby, frowning. Shakes her head. Too bad, thinks Rose.

Wesley says, 'We'd better get going Jo.'

Jo says, 'Look at it Wes, you can see it too, can't you?'

'See what?' asks Rose.

'Nothing,' says Jo. It's Wesley's turn to frown.

Wesley takes Jo's arm. 'Come on Jo, we'd better get on the phone.' As they leave, Wesley says he will do a ring-around for a car-seat pronto. Rose doesn't say thank you. 'Don't forget your mail,' says Jo.

After the door shuts Rose continues to feed George. When he's halfway through she takes the bottle away and holds him over her shoulder to burp. 'You lay over her shoulder like this,' she tells him, 'so where the hell is she?' She settles him in the crook of her arm. 'Who is she?' He takes her intent stare as an invitation to smile and does so. You're romanticising, Rose, it's wind. Watch it.

The packet now holds only a few nappies. She will have to do something, make decisions. George needs a bath, should have done that before the feed, too late now, will have to do it after. The bottles need washing, there are drips of formula on the bench waiting to be wiped up. She will change the baby and while he's lying in the washbasket she will clean the bench and do up some more formula. Rose sniffs. The kitchen smells different. A faint tang of shit and sick and milk on the air. At that moment it doesn't seem to matter. It's not that she doesn't have the energy to move, it's just that she doesn't want to. She is in shock, has to be. She just wants to sit. If only, Rose thinks. Surprising herself, she grins at the baby. Who are you, who are you? His eyes are very blue. There's something about them. Something. 'You can see it too.' What did Jo mean?

'Time to move,' Rose tells herself. But she doesn't. Just one more cup of tea. George will have to sleep out the back of the shop this afternoon and he will have to like it. And if Wesley's ring around isn't successful, he'll have to travel in the wash-basket on the back seat, strapped in somehow. She thinks of Lizzie, Anne and Millie. What are they doing? Leo, Malcolm. Is it one of them? Is it significant that Leo is home this weekend? Come on Rose, she orders, and this time she moves.

ELEVEN

She is rubbing the bench to a shiny gloss with an old tea towel she keeps for this purpose when there's a tap on the door and Claude walks in.

'How did you know I wanted to see you?' asks Rose, 'and why did I only get a postcard from Reefton?'

Claude grins. He nods at George. 'Things been happening since I went away.'

Claude has heard about the baby from Elena who heard it from Olga.

Rose feels her lips harden.

Claude says, 'Something's happened, Rosie.' Rose stares suddenly alert. What the hell now? 'Nothing to worry,' Claude says. Rose makes another pot of tea and some toast. Claude's a great one for toast with his tea. 'Not a bad day,' he says, looking out the window at the dull sky, 'good day for gardening. Not too hot.' Oh get on with it, Rose thinks. She can see he's a bit nervous.

'I was just inside the door at home when the phone rang and it was this woman. Oh boy, toast, just what I felt like.' Rose has a feeling she's not going to like what she hears.

Claude takes a careful sip of the hot tea and bites thoughtfully on the toast. 'You'll never guess what she said.'

'Claude!' Rose warns.

'You sound just like Ada,' Claude grins and all Rose's irritation melts. She smiles. 'Well she just says, "Mr Anthony, I'm Bridget Pearl." ' Nearly dropped my glass.

'I thought you said you'd just got in the door,' Rose says.

'I had,' Claude says and grins. 'She says, "I rang you because your name is Anthony and I'm trying to trace an Ada Anthony." "Oh yeah," I says, I mean she could be anyone. "I wondered," she says, "if you could give me her address." "Be a mite difficult," I says, "unless you've got a hot line to heaven." "Oh," she says, "I'm sorry," she says. Then she says, "I wanted to talk to her about my uncle, Peter Paul Pearl." "Yeah?" I says, I mean you have to be a bit cautious. "Did you know him?" she asks, and I said "Yeah, I knew him." Well what else could I do Rose? And she shouts "Yay!" right in my bloody ear. Nearly dropped my glass. Turns out she's the daughter of Pete's youngest brother. Says her dad didn't really know his brother. He was way the youngest of six and Peter was the oldest. All her father remembered was their mum crying and their father being angry for days when Peter's wife came and told them he'd left her and gone to live in the Hutt with a woman called Ada Anthony. That made me sit up. "Now just a minute," I says, "I'm Ada Anthony's brother-in-law and very proud to be so, she was a wonderful woman, and I won't hear a word against her."' Claude's face was stern and serious. 'I said, "Peter was bloody lucky Ada took him on, never knew what she saw in him myself. Runty little bugger. Always working away in that room he set up as a study. Every spare minute. Not that it did him much good. A reasonable teacher though, so they tell me."' Claude's voice was grudging as though he'd forced himself to be fair. 'Bloody lucky,' he repeated, 'and I set the record straight Rose. Told her, Peter Pearl hadn't set eyes on Ada until he came to inspect the rooms she was letting. What happened after that happened, but that's a different matter. Told her that "Ada Anthony was no pushover. Took her time, kept him waiting. Ada wasn't the type to rush into things."'

'And?' Rose says.

'Well, apparently the reason she wanted to meet me was

that she's working on her PhD thesis.' Claude starts to grin. '"Aspects of Alienation in Peter Paul Pearl's Novels." Aspects of alienation,' Claude repeats, enjoying every word. 'Aspects of alienation. Sounds just like one of those socialist tracts about immigrants your mother used to wave about. Anyway,' he pauses and Rose knows he reached the crux of it, 'she wants to talk to you.'

'How does she know about me?'

'Come on Rosie, don't be like that.'

'Why didn't she ring me then?'

'She did, there was no answer. You must've been at the shop.'

'Why me? I didn't really know Peter. Only that I didn't like him.'

'You didn't give the poor bugger a chance,' Claude points out. 'Anyway, background, she says, background information. She says you're a primary source.'

'I'll give her primary source,' Rose says. 'Do you remember how those daughters of his turned up after his funeral and demanded his furniture? If this Bridget is anything like them she can piss off.'

'Well the thing is,' says Claude, 'I said I'd put it to you and so,' Claude demolishes the last finger of toast, 'I just came along to – sort of break the ice. Find out when you could see her.'

Rose sighs, gives Claude his tea in a cup and saucer, the way he likes it, and pushes her plate of toast towards him. She won't refuse and he knows it, but she'll make him wait. 'How was Dunedin?'

'Dunedin was great. Saw a few mates, had a great time.'

'Ada loved Dunedin,' Rose says.

'Yeah, remember that Southland burr?' Claude smiles and does a bad imitation of Ada's accent. 'My daughterrr, my needleworrrk, my fatherrr.' He looks at Rose. 'Now there was an old bugger,' he says.

When Ada Jones married Sim Anthony in 1949 in the registry office on Lambton Quay, with only Claude there as a witness, she had nothing but the clothes she stood up in plus a purse containing twenty-five shillings. The night before, her father grabbed the suitcase she'd packed, commanded her to leave his house, take that blackguard Sim Anthony with her, and never come back. Charlie Jones then forbade his wife to have anything to do with their only child ever again, and declared his intention of changing his will. He made a phone call and when two workmen arrived, ordered them to remove everything from Ada's room – furniture, bedding, books, clothes, everything. Charlie searched the house looking for any article that had any association with his daughter. He found photos, three tray- and two tablecloths, and a fire screen Ada had worked, her box of embroidery threads, the hussif she'd made to hold her sewing requirements when she sat in that small armchair in the evenings, and the radio he'd bought especially for her to have in the little sitting room so the drone of it didn't get on his nerves while he was reading the newspapers he ordered from around the country. He took the bicycle he'd bought for her last birthday – a big mistake that had been, because it was a flat tyre on that very same machine which led to her meeting that good-for-nothing bastard – removed the wheels, the pedals, the chain, pulled the frame into three pieces and put them into the biggest of the cartons. At the last minute he remembered the bathroom next to her room. He removed the soap, talcum powder, toothbrushes and toothpaste, perfume. When he'd finished, and the five cartons were full and stacked beside the furniture in the downstairs hall by the back door, he did a final check through the house to make sure he hadn't missed anything. He looked in the kitchen where Mrs Bishop, his housekeeper and cook, sat at the kitchen table. He didn't ask for assistance and she didn't offer any. It never occurred to Charlie to wonder whether she approved of his actions or not. He would not have seen it as any of her business although she'd been with his family for ten years, ever since they moved from Gore in the South Island, to Wellington, the capital city and head office of Essex and Sons, Shipping & Freight Company, where he had been appointed manager. He had no idea how fond Mrs Bishop was of Ada. 'The only one in this jumped-up household who treated me as a human being,' Mrs Bishop told her friend who worked next door but one. 'If it wasn't for Ada the house would never be so well run. It was Ada who told him to leave the shopping to me and it was Ada who insisted I get a whole day off and one evening a week.'

Mrs Bishop was a treasure, Charlie was the first to admit it, but he would have sacked her there and then if he'd known she was remembering every detail of his behaviour so she could tell Ada.

Purpose, planning, precision. That's what you needed. Every time. Purpose, planning, precision led to steadily rising profits for his employers and steadily rising bonuses for himself, and it would settle this blasted daughter of his once and for all. Purpose, planning, precision was what Lord Essex had seen in him ten years before; it was why he'd offered Charlie the job and it was why Charlie would hold it successfully in spite of his daughter's behaviour.

Charlie didn't bother to look into his own bedroom where his wife sat weeping, clutching the music of the old Scottish ballad she and Ada had practised for the musical evening they'd held for Charlie's business friends and their wives, last winter.

O wert thou in the cauld blast
On yonder lea, on yonder lea
My plaidie to the angry airt
I'd shelter thee, I'd shelter thee

Once the two men had stowed everything away on their covered truck, Charlie accompanied them on the dark drive around the hills and long winding roads and finally that last pull up the hill to the quarry where the smell told you the dump was close. He was determined to make sure his instructions about dumping everything, liberally dousing it with petrol and setting fire to it, were carried out. Not until the flames darted and strove over the pyre did he hand over the agreed sum. When there was just a pile of snickering, smouldering black and grey with little tongues of red and blue seeking out anything still left to consume he let them drive him back to his house on Karori Road. There he gave them another fiver each to keep their mouths shut. He went inside, up to where his wife still sat, the music on her lap. He said, 'Well, that'll teach her. As far as I'm concerned she'd dead, and don't you forget it. I mean it. Ada Jones is dead.'

'Old Charlie was a verrry worrrried man,' Claude says. 'If his employers in London found out that his daughter had married not just a waterside worker but a unionist, probably a communist, they'd see him as someone who couldn't control his daughter. And if he couldn't control his daughter how could they expect him to manage their affairs in Wellington? He had to negotiate the best possible freight prices with the government, he had to control the unions and not give in to their continual demands for better wages because that would take the cream off their profits. If the Essexes knew Ada was married to one of these lazy, good-for-nothing wharfies, they might replace him with someone whose daughter knew how to behave. So Ada was to just disappear. She'd be visiting her auntie, something like that. Charlie had no intention of scuttling back to Gore with his tail between his legs after his triumphant ten years in Wellington, a goodly sum of money in the bank, his house, the new Chrysler, and membership of the Wellesley Club. Oh no not Charlie. A hard man.'

Rose is glad that Claude is not a hard man. He's direct, doesn't suffer fools gladly, knows what he thinks is right and heads for it. Those who loved Claude called him a determined, principled man; those who didn't said he was a pig-headed unionist with a big mouth. Rose thinks her father was something the same although better looking, judging by the photographs. A lot of men, Claude included, seemed to have difficulty smiling for photographs, but not Sim. In most he was looking out at the world with lively dark eyes and a most engaging smile, a handsome man all right. Rose could see why Ada fell for him.

Men sneaked up on you, Ada told Rose once. They started off being attentive, kind, funny, and once they knew you loved them, they were free to reveal their true selves. There were certain things Sim expected simply because she was his wife. His tea on time, his lunch made every day, meat for breakfast, after a plate of porridge, clean towels and plenty of hot water when he came home from a shift covered in coal dust or blacking and absolutely done. At these times, there wasn't much evidence of the man she'd married, the laughing charmer who'd mended that fateful puncture, and who'd danced every dance with her when she'd sneaked out to go to the social put on by the Watersiders' Social Club at the Oddfellows Lodge Hall. At these times, that Sim was replaced by a weary, resentful and, yes, smelly man who complained bitterly about the conditions he had to work under and of the way some of the men he called 'royals' bribed their way into the easier, less dirty, jobs that lasted twice as long as those that the others got. The bureau system was better than the old auction-block system, but even it could be screwed if the foreman wanted to. Sim and Claude spent most of their mealtimes shovelling food down their throats and complaining about the ship owners, the government, the working conditions, the hours, the dirt and the high accident rate. 'I said to them, why don't you try and get something else? They both looked at me as though I was mad then they looked at each other. "Where?" asked Sim, "this is all we know." I only asked once,' Ada said.

It had come as a surprise to Ada that Claude was to board with them in the dingy flat on Willis Street. 'We've always been together,' said Sim, seemingly surprised that she was surprised. 'I promised Mum I'd look after him.'

'He's a grown man,' Ada said.

Sim shrugged. He'd said all he was going to say. The matter was closed. It was the first chink in the pedestal Ada had put him on. It didn't take long before he fell off it completely, but she never blamed anyone but herself for it. When she told Rose about it, many years later, Ada said, as if excusing her younger self, 'I was young, I fell in love, I put Sim on a pedestal. That's what young women in love do, and young men for that matter. Then, chink by chink, they discover the real person, scars, weaknesses, imperfections and all. If there's still enough left to love, you're one of the lucky ones.'

Claude remembers the first time he really talked to his new sister-in-law. 'What's the matter Ada?' he said when he found her sitting at the wooden baize-covered kitchen table, frowning over a small pile of accounts, pencil in hand, staring at the piece of paper with figures on it. Ada, cheerful, confident Ada, burst into tears. 'I don't know where the money goes,' she sobbed.

'Let's have a look,' Claude said. He flipped through the bills. 'Why do you have accounts at the butcher's and the grocer's and all?'

Ada frowned. 'I thought everyone –'

Claude shook his head. 'Too easy to get out of hand. Look Ada,' he said, 'it's really very simple. You have priorities. You pay the rent, the electricity, insurance; they come first. You've got to have a roof over your head and you've got to have insurance in case Sim has an accident. OK?'

'Insurance is so dear.'

'The job's dangerous, the conditions terrible. Lots of accidents. That's why the premiums are second only to jockeys. They've got you over a barrel because you've got to have it. OK?'

Ada nodded.

'Then,' Claude said, 'as well as setting money aside for those, you put a regular sum in the savings bank. You never miss. You never know when you might need it. Then, you pay cash for everything else. If you haven't got the cash, you can't have it. It's easy, you don't have to be an Einstein.'

'What about when there's no money coming in?'

'Only happened once in the last year. Doesn't happen much now. Not like the bad old days. Just the opposite in fact. Twelve – fourteen-hour days are the norm. No wonder we do a bit of go-slow or spelling. Most of us are absolutely buggered – sorry – by week's end. But no money's always a possibility in this job, that's why you've got to save, and regularly.'

Ada said, hesitantly, 'Sim wants money, you know, for the pub.'

'Too bad,' said Claude, 'what you want and what you get are two different things. You give him his cut out of the wages when he brings them home, and that's it. When he comes round for some more, you say you haven't got it. Because you haven't. Oh you might have a purseful, but it's spoken for see? So it's not yours and it's definitely not Sim's.'

Ada nodded again. It was all so obvious.

'Now look,' Claude said, 'I owe you for my board. I know, I know what Sim said, but Sim doesn't have to worry about the bills. He's a good brother, likes to think he looks after me because I'm the younger one, and he did look out for me, and I did need him to, but I don't need free board.'

'But what'll he say when he knows you're paying board?'

'Who's going to tell him?'

Ada opened her mouth and shut it again.

'Here,' Claude passed over a roll of notes. 'That's what I owe you, and from now on you can count on thirty shillings a week and if it needs to be put up just say, for God's sake. There's a lot of rubbish around money. I always find it best to just say straight out what you want, saves a lot of grief.'

'What's a hold?' asked Ada.

Claude laughed. 'A bloody great hole under the deck of a ship where they store cargo.'

'Sim said that one of his gang fell into the hold and hurt his back, and I didn't know what he was talking about.'

'Well now,' Claude said, 'if Sim says something you don't understand, ask him what he means. Ask me. I don't know anything about keeping house so if you say something I don't understand, I'll ask you, OK? Same thing.'

'I feel such a fool,' Ada said, 'sometimes I wonder what I was doing all those years at school.'

'I think Sim's a very lucky man.' Claude grinned at her.

They both heard the sound of the back door opening. 'Ada!'

called Sim. Ada quickly tidied away the bills and put Claude's money in her apron pocket. 'Thanks Claude,' she said, 'I think I'm a very lucky woman. I've got the best brother-in-law in the world.'

Claude peers at George in the washbasket and says, 'You were just about this fella's age, Rose, when your father and I were locked out. Ada brought you home the same day the employers put the notices up. By God she was glad she'd kept up the savings. The union did its best, and lots of people donated stuff, some farmers, surprisingly, but it was a hard five months. Changed Ada. Something did anyway. It was hard on both Sim and Ada, hard on everyone.' Claude's eyes look inward, back to that time. He nods to himself. 'I think the trouble between Ada and Sim started before then, but I can't be sure. They were both very close-lipped.'

'You haven't told all this to Bridget have you?'

Claude says, 'She asked about 51 and about the women's role. I told her, us men hadn't really cottoned on that it wasn't just a matter of us all being staunch, we had to have the women on side as well. If it hadn't been for Ada and the other women on the Women's Committee, we'd all have been in Queer Street. Oops. Sorry.' He grins at Rose, who doesn't grin back.

'She's got Peter's books, the *Landfall* articles, she can read up the background, what more does she want? The trouble is that decent reticence has gone out of fashion.'

'R-E-T-I-C-E-N-C-E?' Claude scoffs, 'tell me one person who knows the meaning of the word. Even if they did they wouldn't see the sense of it.'

Rose says, 'Everyone's out to pick on the flesh of reticence these days. They like to tear and scratch and gnaw at it until they get to the bones, and when they get there and find there's nothing but bones, it's too late for the poor old skeleton. There's so much stink and mess it's inevitable large globs of it stick.'

Claude doesn't pretend not to understand. 'You'd have had your say,' he says, 'you'd have had your say. You'd have established your outrage, your firm rebuttal. There'd be a record. There should be a record, Rose. If I've learned nothing else, I've learned that.'

'You sound just like Mum.'

'Thank you,' Claude says.

Claude and Ada were as one about Rose's action, or lack of action. They both adhered to the publish and be damned principle. Except that, as Rose pointed out to them more than once, these days there are television cameras and journalists, radio journalists with tape recorders, all of whose jobs depends on their capacity to dance on someone's bones. Even when they know that what they're reporting is not strictly true and that the next morning's papers et al will carry the truer version, albeit buried on a back page or placed at the tail end of the news. All that matters to them is getting the top slots. If innocent people get hurt, slandered even, in the process, too bad, they've got the top slot.

'Claude,' Rose stops. What could he say?

'What?'

Rose speaks quickly. 'I can't help wondering if Ada did as she threatened and went and saw the principal.'

'If she'd been to see him we'd have heard by now.'

'The thing is,' Rose swallows, 'I said when she was leaving that if she did that, I'd never forgive her.' Rose doesn't look at Claude.

There is a little silence. Claude says, 'Thought there was something. Thought there was something. Oh well Rosie, we've all said things we regret. Keeps us humble. I bet Ada didn't think another thing about it.'

'I wish I thought that was true,' Rose says, 'Claude you don't think –'

'No, I don't,' Claude interrupts, 'I don't think it was on her mind so much that she had an accident. If a bloody carload of idiot tourists comes round the corner on the wrong side of the road there's not a lot you can do about it. Ada loved you Rose, she'd be the last one to hold a grudge.'

'Mum? Come on Claude, forty years after the 51 Lockout she still carried a grudge against Patrick Fintan Walsh! I was just remembering that last night. The only one who did her a bad turn that she forgave completely was Thelma Millett.'

'I meant against you,' says Claude, 'but you're right about Thelma. Never quite worked that out.' He looks at Rose, judges the time is right. 'You will see this Bridget Pearl, won't you?'

TWELVE

Wesley is successful. He turns up with a car-seat, a stroller, a suitcase of assorted clothes and a box of real nappies. Rose does say thank you this time.

'Don't thank me,' smiles Wesley, 'thank God.' He moves from one foot to another. 'Just want to say,' he beams at her, 'Jo's a bit worried at the moment, wouldn't want you to think – well … ' He pauses, then goes on, 'It's Lizzie, you probably realised, they had a falling out. Some months ago now. She won't talk to Jo. Or me. Although we've always got on.' He shrugs. 'Jo's tried ringing, Lizzie just hangs up. Me ditto. Jo's sent letters and cards, but no replies. It's too bad of Lizzie. She knows her mother is a bit tetchy sometimes, but she doesn't mean anything. And Lizzie's inclined to fly off the handle herself. She feels things. Always been very sensitive. Jo's worried. That makes her a bit – sharp.'

'I'm sorry.' Rose is at a loss so she latches onto something innocuous. 'It was a boy wasn't it?' Oh great Rose. A great line. Not only have you not bothered to find out what's been tearing Jo apart for months, now you're saying you weren't even interested enough to remember what sex the baby is.

'A boy,' Wesley says. He sighs, looks uncomfortable. 'She called him Simon.'

'Simon?' Rose is astounded although why she should be she can't imagine. She doesn't have a lien on the name. Just because her father was called Simon doesn't mean she owns a copyright on it. But you'd think given that old business with Thelma and Sim, the way he died, you'd think Lizzie would have chosen a

million other names over that. Maybe the feelings of a generation ago don't matter, even if she knows about them. Probably
doesn't know. Who would tell her? Thelma's dead and Jo always
shied away from the whole thing. Who can blame her? Rose
doesn't broadcast that old calamity either. In any case it could be
Royston who wanted Simon. Rose knows more about Elmore,
Royston's great-grandfather, than she does about him. 'What
does Royston do?' she asks.

'Works at a supermarket in Wellington. Assistant manager.
Supposed to be going into his father's supermarket eventually.
They're renting in Karori. Lizzie didn't want to live in the
Hutt. Jo wants me to ring Royston at work, but I don't like to
interfere. It's hard,' Wesley sounds as though he's searching for
the right words, 'but we'll just have to wait until Lizzie decides
to get in touch with us. I suppose I'm putting off doing
anything because it might make things worse. Have to think of
the boy. I don't want to be a stranger to him.'
'I'm sorry,' Rose says again.

With an effort Wesley plasters a smile to his face. 'Not to
worry,' he says heartily, 'not to worry. Leave it to God, it'll all
come out in the wash.' Rose wants to say something, but
everything she thinks of is so patronising – it'll be all right,
time will sort it out, maybe you both need a holiday – or
insulting – has Jo seen a doctor? – that she says nothing. There's
nothing anyone can say, really. Sometimes people do things.
Sometimes there's just nothing that can be done about it.

When Ada began making a habit of coming home late on
Fridays and Saturdays, slurred in her speech and smelling
strongly of beer, Rose didn't know what to do.

'But why?' she heard Claude ask Ada one day, a Sunday,
'why for God's sake?'

'Mind your own business Claude,' Ada said.

'It's not right,' Claude said, 'there's talk. And you should think of Rose.'

'One more word and you can bugger off,' said Ada, so Claude shut up and she went back to basting the roast mutton she always cooked for too long in too hot an oven so it ended up tough and stringy.

Rose hated it when Ada came home drunk. She hated seeing her at the pub, hated the way she sat in the small private bar and drank glass after glass until she was weaving on her feet, hated the way she was unable to get her tongue around the simplest of words. Rose thought the regular drinkers at the pub were probably a bit scared of Ada. She looked at them all as if they were scum although when sober she was pleasant and polite. They knew her story though, so they put up with it. Ada expected Rose to call into the pub during the day to let her know what she was up to. Harry Oliver, the manager, always barged in and wanted to know what Rose was doing, what she was reading, how she was doing at school. He stood too close and made silly remarks about how clever she was and what a big girl she was, as though she was three and not practically thirteen. Rose didn't tell Ada how she felt about Harry. Ada needed the job. There weren't many places in the Hutt that needed a cleaner full-time. Mainly Rose didn't tell her because she wasn't Ada any more. She was a stranger who lived in Rose's mother's body, who spoke curtly at best, snarlingly at worst. It's not my fault, Rose wanted to say, it's not my fault Sim got into Mrs Millett's bed. For weeks she and Jo hadn't even said hello when they passed on the street or in the corridors at school. Jo must have known about Sim and Thelma, she must have. Perhaps she hadn't wanted to betray her mother. Perhaps she just didn't know how to tell Rose. Rose missed her company, her jokes, her presence in her life in a much more intense way than she missed Sim. If she thought about him it was to blame him for Jo's absence in her life. It was all too much.

One day Rose decided to hell with this, and when she saw Jo, she said hello. Jo said hello back, and Rose didn't have to wonder any more who Jo was laughing with, who she exchanged secrets with, because it was her. She loved the hours when she climbed through the window of Jo's bedroom and they lounged on Jo's bed talking about anything that came into their heads. Love, other people's behaviour, boys, dances, favourite film stars, what they think about church, why their mothers voted Labour. They agreed that neither of them believed in God, although they thought He served a purpose for old people.

'Gives them something to do like the vases of flowers on Sundays, or singing in the choir, or teaching Sunday school like long-faced Miss Graham.'

'I like Miss Graham,' Rose said.

'She's all right,' Jo said, 'but why does she always look as though if she smiled it would crack her face?'

They wondered why Miss Graham taught Sunday school classes after teaching at school all week, especially when half the kids didn't want to be in either place. They didn't talk about Ada or Thelma, and Sim's death was never mentioned. They planned what they would do when they were fourteen. They'd sneak out to that milk bar everyone talked about and have a look for themselves. They'd been in there in the daytime, but as far as they could tell there was nothing going on. Must all happen at night. 'Booze,' Rose said, 'booze and sex. So *Truth* says. That's where all the milk-bar cowboys hang out. That's what it said.'

'Where did you see *Truth*?'

'At the pub.'

Saturday nights Rose always heard Ada before she saw her. Which was good because if she was over at Jo's it gave her time to scoot back home. Rose knew Ada would be furious if she knew that Rose'd been in Mrs Millett's house, but she hadn't been able to say to Ada that when she was in their house on her own it took on a presence. It crackled at her, it moaned and creaked. It sighed when Rose moved, and there were rustles on the roof as though something with big feet had landed on it. Whenever she went out to the lavatory she got scared the house would shut its door and not let her back in, because one night when she got back the door was shut and she definitely remembered leaving it open. She stood outside the door for some minutes, stiff with anxiety. She had this feeling she was on the edge of something awful and that when she opened the door that would be the signal for whatever it was to happen. When she did open the door with a sudden frantic heave she shut it again quickly so the house wouldn't notice. There was dead silence. Then the house shivered. Rose didn't know whether this was with anger or laughter. She spent the rest of that night, until Ada came home, crouched under her bedclothes dreading the moment when the house would shiver again. She told Jo who said to come over to their place.

'*I'm only a poor Cinderella, nobody loves me it seems.*' Ada sang beautifully in tune, but with that drunken slur which spelt trouble. Rose leaped out of Jo's window, across their back yard, swerved round the big old pepper tree and heaved herself over the sagging, never-opened gate in the hedge.

She only had time to get her dress off, replace it with her nightdress, and slide between the sheets before Ada was on the path that led to their back door. '*I'm only a poor Cinderella, I'll find my romance in dreams.*' Suddenly the song was cut off by a loud shout of pain, some angry swearing. Ada must have fallen over. Should Rose get up? See what was the matter? She decided not. Falling over always made Ada angry and being helped up by Rose made her even angrier. No, best to lie still and let her mother get herself inside and into bed. In the morning she'd have forgotten all about it. Or she'd pretend to.

Bang! The noise made her jump. Ada was banging something on the concrete path. Bang, bang, bang. It came closer. The next minute there were three hard bangs on the back door and Ada was yelling, 'Rose! Rose! Open the bloody door!'

Rose wanted to pull the blankets over her head and pretend she couldn't hear, but in this mood Ada would keep it up all night. Thelma and Jo would ignore it, thank goodness, and their house was at the end of Little Salamander, so there were no other close neighbours. The houses opposite were set a long way back from the road so maybe they wouldn't hear.

Ada was so intent on yelling she didn't notice Rose had opened the door until she lifted the shovel in her hand to give it another belt. 'You deaf or something?' she demanded, 'look at my leg!' She pulled her dress up and Rose saw a horrible gash. It was starting to swell and where the skin was broken blood was dribbling, running down her front leg and into her shoe.

'If I've told you once, I've told you a thousand times, put the tools away!'

'I did Mum, I did. I hung it up in the shed when I finished.'

'Liar!' bellowed Ada. She pushed the shovel at Rose. 'Now put it away and this time do it properly.' She limped heavily inside, whimpering and swearing. It did look painful.

Rose slipped outside quickly and hung the shovel in the shed where she'd hung it before. A dark shadow reached out and touched her arm. 'Rose.'

'Aaah!' The noise was out before she could stop it.

It was Maisy Beacon. 'Gee your Mum's wild eh.'

'What the hell are you doing here?'

'Got something to tell you.'

'I have to go inside,' Rose said, 'and you should be at home. Can't you tell me tomorrow?'

Maisy was tall and large. Rose was medium height and thin. If Maisy didn't want to move, Rose couldn't make her. It would be like a lamp-post trying to move a mountain.

'Rose!' Ada's voice roared from the house.

'You wait there,' Rose said, 'I'll be back. Understand Maisy? You wait here.' Before Maisy could argue Rose darted around her bulk and back inside very fast.

'About time,' Ada said, 'what the hell were you doing?'

'Couldn't see the hook.'

'Couldn't see the hook,' Ada repeated sarcastically, 'if you'd put it away when you were told you'd have seen the hook all right because it was daytime! Now make yourself useful and get some tea going.'

Rose filled the kettle, put it on the stove and shovelled some coal in carefully – just enough to get it going but not too much so it would drown the embers. If she didn't judge it just right the kettle wouldn't boil for ages. The fall had sobered Ada. With any luck she'd take a cup of tea to bed and Rose could get out to the shed and find out what was going on with Maisy.

Behind her Ada hobbled back from the bathroom with a bucket of hot water. The air in the kitchen was acrid with Jeyes Fluid. She put the towel she carried on the floor and stood the bucket on it, sat down and gingerly put her leg into the milky water. Rose heard Ada involuntarily breathe backwards as the hot water bit into the wound. Rose was fed up with Ada, but as she looked at Ada's bent head, the short hair at the nape of her neck seemed very fragile and vulnerable, like a child's. 'Want a hand?' she asked.

Ada looked up, her eyes wet. 'Sorry Rose,' she said, 'sorry – it's just I got a hell of a shock. And it hurts.'

'It looks really bad.'

'Mmmn.' Ada rocked for a few minutes then she said what she always said. 'What time did you get to bed?'

'About half past ten, I think.' Rose was always deliberately vague. As she handed Ada the tea she got a good waft of booze and smoke. Ada didn't smoke, but there was always a lot of it at the pub. The pub was supposed to close at six, but on the Saturdays Sergeant Hartley was over the other side of town closing time was a moveable feast.

'Saw that girl from your school, the one who's not quite right,' Ada said.

'Who?'

'Who what?'

'Who did you see?'

'Maisy. Maisy. That's her name isn't it?'

Oh shit. 'Maisy's all right. The kids tease her.'

'Toads. Kids can be real bloody toads. How old is she?'

'Same as me.'

'She's big. You should've seen the jokers at the pub pretending not to look.'

'Maisy was at the pub?'

'Far from clean too,' Ada said.

'It's just her dress. She's really clean underneath. She's only got one dress that fits.'

'Hard up are they?'

Rose shrugged. 'You want a biscuit Mum?'

'No!' Ada moved irritably. She lifted her leg out of the bucket and carefully wiped it dry. She wound a piece of old sheet around the gash. 'I want my leg to stop hurting!' She took a big gulp of tea. 'That's good. This Maisy, are you sure she's only thirteen?'

Rose nodded. Ada shook her head. 'Looks eighteen at least. Her dress is too small. Too short. And that hair! Be lucky if it's seen a comb in six months. What's the matter with her mother letting her go out like that?'

'She's dead,' Rose said, 'Maisy's mother is dead.'

Ada gasped. 'That's right, what's the matter with me, how could I forget? Couple of years ago, something wrong with her stomach wasn't it?'

Rose nodded again.

'Poor little thing. What's a girl like that doing at the pub?'

'Might've been looking for her dad.'

'Losing her mother just when she needs her. You don't know how lucky you are Rose.'

Ada meant it too. 'She Frankie Beacon's daughter?'

'Yes.'

'Frankie Beacon. Well she was looking in the right place.'

'Shall I give you a hand to bed?'

Immediately Ada looked suspicious. 'What's the hurry?'

'No hurry. Thought you might be tired.'

Ada smiled, and it wasn't entirely maudlin. 'Good girl. You look after your mother and she'll look after you.' She gave a huge yawn. 'You're right. I'm dropping off as I sit here. You take the tea and I'll bring up the rear.'

Rose waited a minute or two by Ada's bed while she settled. Ada looked up at her. 'I did the right thing,' she said, 'I'm a good mother to you,' then she added, 'most of the time anyway.'

When she heard Ada start breathing heavily Rose tiptoed outside to the shed. Maisy loomed up out of the shadows. 'Now,' Rose said, realising with a shock that she sounded just like Ada when she was on the warpath, 'what the hell are you doing here?'

'Gee she was wild wasn't she?'

Rose had been thinking. 'The shovel. It was you wasn't it?'

Maisy's head went up and down in agreement. The moonlight made her bulky shadow look as though it was dancing to some heavy beat. 'Someone was following me. I was scared. I'm starving. Got anything to eat?'

Rose sighed. You're an idiot, she told herself, but she took Maisy inside, got out the bread and plum jam. Ada should be OK what with the booze and the shock of hurting her leg. No butter for Maisy though, they only had enough butter to last the week. Not that Maisy minded jam on plain bread. She wolfed the thick slices down as fast as Rose could spread jam on them. 'Tell me about the shovel,' Rose hissed.

'Someone was following me.' Maisy spoke through her mouthful of bread. Rose could see bits of half-eaten bread and blobs of jam all mixed up with saliva. She felt sick. 'I was scared,' Maisy said.

'So you were scared,' Rose said. 'What's that got to do with leaving the shovel on the path?'

'So I belted him,' Maisy said.

'What?'

'I belted him.'

'You hit someone with the shovel?' Rose sounded as thick as Maisy did when the teacher tried to explain *Romeo and Juliet* to her.

Maisy grinned. 'Boom boom,' she said and began to giggle. She giggled and giggled. The more Rose tried to shush her the worse she got. In the end, because Maisy was weak with laughter, Rose managed to push her outside, back to the shed, where she realised to her dismay that the giggles were now infecting her. She must not laugh. The effort made her shoulders shake and tears come into her eyes. It was no good anyway. The laughter rose and danced and danced and rose. So she gave. One good burst, she thought, to get it out of my system. Then it'll be over. But every time she got herself under control Maisy, happy she'd made Rose laugh, said, 'Boom boom,' and started her off again.

Eventually though, fear of Ada's reaction if she heard something seeped in like rain edging in under the back door when the wind blew hard from the south. Rose's giggles stopped.

Maisy said, 'He got a bit sick of following me after that,' and Rose nearly started up again. She made her voice very firm. 'Did you hear anything after you stopped?'

'Only someone being sick. Someone was,' Maisy hiccupped loudly, 'being sick. Bet he got a surprise eh. Just sneaking along and then boom boom!' She waited for Rose to start giggling again. Maisy never knew when you'd had enough, when the joke was over. When she was enjoying herself she tried to make it last forever.

'Who was it?'

Maisy moved uneasily. 'Dunno. He goes, "Come on girl," that's what he said. Come on girl. He goes, "I won't hurt you." I think he wanted to take my pants down. That's what I think.'

Must have been one of the jokers from the pub, one of the men Ada talked about. 'You'd better be off home,' Rose said. She couldn't see Maisy's face properly, but Maisy's body shifted and Rose just knew she had that look on her face like she always did when she didn't want to do what she was being asked to do.

'I'm not going home,' Maisy said. 'I'm not going home.'

'Listen,' Rose said, 'if you're scared, I'll walk with you.' And pray that Ada didn't get up to the lavatory and check in on her on the way.

Maisy shook her head. 'Not going home,' she said, 'home's horrible.'

And that is all she would say. After twenty minutes of sneaky questions, sudden questions, direct questions, all of which got nowhere, Rose gave up.

'OK,' she said, 'you can sleep at the end of my bed.' Rose

sounded grumpy because she was, and she was tired, and worried that Ada would wake. And Maisy was so big. The thought of her bulk taking up space in Rose's single bed wasn't great, so she stopped thinking about it. That was the best thing to do when you were faced with something you couldn't change. Like her mother. Her father. The hotel. Ada's drinking. It was all so horrible. So stop thinking about it Rose and start thinking about something else. Something good. If there was anything good.

'You'd better go to the lav,' Rose said. They crept through the wash-house to the lav. Well, Rose crept. Maisy lumbered. Their piddle sounded very loud. Don't think about it, she told herself. She was spending half her life telling herself not to think about things.

'What's going on?' Ada's voice sounded loud and fierce. The suddenness of it coming out of the dark made Rose jump and Maisy gave a terrified yelp. 'Come on Rose, what's going on. Who's this?' Ada peered at Maisy, then shone the torch. 'Jesus, God,' said Ada.

Maisy put her hands over eyes and tried to shrink behind Rose.

'She hit someone with the shovel.' It sounded so bald when said out loud, but it was the truth and that was the only thing left now. You told your mother the truth only when anything else was plain useless. Jo and Rose agreed on that.

'Why?' Ada's voice was sharp and disbelieving. She addressed Maisy. 'Well girl, why?'

Maisy shook her head and said nothing.

'She says he was following her and saying things like, "Come on girl I won't hurt you."'

'He wanted to take my pants down,' Maisy volunteered.

'She says she hit him, then she heard someone being sick.'

'Boom boom,' said Maisy.

'Shut up!' Rose was angry with Maisy, angry with Ada, angry with everything. 'Just shut up Maisy Beacon!'

Maisy cowered back and Rose felt mean, but she was sick of everything.

'Oh Jesus,' said Ada, 'where is the bugger then?' She limped around the backyard, the torch swinging in a wide arc in front of her, the two girls following. Rose heard Maisy's hoarse breathing, loud in the night air. Ada peered into the shed, nothing stirred. 'He must have gone,' she said finally.

'What's up?' yelled an indignant voice from the fence, 'who are you? What do you think you're doing?'

'It's me Mrs Millet,' Rose said, 'and Mum.'

'What are you doing at this hour of the night for God's sake? Nearly had a heart attack when I saw that torch! Oh Jesus, sorry, shouldn't have said that.'

'What is it Mum?' Jo joined her mother at the fence.

Ada never said more than hello to Thelma Millet anyway, but she hadn't even done that since Sim died in Thelma's bed. Rose saw Ada open her mouth to say something like mind your own business, when Jo gasped, 'Mum! Mum! There's a man lying on the grass! There! By the tree!'

Thelma scrambled over the fence, but Ada was at the tree before her. A man was lying there all right. Ada shone the torch on him. He lay very still as though he was playing dead. Rose couldn't see his face, just his reddy-purple hands. She knew those hands.

'Christ almighty,' Ada said.

'Holy hell,' said Thelma.

'I didn't mean to,' Maisy burst out crying, 'I didn't mean to! He shouldn't have, he shouldn't have. All I did was give him a belt with the shovel.'

Looking as though she wouldn't mind giving Maisy a belt with the shovel, Ada knelt down by the man. Maisy snivelled and huge trails of snot run down from her nose. Just as they got near her mouth Maisy gave a huge sniff and dragged them back part of the way. Rose's stomach heaved violently.

'Here, Rose, give her this,' Ada ordered sharply and holds out her handkerchief. Ada and Thelma looked at each other across the man lying on the ground. 'Oh for God's sake,' Ada rasped irritably as Maisy floundered, 'can't you even wipe your nose properly?' Ada got up, grabbed the hanky and wiped Maisy's face. 'Now blow,' she said, holding the hanky to Maisy's nose. Maisy blew. 'Get rid of this,' Ada said to Rose. But that was too much. Rose turned away and was sick onto the lawn. 'Oh for God's sake,' Ada said. She looked at the used hanky with sick disgust. 'Now stop it at once Rose,' she said. 'If this is the worst you ever see you'll have a very good life, believe me.' She threw the hanky on the ground.

'I'd just like to know what I've done,' Thelma said, looking up at the sky. 'I'd just like to know what the bloody hell I've done.' Ada looked at her contemptuously. Thelma bent over and listened to the man's chest. Then she stood up, looked at Ada, didn't say a word.

'Oh for Christ's sake,' Ada said.

The two women looked at each other for what seemed like a long time. Thelma's eyes were shadowed and she looked tired, as though she hadn't slept well. Ada's eyes were brighter, fiercer, the way they'd been since Rose told her about Sim. As she and Thelma looked at each other, something of that sharp intensity spread to Thelma. She nodded.

'What are you standing there for?' Ada said finally, as if just remembering that Rose, Jo and Maisy were there. 'Get her a clean hanky Rose.'

'Pooh,' Maisy said, 'smells like he's pooed his pants.'

'Mum,' Rose said, 'is that Ha – '

Thelma overrode her words. 'Jo, you get Maisy a hanky from

our place. Go on. Take Maisy and Rose and go home and make some tea. Then stoke up the fire, stick the girdle iron on and make some scones. The girls can help. And watch the noise eh? Any more people here and we might as well sell tickets.'

'What are you going to do?' asked Jo.

'I'm going to wake up this rooster and give him a piece of my mind. And then I'm going to see him off the property. And Mrs Anthony's going to help me. Right Ada?'

There was a tense pause. Slowly Ada nodded.

'Then I want to talk to Mrs Anthony.'

They had made the scones and cleaned up, set the table and had the kettle well boiling when Thelma and Ada came into the kitchen. They both looked even tireder now. 'Thank God,' Thelma said, 'a cup of tea. We'll just wash our hands.'

'What about the man?' Maisy asked.

'He's gone,' said Thelma, 'buggered off and, hopefully, fallen in a ditch somewhere and drowned himself. You just forget all about him. If we never see him again it'll be too soon.'

'Who was it Mum?' asked Jo.

'Don't know,' said Thelma, 'and I don't care. Some tramp I suppose. Now hurry up and eat your supper, then I suppose we'd better see Maisy home.'

'She won't go,' said Rose. She must have been wrong about the hands. If it had been Harry Oliver from the pub Ada would know him. 'I tried to get her to, but she won't. She just keeps saying home's horrible.'

'Oh Christ,' Thelma said, addressing the ceiling this time, 'where does it end? That's all I want to know. Where – does – it – end?'

No one answered.

'She can sleep at the end of Rose's bed,' Ada said, 'I've had enough for one night.'

'Which reminds me,' said Thelma, 'I'd better have a look at that leg before you go. I'd rest it if I was you. Better let them know at the pub that you won't be in to work on Monday.'

'It'll be fine,' Ada said. Then Rose saw something that only later did she realise was one of those moments of clarity that came after times of great tension. Whatever Thelma had said to Ada had taken away the hatred and disgust and sense of betrayal which had been in her mother's eyes for months. Her eyes were tired but calm. Even her voice had changed. 'My leg'll be fine. And I'd better turn up.'

'If you're sure,' said Thelma who looked different too. Still tired but somehow more alive. Rose had heard her dragging her feet around their house, but now she walked purposefully to the stove, grabbed the coal scuttle and filled the fire.

'I'd better,' Ada repeated, 'in fact I was wondering –' and she moved closer to Thelma, lowered her voice and spoke softly.

Thelma nodded. 'Right,' she said, 'yeah, you're right.'

In the morning Maisy had gone. Rose heard Ada in the kitchen. She stretched luxuriously then felt underneath her pillow for the old movie magazine Jo loaned her, looked at the pictures of Ingrid Bergman and Marilyn Monroe. Rose loved Ingrid's face, Jo preferred Marilyn's. Rose felt sorry for Ingrid, falling in love with Roberto and being gossiped about, but at least she's happy now with all those twins, her large family. Her bed felt good without Maisy in it. Maybe she missed her mother, maybe that's why she didn't want to go home. Rose could understand that. If it had been Ada who'd died, she would have missed her so much she didn't want to even think about it. Really she wasn't missing Sim at all. He had died, he was gone. When he was alive he made it obvious he'd have preferred a boy. 'Don't be too worried about that,' Ada told her many times, 'men often want sons. Doesn't mean he doesn't love you.' Rose couldn't say he was a bad father. He was kind, didn't hit her, didn't even growl, and sometimes he was so funny, you couldn't help laughing.

Rose remembers being in a car Sim borrowed to take Ada for a Sunday afternoon drive. Rose sat in the back. Ada hadn't wanted to go, but in the end she gave in. He'd driven out into the country to find a possie to have the afternoon tea. They had a thermos and a bottle of milk and a jar of sugar, a packet of bought biscuits for a treat, all packed into a wooden box.

'Shagger's Hill,' her father said, indicating a hill on the right. He was grinning.

'Sssh,' Ada said, frowning.

'Lots of shags there,' Sim said, 'that's all I meant. Big birds, Rose,' he added helpfully. Ada started to giggle, tried to control herself, but they were too strong for her. She laughed helplessly and Rose saw her father look pleased with himself. Rose knew, of course, exactly what Shagger's Hill meant and knew it was another of the things adults say that children aren't supposed to catch on to. As if kids didn't know about people doing it. Rose wondered who would make her mother laugh now? Not that it had happened much. Ada was always, at least in Rose's presence, perfectly pleasant to her husband, but years later Rose realised that what was missing between her mother and father was the day-to-day spontaneity which happens between two people who live and love together. There were no sudden surges of laughter, no flare-ups of argument, none of the ups and downs Rose knew happened. At the time, though, all Rose knew was the politeness on Ada's part and the carefulness on Sim's. It was normal. She thought nothing of it.

'You going to lie there all day?' Ada didn't sound angry. Rose relaxed, yawned, got up and wandered out to the kitchen, screwing her eyes as she went to make stars in the air. Ada had cooked pancakes, Rose's favourite. They were a bit burned, but there was golden syrup, lemon juice and sugar on the table so that would all wash down the burned bits. At the end of the table sat Maisy, her face smeared with golden syrup and sugar. 'Wipe your face Maisy,' Ada said, and Maisy grabbed the old tea towel sitting beside her and wiped her face.

'Good girl,' Ada said and Maisy lit up like a lamp. She wiped her face unnecessarily hard, unnecessarily often, after that and smiled all the time. It took a bit of getting used to, but at least it didn't make Rose feel sick.

'Have your breakfast Rose, then get washed and dressed. When you've finished I'll run the bath for Maisy. She needs a good do. Something will have to be done about that hair. When you're dressed you can go and ask Mrs Millet for the clothes she said would fit Maisy.'

Last week Ada had told Rose that Harry Oliver had offered them the downstairs flat in the pub he and his wife shared when she was alive. 'Says he doesn't need a whole flat now,' she said, 'he has all his meals in the pub kitchen and, as far as the evenings are concerned, by the time the pub shuts and he's cleaned up, all he wants to do is lie on his bed and enjoy a read. He's sick of cleaning so we'd be doing him a favour. I've been thinking of selling this place, been paying it off ten years now, should get a reasonable whack in my hand and with your father's insurance I thought I could afford something else in a better neighbourhood. But if I took up Harry's offer I could leave it in the bank and save even more. Only be a nominal rent, electricity and food thrown in, might be a good thing.'

'Where would you be,' Rose asked, 'at night?'

Ada didn't answer.

Rose carried her yesterday's clothes out to the wash-house. Ada was already bent over the tub rubbing Maisy's clothes against the ribbed board. 'I'll soak these overnight,' she said. 'Wait till I see that father of hers.' She added, 'Rose, just a minute. I've had a good think about it and the pub flat wouldn't really be suitable. And the drinking – I know it's been a worry. I'm putting a stop to it.'

Rose couldn't answer, she wanted to cry. A voice rang out. 'Are you there Ada?' Thelma Millet. Behind her stood Jo.

'Yes?' Ada said, her voice alert, edgy.

'It's OK,' Thelma said, 'it's OK. Just thought you'd be interested to know that Harry Oliver hopped town last night. Doesn't appear to be any hanky panky with the pub takings, but he's let the place get a bit run-down since his wife died. Apparently the owners had a word with the sergeant. If you hadn't gone to work there Ada, he'd have probably been asked to leave months ago. Anyway, according to the sergeant, some-one was seen leaving the pub in the early hours. It was still dark, so they couldn't see who it was, reckoned there were two people, one carrying a suitcase and a bag. The sergeant reckons it was Harry, thinks the second person must have just been his shadow. His stuff's gone anyway. I took the opportunity to have a word with the sergeant about Frankie Beacon. He says he feels sorry for the man, but he'll have a word.'

'I could take Maisy I suppose.' Ada said it unwillingly, but she said it.

Thelma looked startled. 'Christ,' she said, 'I know how you feel, but you don't have to go that far.' Then she said, 'See what you mean. OK. Good idea. You won't have to do it all on your own. I'll give you a hand.' She turned to go. 'President Kennedy has been shot. Dead. Terrible mess apparently. His poor wife!'

'There's always someone else,' Ada said.

'Yeah?' said Thelma sarcastically, 'no kidding.'

Ada started laughing. She laughed and laughed and laughed even more than she did that afternoon when they passed Shagger's Hill. Thelma grinned, pleased. Rose rolled her eyes at Jo. Adults!

'Boom boom,' said Maisy.

Ada and Thelma stopped laughing. Thelma looked at Maisy then up at the sky. 'I just want to know what I've done,' Maisy said.

THIRTEEN

Rose says, 'That's the river, George.' George is supremely indifferent. The rain last night has left the grass wet so she walks along the path at the top of the bank. George enjoys being moved along in the stroller, but does not enjoy stopping in the stroller. He doesn't care for views, is indifferent to the kingfisher on the wire or the ten big white geese who stare at them superciliously as they pass. Every time Rose stops to look at the river, or a bird, he waits for a moment and when the stroller doesn't move, gives a protesting cry. 'Look, George, a big bath,' Rose says, hoping to God no one can hear her. No one except a few-months-old child, that is.

Earlier, Rose had phoned Sibyl. Kitty answered. She sounded subdued. 'Sib's in the shower. We're off to the mall. Retail therapy she reckons. Then we're going somewhere for lunch.' 'It's all right,' Rose said, 'you can say Olga's. How's Sib?'

'Louise,' Kitty hesitated, and Rose knew exactly what she was going to say and that she didn't want to hear it, but she was going to have to. 'She rang Sib last night. She's really sick. They can't do chemo even, it's too late. So after lunch we're going to see her.' Kitty sounded close to tears. She changed the subject abruptly, as though she couldn't bear to say any more and said, almost truculently, 'Have you ever heard of memory boxes?'

'Yes,' Rose was surprised to hear her voice sounding so calm, 'in a book Sibyl and I both read. *Before I Say Goodbye*. Ruth Picardie.'

'Sib wants to do one. She says find her a trunk, a box is too small.'

'I've got a trunk,' Rose said, 'one of Ada's. You can have that. Pick it up tomorrow. Give my love to Sib. And Louise.'

'Will do,' Kitty said.

Louise, thought Rose, Louise. Two of us, there's just me left. I wonder when it will happen to me. She felt an immense tiredness as she stared out the window still holding the telephone. I wish I hadn't rung, she thought, first Sib, now Louise, soon it'll be me.

Now she thinks how lucky she is to be able to see those white, white geese and the blue-green kingfisher. It's not just that given the mess industry and successive councils have made of the river mouth, it's a miracle even this little patch has survived, but that she's here right now, that George is here; that at this very moment the white geese are honking and the kingfisher is so intent on that shape in the water it doesn't even turn its head; that so far, she hasn't been given the bad news. Monday, she thinks, Monday, they'll tell me Monday.

The spit where the Waiwhetū Stream separates from the river is haven for all sorts of ducks, geese and swans that congregate here all year, whose colonies are hugely increased as May, the duck-shooting season, approaches, and then reduce again as the danger passes. It never ceases to amaze Rose how many varieties of duck and other birds might be seen here. She has even seen quail scuttling away. Out on the river she counts five pairs of geese. One lone goose is skulking a little way back from this main group. Every time it gets close to the others one of them turns and honks at it, and it falls back again. They don't want it now, although it was probably part of the group before its mate vanished.

'Aha, aha,' says George.

'Once upon a time,' Rose tells him, 'there were several tracks to the sea through the forest from the Akatarawa Range, but most were only used by bird hunters or by war parties. On their way was a big raupō-fringed lagoon which was the home of two man-eating taniwha. These two taniwha terrorised and ate anyone who came their way. So eventually the hunters stopped using the area and the warriors decided it was safer to make peace, which was all very nice for them, but the taniwha soon became very hungry without juicy humans to eat. So they began eating the shrubs and the bark of trees around the lagoon, and pretty soon the water was fringed not with healthy, vigorous raupō and giant kahikatea, but with grey, dead trunks and grey, dead places. The taniwha, who couldn't leave the water for too long or they would die, grew thinner and thinner as their food supplies dried up. Then along came some little boys exploring the lagoon. The little boys had been told not to go near the taniwha, but when did little boys take any notice of such commands? The two taniwha couldn't believe their eyes as this group of juicy morsels arrived on their doorstep. They crept up on the boys and lunged. But the little boys had seen them in the nick of time and jumped away, and the two taniwha crashed into each other. They charged and lunged and bit and ripped at each other with such force that the bank of the lagoon collapsed and its waters began gushing out all the way to the far-off sea in Te Whanganui-a-Tara, the Great Harbour of Tara.

The taniwha were appalled. With great cries they stopped fighting and charged after the water, tearing a deep channel in their wake. This channel soon filled up with water and was given the name Waiwhetū, because the water was so clear you could see stars in it.

When these two fierce taniwha finally reached the deeps of Te Whanganui-a-Tara these two, who had everyone who met them shaking in their skins with fear, now discovered what it was like to be really really frightened themselves. Te Whanganui-a-Tara had a big, fierce taniwha of its own. He made short work of the two interlopers and they disappeared inside his big fat stomach, never to be seen again. But the power of those two taniwha never quite left the Waiwhetū and when in 1839 the big river, called Heretaunga for at least one thousand years, was renamed Hutt (after the founding member, director and chairman of the New Zealand Company, Sir William Hutt), and the valley was given an Upper and Lower Hutt just like they did in England, and the creeks, islands, bays, headlands, straights, reefs, all were given new names by the new settlers, but the channel forged by the two taniwha, with the waters flowing through it to the sea and back, remained Waiwhetū, Starry Waters. And sometimes on a very clear, still night, you can see the two once-fierce taniwha glide and play among the stars of the waters they loved, and that is why the waters will always be called Waiwhetū, the water of stars.'

George is asleep. Rose pushes the stroller back along the stop-bank path. There's a move on at the moment in Lower Hutt to change the name again. In fact, there's been debate since the 1940s. The proposers want to drop the word 'Lower' and have Hutt City as the main name. There have been letters in the *Hutt News*, both for and against. Some have been very eloquent about sticking to tradition and keeping the present name.

Now, thinks Rose, can't put it off any longer. Just open the damned thing Rose. She steers the stroller over the rutted grass and weeds and down towards the river. The water's very clear today, the mass of it seemingly quite still, waiting. She stares into it and thinks for the millionth time, I wonder how I could reproduce this in fabric? What colours? What fabric — silk?

Silvery satin? Grey shiny cotton? She pulls the envelope from her pocket and takes out the letter. It's quite short.

Dear Rose,

I write to apologise for being such a coward four years ago. I should have supported you and not allowed my anxiety about losing my job to take over. I also realise now, that I had other anxieties which I hadn't faced. It's been on my mind ever since. I have recently told Mr Gerrison that I feel a grave injustice was done and I've contacted John Nelson, chairman of the Board of Trustees, and told him the same. I am deeply sorry and ashamed of the hurt I caused and for being partly the cause of you leaving as you did. I am hopeful you will be generous and allow me to come and see you, briefly, to apologise in person.

Yours sincerely, Marcy.

Rose's hand shakes as she tears the letter into tiny pieces and throws them in the river. 'The cheek,' she says to the little white scraps as they float away towards the sea, 'the bloody cheek!' In the water there is a blackboard in a classroom. There is graffiti on it. Dirty dyke. Pervert. Lesbians are Filth.

She humps the stroller back over the grass and up the stony track. 'You'll be all right,' she hears her mother saying, 'you'll be all right. I was.'

FOURTEEN

The first thing Ada knew about her husband's death was when she came home from choir practice, saw the doctor's car outside Thelma Millet's place and Rose waiting at their own gate. Waiting for Ada, Rose imagined her father, naked, sprawled face down, stiff, among Mrs Millett's sheets. She wonders if his thing was inside Mrs Millett and what it was like for her. Did he give a tragic cry and fall back moaning? Maybe death gave him such a fright he yelled out his favourite bad expression, 'Christ almighty!' as he died. As he realised. If he had time to realise. Did he think of her mother? Of the moment when she would be told? Of who will have to tell her? Of his daughter? Perhaps he did. Perhaps that was why he said Christ almighty! For quite a long time Rose never thought of Sim without seeing him arching back on top of Mrs Millett yelling, 'Christ almighty!'

'Shall we go down to the church hall and get your mother?' Jo said, her face white, her eyes staring past Rose as if she couldn't possibly risk looking into Rose's eyes.

'No,' Rose said, 'no.' Her mother would not want to get this news while the choir looked on.

'Shall I stay with you?' asked Jo.

Rose shook her head.

'I'm sorry,' Jo whispered, 'I'm sorry.'

'What's up?' Ada asked, smiling in spite of the sight of Doctor Carson's flash Citroën, much too low slung for our country roads so Claude said, parked outside her neighbour's house. Rose could see the elation a good sing always arouses bubbling away inside her mother. Ada reckoned a good sing sent notes buzzing round her veins like bees in the height of summer, drunk on nectar from the blue borage flowers. It was that exhilaration that kept Ada singing in what was virtually a church choir. Rose didn't want to quench that, didn't want to tell her, but there was no one else to do it.

She never forgot how her mother's face changed. The skin on it stretched tight and then tighter across her cheeks and her chin, and somehow, it seemed to Rose, she grew leaner and taller. Her nose, which had always been in proportion, grew longer, her eyes got smaller and her lips disappeared. She was ugly. Her music book was clutched so tightly the bones on her fingers looked as though they would pop out of her skin. Ada stayed immobile for some minutes that seemed like hours then, shaking her head sharply once as if to clear it, she turned and marched up the old concrete path and inside their house.

Rose didn't know what to say when she got inside. 'Shall I make a cup of tea?' seemed a bit funny, but she said it anyway.

Ada nodded. Why not, the nod said, make a cup of tea, don't make a cup of tea, what difference does it make now? Rose put a piece of wood in the range then a few pieces of coal and the embers blazed into life under the kettle. When the water in the kettle trilled she put some in the pot, swirled it round, emptied it in the sink and put two teaspoons of Bell tea leaves in the pot. She poured boiling water over the leaves and left it to draw, got two cups and poured some milk from the bottle in the fridge into the small white jug. Ada didn't allow the bottle on the table. No sugar. Ada didn't take sugar in her tea so the only time Rose had sugar was when she sneakily made a whole pot of tea for herself and drank it all, thick with sugar, when Ada was out.

Ada sat in her old varnished bentwood chair at the top of the scrubbed wooden table with its floral baize cover, one of her hands rested on the table, the other curled in her lap. She stared ahead straight at the framed photo of Sim and Claude aged twenty and seventeen – their mother between them, black hat, black coat, severe expression – but Rose doubted she actually seeing the photo. Rose poured a cup of tea and pushed it towards her mother who blinked at the movement, breathed deeply, and then turned her head and looked at Rose as if wondering who she was. 'Your tea,' Rose prompted when Ada made no move to drink it. Ada picked up the cup and sipped. After that first taste she drank quickly. She was always parched after choir practice. 'Another one?' Rose said, more to break the silence than because Ada might really want another cup.

'What?' Ada said.

'Do you want another cup of tea?'

Her mother shrugged so Rose quickly poured her another and one for herself.

'You'd better go to bed now,' her mother said. After a few minutes she said, 'What's the time?'

'Five past ten.'

'You get off then. You've got school tomorrow.'

Rose didn't argue. 'What about you?'

'Soon,' she said, 'soon.'

'Can I sleep in your bed?' Rose didn't know why she asked, the words just came out. She hadn't slept in her mother's bed since she was little.

Ada made a noise like a groan. 'Why not?' she said.

There was a knock at the door. Rose stood up to go and answer it.

'Leave it,' commanded her mother in a fierce whisper, 'leave it.'

The knocking sounded again, louder. Whoever was at their door must have known they were up because the lights were on, must have known Ada didn't want to see them. But whoever it was knocked a third time. 'Mrs Anthony,' a man's voice said, 'Mrs Anthony, it's Harvey Hipp here. I need to talk to you Mrs Anthony.' Ada, always so intent on good manners and behaving yourself, sipped her tea, shut her eyes, and sat as though there was no knocking, no voice saying just five minutes Mrs Anthony, just five minutes, please Mrs Anthony.

Rose's eyes were wide open, staring not at the door where the knocking sounded, but at Ada, asking a question without actually putting it into words.

'The undertaker,' her mother said, 'Harvey Hipp's the undertaker.'

'I know who Mr Hipp is,' Rose said.

Ada looked at her daughter impatiently. 'He wants to know how I want your father buried and what sort of coffin I'd like. That's why he's knocking at the door.' She spoke quickly, angrily, as though talking to someone she disliked.

'Mrs Anthony,' the voice was louder, 'Mrs Anthony, just a few minutes. I know you must be upset, but decisions have to be made. We should call the police, sudden death you know, but –'

'Ada!' A new voice. 'Ada! It's Claude.'

Ada got up and opened the door. Rose saw, for the first time, how alike her father and uncle really were. Both tall, dark hair, eyes that smiled, a long nose and an oblong-shaped jaw. If you hadn't seen Sim you'd think Claude was a really good-looking man.

Claude, her mother and Rose sat at the table. The tea got cold while Harvey Hipp, who declined a seat, explained that the doctor reckoned there was no need to involve the police.

'It's obvious Sim died of a heart attack. And if the police are brought in it'll make everything so much more ...' Mr Hipp waved his arms and let his voice fall.

'More?' asked Ada into the silence, more to be a nark than really wanting to have it spelled out.

Harvey Hipp looked uncomfortable.

'Spit it out Harv,' said Claude.

Mr Hipp spoke in a rush. 'As it happens, Mrs Anthony, I owe Thelma a favour so if it's all right with you, I can – ahem – remove the body and – ahem – see to everything.'

'I'm not paying, I'm telling you that right now,' Ada said. 'If she wants a coffin she can pay for it.'

'I'll pay for my brother's coffin.' Claude sounded angry.

Ada looked at him. 'As far as I'm concerned you can just drop him in a hole and forget him.'

'I'll pay,' repeated Claude. He looked at Harvey Hipp and said, 'What did Doctor Carson say?'

'He said it would be – upsetting – enough for Mrs Anthony without the police.'

'Huh,' Ada said, her voice as dry as an old bone, 'the sergeant will know anyway, you know what this place is like.'

'He'll know all right,' Mr Hipp said, 'but not officially, if you get my meaning. Not officially. If he's not informed officially, then he doesn't have to take any action.'

Mr Hipp frowned and darted a quick glance at Rose.

'Rose is twelve,' Ada said, 'she might as well find out what life's about. Do what you like,' she added to Claude, 'just don't bother me with it. Is that clear?'

Claude cleared his throat and moved impatiently, but didn't say anything.

'Quite,' said Mr Hipp, 'quite. And may I say how sorry, ahem, how sorry I am.'

'Why?' asked Ada, 'it's more money coming in isn't it? Can't be that bad.'

Claude said, 'Ada! For Christ's sake! It's not Harvey's fault.'

Mr Hipp looked more hurt than angry. 'Mrs Anthony,' he said, 'Claude's right. It's not my fault.'

'What was the favour Thelma Millett did you?' Ada sounded really nasty.

Harvey Hipp's face and neck, even his hands, were instantly flushed with red. 'How dare you,' his voice trembled, 'how dare you! I'm trying to make allowances – but – here we have the doctor and me falling over ourselves to make it ahem well, as easy as we can for you in the circumstances and –'

'And all I can do is be angry and deeply offended?' said Ada. 'Mr Hipp, if you wanted grateful snivelling, you've come to the wrong house. I don't think for one minute that not calling the police is purely for my sake and you can tell the doctor I said that. He probably owes Thelma Millet a favour too. Perhaps even the sergeant is not above owing her a favour. Probably, when it's all boiled down, I owe her a favour. Well, you all do what you must. Just leave me out of it.'

'We can't do that Ada,' Claude said, 'you must see, we can't do that.'

'Why not,' said Ada, 'he did.'

Harvey Hipp looked at Claude, and Claude looked back at him.

'I'll see you tomorrow Claude,' Rose's mother said in a way that meant, go now, no argument.

'If you're sure.' Claude sounded doubtful.

She didn't answer. Mr Hipp wished them goodnight. Rose accompanied them to the door and waited until they had enough time to get to the front gate before she turned the out-side light off.

'Right,' Ada said, 'bed.'

It was then, lying in the dark, Ada told Rose about Manny. Emanuel. Emanuel Jonis. Emanuel Jones. A small, stocky man who liked to stand in the rain in the dark green of the Catlins.

'Now I'm the immigrant in a new country, Rose,' Ada said after. 'Now I know how it feels.'

George burps. Thank God for George. He has a solidity and warmth that, for all their short acquaintance, seems hugely familiar and calming. His eyes are closed and his mouth around the teat is smiling as if at a joke only he understands. His faintly blue lids are creased along the lashes' end. They are dark, the lashes. They match the soft cap of dark silk that covers his head. Was it only fifteen or so hours since she'd first set eyes on him? As she lifts him to put in the carrycot which will be strapped in the car, he opens his eyes and they stare at each other. Suddenly he wrinkles his nose and smiles at her. Instantly Rose's heart surges with pure pleasure. She smiles back. There is a moment of wordless delight in each other, and in that instant Rose falls like a stone into love. It is a remarkably clear-sighted experience. She knows exactly what is happening and is unable, does not even want, to stop it. I've been here before, she thinks, remembering Olga and that meeting when she wandered in. Irrevocable, this is irrevocable. George farts in a bubbling growl and Rose laughs. Who are you? she thinks. Who left you on my porch? When are they coming back? I must find them. How will I bear it when they come for you?

FIFTEEN

The phone rings on and on. Lizzie must be out. Rose will ring again later.

'Heard Lizzie had post-natal depression,' Olga said hastily, before she dashed off to her café. Their whole meeting had been totally unsatisfactory. Rose and George arrived at the bookshop, Rose said thanks, Olga said fine, that Rose would probably need someone to hold George while she shopped so she'd come back at three and go with her to the supermarket. 'Make it half past?' Rose asked, 'I want to have a word with Betty.'

'Half past,' agreed Olga, 'sorry Rose, must go, Leo says he's run out of space for the meat. Bye.'

What did you expect Rose? A passionate embrace, a plea for forgiveness? Fortunately she didn't have a lot of time to think about it. The shop was busy with people who browsed and didn't buy until five to three, George wakeful, and she was glad when finally the last one left with three collections of Lou Johnson's poems under his arm and she could lock the door. She shovelled the innards of the till into the canvas bag and hastily entered the orders she'd recorded in her diary on the computer, secure in the knowledge that they'd pop up when she opened up the computer on Monday morning. 'You're going to have to put up with a visit to Betty and then a trek around the supermarket,' she informed George, 'so you might as well put a good face on it.' He didn't appear to mind this straight talking. A bubble came out of his mouth, collapsed and dribbled down his chin. As she wiped it she thought of George Byron and his daughter, another Ada. One thing she would bet on with certainty was that Byron never wiped the dribble away from his daughter's chin. '*The Assyrian came down like a wolf on the fold.*' It sure did. Both Ada Byron and her father were certifiably mad at times. Some tiny genetic connecting thing in their brain didn't work, or worked too much. Bipolar it's called these days.

George needs to be changed. Rose can't understand where all this piddle comes from. She didn't pee half as many times as George did and surely, on the basis of size alone, her bladder should produce more. He must have the bladder of a camel without the ability to hold on to its contents. 'Never mind,' she tells him, 'as long as your brain works, that's the main thing.' He seemed bright enough. He knew what to do to get fed, that was obvious.

Rose's brain works very well. It organises her actions, nerves, reactions, darts here, darts there. Some people describe the brain as a warehouse, but Rose thinks hers is a series of files, all of which hold different Roses. When the right buttons are pressed one of the Roses is brought up on the screen of her mind. Whether from the past or future, none of them resembles the present Rose. Randomly they surface, triggered by an image, a memory, some words, the sight of a tree, a sound or a smell. These other Roses, whatever their role in the actual happening they bring to the surface, now feature in the middle of events, incidents, images. It is other people who are on the margins, although the words they speak live forever in Rose's files.

'Is your mother home?'

'Of course I believe you – it's just – I can't afford to lose my job.'

'Miss Anthony said if I wanted to be Juliet I must be nice to her. And she touched me. There.'

'Once upon a time in a far distant land there lived a race of people composed solely of bones.'

'I'm very sorry Miss Anthony, there's been a terrible accident.'

'Sorry Rose, it's definitely cancer.'

'If I didn't know you were anti all people I might think –'

'They can't do chemo, too late apparently.'

It is alchemy the way thoughts, incidents, memories are changed once they are secure in her files. None of them exact, all bearing exaggerations, wishful thoughts, dreams, fears, all essential because they tell her who she is. One of Rose's fears is that when she's really old all these Roses will crash and the real Rose will be lost. She sees an old Rose crouched in a cane chair giggling to herself and dribbling. With no one there to wipe her chin. Pretty depressing. She could live until she's ninety or even one hundred and there's no point spending the next forty or so years wallowing in worry about her brain's possible disintegration. She just hopes she knows who she is when she lies dying.

Ada Byron was a genius. She had a way, not with words, but with numbers; a talent she'd inherited from her mother whom Byron called, not admiringly, the Princess of Parallelograms. Rose is given to these enthusiasms for characters she finds in books, she enjoys them, and like old friends, she's always pleased to hear or find something new about them.

'There you are,' she says to George, 'please make that last for half an hour. Think you can do that?'

He stares impassively.

'OK,' Rose says, 'please yourself, if you get a rash don't blame me. It's your bum.'

Poor Lizzie. Post-natal depression. But she must be well enough to go out. Probably needed to go out. Better than staying home feeling sorry for yourself. Oh well, on with the dance Rose. She locks the canvas bag in the car and walks quickly into Calico and Cottons. She introduces George, and Betty smiles at him. Everyone smiles at George.

'How's Anne?' she says to Betty who looks startled, as well she might. Rose has never shown the slightest interest in Anne before.

'Tired,' Anne's mother says, carefully placing her ruler on the fabric and running the rotary cutter firmly along the side. She pats the fat quarter she's cut and folds it deftly into a small square. It's an unusual teal blue. Be good if you wanted to do the sea over at Evans Bay on a fine day. Sort of picture post-card, but striking. Rose wants it. 'Haven't seen her for a couple of weeks because my husband's had the flu, but we've spoken on the phone. She sounds a bit tired, a bit frazzled. It's not easy on your own.'

'No,' says Rose, 'and she's managing all right? Baby OK?'

Betty frowns and nods. 'Bit peaky. She says the baby's a bit peaky. Crying a lot. I said why doesn't she get the doctor, and she said she can't afford it. I said what about the subsidy, and she said you still have to pay something. She's only got enough for food and rent this week. So of course I said I'd pay.' She sighs, shakes her head, and as she automatically cuts two more fat quarters, out it pours. 'Sometimes you wonder about them, don't you. I thought the one thing my daughter would never do was get pregnant like this, no father around, but she did, she did. She was so sensible. That's what I thought. She had that good job. I do what I can, but with the shop, it's not as much as I'd like. She lives in this awful flat, honestly Rose, I nearly cried when I saw it. I think she's finding life very hard,' Betty tries to smile, 'if her bad temper's any indication.' She sighs, unfolds some more fabric. 'Sorry. Sometimes it just gets me down. I'd have her with us, but my husband is adamant. She's made her bed, let her lie on it, is his attitude. He's just so disappointed. She was his favourite. I don't know, you do your best for your kids and where does it get you? You think they're grown-up and then this sort of thing happens. Oh, I put a good face on it, but really Rose, sometimes it's just too hard.'

'Sorry. I just wondered.' Rose has a brainwave. 'How's your other daughter? The one who works in Wellington?'

'Been made redundant,' says Betty, 'but it's not the end of the world, she says, reckons she'll soon find something. Always been an optimist. She will find something too. In the meantime she's going to stay with Anne, sleep on her sofa. Should help Anne and she reckons she'll save money. That's all she cares about, saving money.'

'What does she think of Anne's situation?'

'She thinks the baby's wonderful, but swears she's never going to have any herself. She wants some land somewhere, she's always on about permaculture and sustainable gardening. It's a funny thing, Rose, she's more like my husband than Anne ever was, but he's never really taken to her. It'd break my heart if I let it. He only had eyes for Anne and now she's, as he sees it, let him down, he's shattered. Sometimes I wish I didn't have to go home and that's a fact.'

Betty sounds so desolate, Rose wishes she'd never started this conversation. 'I'll have one of those fat quarters, please Betty.'

Betty brightens immediately. 'Did you see that new silver fabric? Just came in yesterday. It's pure cotton but looks like satin. Beautiful.'

'OK,' Rose says resignedly. She has to smile.

'Even in the midst of her anxieties Betty never misses a trick,' Rose says to Olga, as they wait in the queue, 'but she looked better when I left.' The woman ahead of them grabs sugar and eggs from the trolley and puts them on the counter. She adds milk. Bread. Coffee. A chicken, potatoes, kūmara, pumpkin, broccoli. Must be planning a good old-fashioned roast dinner. Followed by the peach and passionfruit ice cream for dessert. They all wait for the assistant to install her till. It's Millie. The spiky hair has changed colour, but it's the same smile. 'Hi Rose!' she says, 'hello Olga!' The woman in front, still transferring goods from the trolley to the counter, stops, looks, raises her eyebrows and gives Olga that East Coast hello, grins and continues transferring her groceries. Millie looks at George then looks at Rose. 'Just looking after him for a friend,' says Rose. She's perfected this script as they've gone around the supermarket aisles greeting various surprised faces. 'How long have you been working here?' she asks, 'and where's your baby?'

'With Mum,' Mille says quickly then smiles attentively at the customer who is still unloading. You're not supposed to talk to other customers while you have another one in front of you, but Millie continues.

'Decided it was time I did something about a job. Not much use having UE if it just goes to waste. Didn't fancy university; all those up-themselves noddies telling me how I should think, decided I get on well with people, so I applied for a trainee manager's job and got it, but I have to do my time on the checkout.'

Millie pushes the woman's goods over the barcode patch and slides them into the waiting hands of Marge Have a Nice Day. Out of the corner of her eye Rose sees the store detective, a large Māori woman, ease herself around the back of the checkout behind Millie and stand quietly, apparently looking out the window. Something is up. Olga has noticed too. They look at each other and wait.

The woman turns the trolley in which her bags have been placed by Marge Have a Nice Day, moves to go out the door.

The detective takes a step forward. The woman stops. She holds the checkout slip. 'Excuse me,' she calls to Millie, 'how many frozen chickens are there in my groceries?'

Millie gasps, rolls her eyes at Rose, tries her best to remember. Being a checkout operator is not the sort of job you can do blindfold whatever some customers think, but once you've gone past the checkout, you've gone out of the operator's life.

'Should've been two,' the woman says, 'there's only one on the list.' She walks back to the counter and starts unloading the bags from the trolley. 'Sorry!' she calls to Rose and Olga, 'sorry!' she calls to the queue behind them.

There is only one chicken. 'That's funny,' she says, 'I know I picked up two.' She fumbles among the groceries as though she expects a frozen chicken to pop out of thin air. Get on with it, Rose thinks. 'Well, I don't know,' the woman says, and then a thought strikes her, a blinding light, it seems.

'Coarse acting number sixty-four,' mutters Olga in Rose's ear, 'maybe she'd like to audition for Hutt Rep.'

'Aha!' says the woman. She dumps her backpack on the counter, scrabbles in it and pulls out a frozen chicken. 'Sorry, sorry,' she apologises, 'sorry, I've been really busy lately!' She hauls the backpack towards Marge and says, 'You'd better have a look in it and see if there's anything else there.' She rips open the zip to its fullest and, while Marge is reluctantly peering in, explains to Millie and the supermarket at large that she's had a lot on her mind lately. Some real worries. Everything is all right now, but it just shows how your mind wanders. 'Must have been thinking of something else.'

Marge pushes the backpack back towards the woman, who repacks the trolley and walks towards the sliding doors with a cheery 'Morning!' to the store detective who, with a face like stone, is pretending to study the notices posted on the board provided for customers.

Rose keeps her face passive. Millie has a closer look at George. 'Your mother doesn't mind having the baby?' she asks Millie.

Millie laughs. 'She prefers them that age, says she knows where they are,' Millie snorts, 'and my ex-boyfriend helps out.' She lowers her voice, but Rose can almost hear the ears flapping in the queue. 'Still wants us to get married,' she says, 'but I told him he has to grow up, get a good job, get some attitude, you know? There's more to being a good father than playing ball.'

Rose nods, as though she understands what Millie means. How do you 'get' attitude? Maybe you go to an attitude shop and buy some. If so, I'll have a kilo, please. She pays and takes the receipt, and Olga pushes the trolley out.

'I'll get Mum to bring the baby into the shop,' calls Millie, 'and you can see how she's grown!'

The woman with the frozen chicken is unloading her goods into the boot of a large old bronze-coloured car. She smiles at them, winks, shuts the boot. 'Hello Olga,' she says and laughs. 'Just saw the D in time,' she says and gets into the driving seat, smiles and backs out, and drives away.

'Who's that?'

'Oh, just someone I met once,' says Olga.

One of them, thinks Rose. One of the women who stay in Olga's spare room. That room which is available for desperate women. George's mother is probably in that category. God, thinks Rose, I hope she surfaces soon. After they pack up the boot, strap George securely in the seat, get into the car, Olga is still smiling.

'I know the statistics,' she says, just a little defensively, 'shop-lifting creams off three percent of any profit (or loss) and that it's a big no-no. But the last time I saw her she had a broken arm, bruises all over, and she'd been raped by two men. Somehow I can't judge her.'

'I got a letter from Marcy,' Rose says. She hasn't meant to tell Olga but the words come out.

Olga turns sharply. 'What did she want?'

'To say she's sorry.'

'Huh,' says Olga.

George makes a sound and they both turn and look at him. 'Aha,' he says.

'Yes, well, I'd better get him home,' says Rose.

'You OK?' asks Olga.

Rose nods. She'd like to have talked about the letter; whether she'd made a mistake ripping it up, whether she should have kept it. Whether she should forgive. Whether she could. Nelson Mandela had, and God knows he had more reason not to than Rose does.

George mews warningly. 'Soon,' Rose says to him, 'soon.' She turns to Olga. 'I hope his mother turns up soon. I don't want him to go, but she must be frantic.'

'Have you thought –' Olga stops.

'What? What?'

'Maybe she's not able to. Turn up.'

'Not able to? Oh shit. Oh no. Oh no. You mean badly hurt?'

'Either that, or –'

Rose is appalled. Although why she should be, she can't think. Of course it's a possibility. She's read worse, heard worse.

'Olga,' she says.

'Yes?'

'Why did you put up with the one night a week if you didn't like it?'

'I wanted to be sure,' Olga says, 'I thought that's why you suggested it. Because you weren't sure either. Now I am.'

'I'm sorry,' Rose says.

'Me too,' Olga says. She says it cheerfully, as though it's of no moment.

'Louise is very sick.'

'Mmn,' says Olga, 'Sib told me.'

Rose drops Olga off at the café and as she drives home she sings to George. 'I'm only a poor Cinderella,' she sings, 'nobody loves me it seems.' Cheer up for God's sake, she tells herself, cheer up.

Turning into Little Salamander, she hears the boom box. Bugger. Bloody Knock-Knock has started afternoon sessions again. Bugger, bugger. The noise is unbearable. George starts aha-ing and in a couple of seconds has wound up to full volume. Rose is immediately intensely, furiously, passionately angry. A thermometer inside has just shot up a couple of hundred degrees. She can't remember ever being so full of rage. Her whole body is on fire with it. 'Right,' she says to the now-screaming George, 'you're going to bed my boy, and I'm going to do something about that noise. Time I got some attitude.'

SIXTEEN

It's only a few metres, but it feels as though she's walking a marathon through thick treacle. The wind is increasing and will get worse. Run its course. As it always does. The trees are crackling and swishing in a sinister fashion, as though warning of worse to come. Over the road a man walks along muttering and shaking his fist upwards. He's absorbed in his own murky world, hardly likely to notice Rose. He must be squatting in one of the houses. He stops and laughs, doubled up, and as he straightens, still laughing, he sees her. His face changes and he walks quickly on, pushing against the wind, muttering to himself and firing quick glances over to where Rose is also straining against the wind.

Rose remembers that man at the dump, or the Refuse Recycling Station as it's now called. Much nicer to visit than when it was called the dump. In those days you smelled it and heard the noise of the seagulls before your vehicle reached the place where you dumped your rubbish. A name change in this instance was not just cosmetic. It signalled a completely different environment. No smell, no seagulls, no noise. When people moan about the good old days Rose always thinks of the dump or the days without washing machines.

She'd backed in between a four-wheel drive and an old station wagon. As she was unloading the boot and emptying the heavy plastic compost bags she kept to stow garden rubbish in, the man from the four-wheel drive – large, big face, huge arms with a tattoo of a boa constrictor writhing up one forearm –

was attempting to lift the trailer so it would tip its contents in the big channel where a man on a front-end loader was pushing rubbish into a large cavern down the end. He gave up, muttering to himself, and yelled over her head at the man unloading his rubbish from the back of his station wagon, 'Give us a hand, mate?'

The man said, reluctantly, it seemed to Rose, 'OK. Better not be too long. My son gets upset if he can't see me.' He clambered in front of Rose, 'Excuse me, sorry,' he said, and the two men lifted up the end of the trailer so that its other end tipped over the edge of the concrete retaining wall. All the bags, branches, an old couch, a broken chair, newspapers, plastic bags, slid into the pit. 'Thanks mate,' the fat man said, wiping his forehead with his hand, 'thanks. My 24-year-old son, who should have been here helping, is sitting at home hoping I'll drop dead so he'll get all my money.'

The other man ducked past Rose and gave her a look from under his brows. She pretended she hadn't heard. 'Yes,' he said, 'it's always hard.' He laughed, 'Daddy's coming soon boy, don't worry, Daddy's coming.' He laughed again, not happily. 'I know how you feel. Sometimes when I'm at home and there's no one else to help −' He shook his head. 'You OK boy? Good boy, Daddy's here.'

'Anyway mate, thanks for your help. Appreciate it.'

People, Rose thinks, people.

Good, here's the open gateway. How many times she's walked up this drive. She and Thelma got on better and better as Rose got older. Unlike Rose and Jo. Which is weird but there you are. We're all weird when you get down to it. The good thing is that somehow, as you age, another person's age doesn't matter. It's whether you click. That famous feminist verb. Well, Rose had 'clicked' with Thelma. Just another way of saying they looked at the world the same way. Rose thought Thelma had been surprised and pleased that she and Rose developed into friends in their own right. Thelma shared Rose's suspicions of Peter Paul Pearl but was won over, as Rose was (albeit even more reluctantly than Thelma), by Peter's genuine love for Ada.

Whether Thelma had any long-term guilt over Sim, Rose didn't know. She had never discussed her father with Thelma. It was a no-go zone, one that Rose was happy to leave undisturbed. She and Jo had never discussed him either. Dying in Thelma's bed put him beyond discussion, beyond even memory. Somehow though, Ada and Thelma found their way to that rough area which lay between a rock and a hard place. Only they could have surmounted the obstacles which lay in their path, only they could have done that. Whatever they said to each other, however the rapprochement was arrived at, they kept between them alone. And the Skeleton Woman.

Thelma had lived in this house as long as Rose could remember. She'd actually moved in when Rose was nearly a year old. Her husband had died or been injured or something after an accident on the wharf. So many things about Thelma she'd never got clarified. Rose knew that she'd used the insurance money as a deposit on the house. Rose had no idea whether Thelma had any other affairs after his death. Probably someone dying in your bed in the middle of a fuck was enough to put you off affairs for life. Rose wished she'd asked Thelma how she coped through all this, but it was too late now.

Four years ago, when Rose had come home, Thelma seemed to be the only one who understood her fear. The only one who didn't say Rose should have stayed and faced it out. Thelma said that Rose took the option she took. She said there were no rights or wrongs, or shoulds and shouldn'ts, there were options, and Rose had taken the one she had taken. An airy-fairy position, but at the time Rose had been grateful.

After a careful survey of the area, Rose scuttles up the driveway and leans thankfully into the safety of the old mutabilis. She's wearing gloves and long sleeves so the prickles could bite as much as they liked, it wouldn't be a worry. So far so good. Her breath is harsh and loud but the boom box effectively tops any other noise for miles. It's deafening. How can Knock-Knock stand it? She's read that powerful noise close up can kill and there's that Dorothy Sayer novel about church bells based on the same premise. The murderer shuts his victim in the bell tower, and the heavy giants crashing and booming in such close proximity kill him.

'Are you sure you want to do this?' Olga had asked when Rose rang her.
    'Certain,' Rose said, 'this is the time.'
    'If you're sure,' Olga still sounded doubtful.
    Rose didn't answer.
    'OK,' Olga said, 'I'll get the gear.'

'Right.' Rose lunges away from the bush, up the steps, grabs a brick from the small pile on the verandah and bashes it on the front door. So far so good. Everything according to plan. She bashes the brick on the door again. Nothing. They must all be deaf. She bangs the brick on the door so hard she thinks it will break, but it's an old strong wooden door. It shivers but doesn't yield. The noise inside goes down a fraction. There's some shouting and then the sound of heavy footsteps. She drops the brick and transfers the can to her right hand.

The door opens and there stands Knock-Knock. Even he looks startled when he sees the balaclava-clad head on top of a long pale-blue smock. 'Yeah?' he growls.

She sprays his glasses first then the rest of him in one wide swathe of red, not caring if she showers the door behind him. 'Fuck!' he yells in disbelief, 'Ding! Fucking hell!' He staggers back, his hands to his glasses, and she runs inside, into the sitting room, spraying as she goes. Sorry Thelma, she says in her head, sorry. She pulls out any cords she can see and then sprays the sound system for good measure. On her way out she gives Knock-Knock one more burst. Fumbling at his glasses only makes the mess worse. 'Ding!' he screams, 'Ding!'

A shout echoes from somewhere but Rose is out the door and on her way.

She scoots across the verandah, down the steps, and then she runs. She runs like she's never run before. The wind is at her back and she's flying. Back down the footpath, no time to know or care whether anyone sees her. Up her own driveway. Nearly there. She pants inside the open back door and on to the sheets of newspaper spread out over the floor. She drops the can, the gloves, and carefully, very carefully, strips off the balaclava, the smock, the socks and shoes. In her underwear she heads straight through to the bathroom, surveys herself in the mirror. No splashes, no dots, nothing. Good. No time to gloat. She pulls on the track pants and top she's left ready and pushes her feet into her ankle gumboots. Back in the hall she sees the newspaper has been rolled up and taken away to be safely stowed in the freezer. A minute to go in the time frame she's worked out. She shuts the back door and walks quickly towards her small vegetable garden, picking up the hoe on the way.

When Knock-Knock and Ding come tearing up her driveway she is hoeing the weeds around a row of carrots, her eyes squinting against the little grains of soil tossed up by the wind. 'Yes?' she says, wiping her forehead. Coarse acting number seventy-two, she hears Olga say in her head.

Knock-Knock looks as though he has a bad case of sunburn. Someone must have given him a towel to wipe the worst of it off but there's still enough to enjoy.

'Bloody bitch,' he says, 'I'll teach you.'

Ding says, 'Hold on Knock.'

'Shut up.'

'But there's no paint on her.'

'Shut up. Where were you anyway? You should have come when I yelled.'

'I couldn't. It's the chinese. It always does that. I had to stay sitting.'

'You got a problem?' asks Rose.

'You and me, we're going to have a little talk,' says Knock-Knock.

'I'm a bit busy at the moment. Want to get this weeding done before it's dark. You know what weeds are like when the carrots are small. If you let them get away on you the carrots are smothered.'

Knock-Knock is not in the mood to discuss gardening. He grabs the hoe and throws it away.

Ding says, 'Look Knock-Knock –'

'Has to be her. Who else has complained? It was her.' He reaches out and seizes Rose's arm. His fingers dig in. I'll have bruises there tomorrow, she thinks.

'I wouldn't if I was you,' she says.

'And who's going to stop me? Inside bitch. I think I'm gonna enjoy this.'

He pushes her ahead of him and as he does so a figure appears on the back porch. 'Something wrong?'

Standing on the porch is a policewoman. For a second Rose thinks Knock-Knock is going to pass out. He wipes his hand over his face, but when he takes his hand away the policewoman is still there. Ding doesn't hang about. He might not be the sharpest knife in the drawer but he knows when to make himself scarce. They hear his voice calling behind him, something about having to get back. 'Sorry it's the chinese,' floats back.

'Everything's OK,' says Rose, 'isn't that right?' She beams at Knock-Knock who gives her a filthy look. 'This is my neighbour, officer, we were just discussing music. He's a great lover of music.'

'Right,' says the officer, 'well I wanted a word with you Miss Anthony if you have a moment.'

'Sure,' Rose is annoyingly effusive, 'sure, always ready to help the police.' She turns to Knock-Knock. 'If you'll excuse me.'

Knock-Knock looks the officer up and down. He would like to say a number of things to this Māori woman in uniform but he doesn't. He doesn't need to. It's all there on his face. He snorts, gives her another look and walks away down the drive.

Rose goes inside followed by Olga in the policewoman's outfit.

'Done it!' She sits on her William Morris chair and laughs until she cries. She feels as though she is gliding across the skies in one of those big, highly coloured balloons, her rage completely gone, swept away in this euphoric soaring flight. 'I'm getting too old for this sort of thing,' she says finally.

Olga looks at her silently for a moment then says, 'Why is he called Knock-Knock?'

Rose shrugs. 'Something to do with those old jokes I suppose.'

'There's something else – insurance companies I think – what the hell is it? Oh yes, when two people have an accident, say, and both insurance companies are involved and they both agree to pay for their own client, it's called knock-knock. I think.'

'I don't think Knock-Knock has insurance,' Rose bursts out laughing again.

Olga starts removing the uniform she'd borrowed from the Player's wardrobe. 'He really wanted to have me on. Call me whatever's the latest for someone seen as brown on the outside and white on the inside.' Olga looks as though she might cry. Rose stops laughing. A chill wind is nudging the balloon.

'I'd better get back. The chef will think I'm doing this on purpose today because he's leaving.'

'I'm sorry,' Rose says, 'I shouldn't have asked you.'

'If it wasn't Knock-Knock it'd be someone else. Should be used to it. I talk smart, I'm up myself,' Olga sounds bitter and harsh, 'doesn't matter what I do, I haven't failed in the Pākehā world, so I must have been taken over.'

'I'm sorry,' Rose whispers. 'I'm sorry.'

'Wonder what his real name is.' Olga folds up the police-woman's uniform and puts it carefully in its box.

'Thank you,' Rose said.

'Better get these back to the theatre,' Olga says, and leaves.

George wakes and while she's bathing and feeding him, she thinks of Olga, thinks of that last tangihanga she attended. She'd visited marae before, had attended tangihanga before, but this was the first time as part of a whānau. Previously she would have been in a group of Pākehā work colleagues. She was nervous, she was always nervous. Olga held her hand on one side and Puti on the other. On either side of them walked Sam and Mere. Rose knew that in Puti's case holding the hand of this stranger in their midst was an indulgence because of Olga, courtesy rather than affection for Rose. Rose had never said how extraordinary it seems to her that a people who were coaxed or coerced into Christianity by people who took their land in the name of God, should have allowed it such a prominent place in their lives, should have so willingly grafted it on to their own traditions. She'd never said, but she thought Puti had sensed it. Although looking at Sam, lips moving in silent prayer as he moved slowly forward, you could see, in his case anyway, it was a wholly joyous acceptance. Rose had never told Olga how she puzzled over being talked at by men only, how curious it was that the women, most of whom were perfectly capable of making far better speeches, remained silent during these marathons. The explanations she'd read or heard said each gender has its role, that it's the women who call you on to the marae and it is the women who sit by their dead. In any case she was the outsider here, it was not for her to say anything. Her role was to be quiet and listen.

'Hoki atu ki tō tātou kaihanga. Moe mai i te pō nui, te pō roa, te pō kāhore he otinga,' the speaker addressed the dead woman, bidding her to return to our maker, to sleep within the large night, the long night, the never-ending night.

The dead woman was a daughter of a friend of the Porohiwi family. They didn't know her well, but Mere had been at school with the mother. The woman died of lung cancer. Thirty-two. Speaker after speaker paid tribute to her. Rose strained to hear the one word in ten she understood, made yet another vow to give te reo another go. They were seriously mourning the loss of this beautiful young woman to their iwi, genuinely grieving for the husband and two small children supported now by three older women, one of whom would be Mere's school-mate, but Rose knew that after the meal some of those same mourners would be out the back smoking up a storm. But as Olga said, it's very easy to judge.

'Come on then,' she says and George obligingly opens his mouth like a little gannet and practically swallows the bottle whole. Rose has to smile. ' Take it easy,' she tells him, 'take it easy.'

There was a boy she'd taught once. Under 'Aims in Life' he'd written, 'To join the mini-mongrels'. He'd probably achieved full status by now. He was fourteen when she taught him, had been smoking since he was ten. He had dark, watchful, very old eyes, and a guarded, secretive way of looking out at the world. He'd already been in trouble with the police, many times. She'd never asked him about it, she should have, to hell with privacy. The boy was already lost, Rose defended her old self, in any case what could you, a Pākehā female, do? 'We always teach children something,' an experienced teacher told her when she was on her first section, 'and they always learn something, but it's often got bugger all to do with the curriculum.'

What did she teach that boy, what did he learn? What had she taught Knock-Knock?

Oh shit, she thinks, remembering Olga's face after Knock-Knock left, remembering Ada. Maybe we're all immigrants floundering around in strange countries. Maybe floundering is better than doing nothing. Or doing the wrong thing. Christ, thinks Rose, maybe I've made a terrible mistake. What the hell got into me?

There is a knock at the door. Rose gets up still carrying George, bottle clamped to his mouth. It's Bridget Pearl. Rose knows immediately that it's Bridget Pearl. She's short and round, but unlike her uncle Peter she has a head of thick, black hair, and as she holds out her hand and introduces herself, it's obvious she hasn't inherited his shyness either.

'I thought I'd better come in person and make an appointment,' Bridget smiles, 'Claude said you'd agreed to see me.'

'Reluctantly,' Rose warns, wanting Bridget to disappear, wanting everyone to leave her alone. She shouldn't have done it. For a few minutes of heady relief from that overwhelming rage, and if she was honest Knock-Knock was just the last straw on that bonfire. And what had she achieved? She'd made life harder for Olga, that's what. Why the hell didn't she think? She needs to think now, she feels as if she's on the verge of something really important or something deeply stupid and she needs time to sort out which one it is. She certainly doesn't need Bridget wittering away about time.

'When would be convenient?'

'Seeing you're here,' Rose says, thinking get it over, for God's sake get it over, 'you can talk while I finish attending to the baby.' Rose turns and Bridget follows.

SEVENTEEN

Bridget sits in the black chair. She watches while Rose changes George, washes his bottom, his hands and face. Rose sits down in the Morris chair and George seems quite happy on her knee. Bridget gets a small cassette recorder from her bag. Rose shakes her head and Bridget puts it away. 'Take the tape out,' Rose says, and Bridget, looking a bit surprised, does so. Rose isn't taking any chances.

'Now,' says Rose, 'tell me exactly what you want from me.' Reaction is setting in with a vengeance. It's not just Olga. Rose knows what she did to Knock-Knock is illegal. What if he goes to the police? The real police. I was crazy, she thinks. What they call road rage transformed into loud-music rage. I could be in the cells now. What on earth is the girl saying?

'Some background on my uncle's time here,' Bridget says, 'because it was here that he wrote *The Man Who Loved Rain* which turned out to be his most popular book. I want to look at the changes in his life which made this possible. I mean something obviously happened.'

'He left an unhappy marriage.'

'Yes,' says Bridget, 'but I think there's more to it. His works before then are obviously his of course, but they lack that particular driving force, that intensity and insight that he achieved in *The Man Who Loved Rain*. You can see why the earlier works didn't take off in quite the same way. He was trying to be too clever I think, complexity for its own sake, that sort of thing, but in *The Man Who Loved Rain* he's somehow gained confidence to let it take its time. The first two are, well, overly dense is too strong but – he lost sight of telling the story. *The Man Who Loved Rain* has a very strong story and while it's probably better known than read nowadays, in a popular sense, you can see why, at the time, it sold very well.'

'Maybe he just got better.' Rose smiles at George as she wipes his chin yet again. Do all babies dribble so much? She knows they do when they're teething, but George is too young for that. Oh shit, she thinks, but it's too late. She sees a little Knock-Knock and he's lying in a small bed and he's crying and crying. You're just being ridiculous Rose, it's just reaction, settle down. You did what you did. A bit late now to feel sorry. She feels bad about Olga. You are a selfish bitch Rose Anthony, all you think about is your own petty revenges, not a glimmer of what it's like to be Olga. After three years you've got no bloody idea. And you've got the nerve to grizzle about her.

'Maybe,' Bridget ploughs on, 'but he dedicated that particular book to your mother, so I wondered if it was her, if – their friendship – made the difference.'

'They were lovers,' Rose says, 'you don't have to pussyfoot around. They lived together for years and years.'

'Uncle Peter never sought a divorce?'

'It would have been pointless even if his wife hadn't made it clear she'd never agree. Ada didn't want to get married again.'

'Do you remember the time when he wrote *The Man Who Loved Rain*?'

Rose shakes her head.

'He must have been living here about four years by the time it was published, so it would have been written possibly 66, 67.'

'I was too busy being a student. I only got home in the holidays. And even then I had a holiday job. I was probably too interested in myself, in what I wanted to do, you know how it is.' Just watch it Rose, she tells herself, no need to be rude.

'And I didn't really like him so I didn't take much notice,' she says.

'Claude said,' says Bridget.

Oh really, thinks Rose. George looks as though he's getting sleepy, he's certainly got heavier. Rose settles him in the carry-cot. George immediately opens his eyes and looks around. 'Go to sleep, George,' Rose says, but her voice lacks conviction and the baby continues to stare at her. Does he know what she did to Knock-Knock? Does he know she's the kind of woman who goes mad with a spray-can?

'What sort of woman was Ada?'

Rose smiles at the baby. 'I'm biased. I think she was a great sort of woman.'

Bridget says, 'So does Claude. He nearly bit my head off when I first mentioned her in what he thought was a derogatory way. Do you have any photos? Any other records? Diaries? Journals? Letters? I understand she was a great needlewoman. Maybe there's something of hers I could see.'

'I've got a few photos. None recent. Although if you look through the old *Needlework* magazines you'd probably find a couple. She took workshops.'

'And she didn't keep diaries.'

'No.'

'Claude said something about some tapes.'

'Did he,' Rose says. Trust bloody Claude. Is there anything he hasn't told this stranger? Oh bugger, she thinks, what will Claude say when he finds out what I did? Don't be any sillier than you can help Rose, you're a grown woman, what your uncle has to say about your actions is neither here nor there. Yes, but does Claude know that?

'I was wondering if I could listen to them.'

'I haven't even listened to them myself,' Rose says. Will this woman never go?

The baby starts making noises, aha, aha, aha. Soon he will work these up into a full-scale roar. Good, thinks Rose. Go for it George.

'Peter died suddenly,' Bridget says, trying another tack, 'was he working on anything when he died? That you know of?'

Rose frowns. She must make an effort or Bridget will be here forever. Hell is other people. Sartre, misogynist old bastard, was right. Not all people. There are exceptions. At least one. She hopes Olga is OK. Perhaps, if Bridget ever goes, she could ring her. But she's already asked enough of Olga for one day. Besides, what can she say? I shouldn't have done it? A bit late now. Bridget is looking at her, waiting. 'Peter was always working,' Rose says, 'I don't know if there was anything special. Ada didn't say.'

'That's one reason I'd like to hear the tapes,' Bridget says. 'I can't imagine him giving up writing. I think there must have been some sort of work-in-progress. I wondered if you know where it might be?'

Rose snorts. 'You should ask his daughters. Ada said he was hardly cold before they were here, wanting all his things. Vultures, she called them. They took his desk, typewriter, tables, chairs, everything. Yes. Maybe you should ask them.'

'I have,' Bridget says, 'I talked to them before I put my proposal to the committee. And I rang them again before I came up here. They said if there was anything, Ada must have it.'

'Well they would, wouldn't they.'

'There was nothing like a manuscript among her things? When she died?'

'Haven't looked,' Rose says. She can hear her voice. Un-helpful would be the kindest adjective. What she says is true though. She hasn't even cleaned out Ada's clothes. She dusts and vacuums the room, opens the windows so air can get through, leaves the wardrobe door open to stop it getting musty, but that's as much as she's been able to do. The thought of going through Ada's clothes, through her drawers, ferreting through anything else she kept in her room, is just too horrible to contemplate. I'll get round to it, thinks Rose. I'll have to now. I've said Sibyl can have the trunk for her memory box. At the very least I'll have to empty that.

Bridget's a trier, she's not giving up. In any other circumstances, Rose would have liked her. 'What about Manny's story? Where did Peter get it from? Did he make it up?'

'Manny was my mother's grandfather. She told me about him when I was twelve.'

The baby is still aha aha aha-ing, so Rose picks him up. Making a rod for your own back, she hears Ada say. She sits down in the Morris chair and holds him snugly to her. There's something hugely comforting about the feel of the small body. Like a human wheat bag, thinks Rose, although heavier and with a distinctly different smell.

Bridget is awed and delighted. 'Your great-grandfather! How wonderful! I wonder when she told Uncle Peter.' She writes something in her notebook. 'It's always interesting to find the source of things, don't you think?'

Rose surprises herself. 'Yes, but it doesn't take away anything from the skill Peter shows. He took Manny's life, or what my mother told him of it, the little she knew, and made it into a novel. That's what my mother always said. She said it was only when she started reading it aloud that she knew fully just how clever Peter was. She said it was the difference between keeping strictly to a traditional needlework pattern and taking that same pattern and making it your own, adding your own ideas, allowing your own creativity to take over. I think it was her own talent which made her appreciate Peter's, although they were in quite different fields.'

'So if there's a manuscript, the Skeleton Woman will find it.'

'Eventually,' Rose says. She is surprised. 'How do you know about the Skeleton Woman? Don't tell me, Claude told you.'

'He said I might have to practice a bit of patience, let her do the job for me. But I thought perhaps she wouldn't mind if I give her a helping hand.'

'The trouble is,' Rose says, 'you never know whether you're helping or hindering.'

'No,' Bridget says, 'no, you don't.' She sighs, looks across at the baby and smiles. 'He's asleep,' Bridget says.

'Aha aha aha,' says George.

Go George, thinks Rose.

'Claude says you have a second-hand bookshop,' Bridget says, 'that must be wonderful.'

'Has its moments,' Rose says.

'I just love going into second-hand bookshops.'

Rose says people often say that to her. She says they say that because they imagine all you do is sit and read. She says that after you've done the cleaning, pricing, the shelving, after you've cleaned windows, the floors, done the banking, after you've decided how you'll rearrange the window on Thursday and if there are no customers and the phone doesn't ring, you've checked the mail, the email, and providing you're not too worried about cash flow and overdrafts, it is possible to snatch say five minutes to read.

Bridget smiles.

Rose thinks she's not too bad. She says, 'Apart from being your own boss – which is totally great – if you still feel a certain excitement when you pick up a book, if you're still prone to enthusiasms for a character, a writer, a subject, if you can live during the quiet times on the smell of an oily rag, then you'll do well in a second-hand bookshop.'

'Did Ada like books?'

'Loved them.'

'You must have inherited that.'

'Possible I suppose. I like needlework and she did. I've inherited her liking for being in control I think.'

'All sorts of legacies in families,' Bridget says, 'I was reading about Virginia Woolf's — half of them seemed to be mad, so it's no wonder she had her moments. Did you know her mother's grandfather drank himself to death in India and that his body was sent back to England in a cask of rum? On the voyage the body exploded out of the cask and the shock killed the widow and the sailors drank the rum. So the story goes.'

'Probably invented,' Rose says, although remembering Byron and his Ada it needn't have been. 'Heaven knows what intense suffering and agony I have gone thro'; and how mad and bad and desperate I have felt,' Ada Lovelace née Byron wrote. There, there, Rose says tenderly across a century and a half, there, there.

EIGHTEEN

Rose watches herself in the mirror. She's never really liked her face and likes it less now it's getting older. Those little marks working their way upwards from her lips are deeper, more noticeable; the grooves from nose to the outer edge of her lips are more pronounced. There's a shadow of wriggly lines on her forehead. Her eyes look smaller. She's tired. Is that a sign? She won't think about it right now.

The baby went off to sleep again before Bridget left, but only briefly, and he's been wailing off and on ever since. Rose has fed him, walked up and down with him, tried a bath, changing his clothes, remaking the bed, even singing to him. Maybe you should have tried another song Rose. He's probably getting pretty sick of 'Poor Cinderella'. I could have stood on my head, she thinks, nothing made any difference to his scratchiness. Or to hers. She's on the way to falling out of love with this baby and tells him so. He doesn't seem to heed the warning, although he does fall asleep for five minutes before he wakes again.

Rose is working up to ringing Alice. But it's Saturday night. You don't ring doctors on a Saturday night unless it's a real, dire emergency. And as far as she can tell George has no temperature, he's not feverish. He's flushed, but so is Rose. She's pervaded by disbelief that she did what she did to Knock-Knock. George has swallowed all his food, his stomach is not distended, he doesn't have any spots. Maybe he just feels like a good cry. Rose thinks she wouldn't mind a good cry herself. Perhaps this is why he was left on her porch. Someone just wanted to have a good cry in peace.

She wishes she knew more about babies. She puts the washing machine on for something to do. She drags an old drying frame of Ada's out of the shed and sets it up in the hall. The wind is getting up, but will bring more rain. No good hanging the washing outside. Even if the rain wasn't threatening, the clothes would be ripped to pieces or torn off the line by that onslaught.

At the rate this child is going through clothes, she'll have to beg some more from Wesley. As for nappies, he's rapidly using up all the fabric ones Wesley brought, and it'll be back to the throwaway ones soon. Luckily she's got three packets in the cupboard. If only he would just stay asleep – even an hour would be heaven. Rose thinks she'll have to get some sleep soon, she'll just have to. I'm fifty tomorrow, thinks Rose, I'm too bloody old for this. Too bloody old to be rushing around the streets with a spray-can full of red paint. She peers at her face in the mirror, the face of a petty criminal. Maybe a bit of moisturising cream might help.

While she smooths on the cream (always such a comforting feeling) she thinks of the gallons of this stuff she's used over the years. It's not that she really believes it works any of the miracles its makers claim, it's more basic than that. Like massage, the touch of hands, fingers on one's skin, the soothing repetitive actions, have a sort of settling effect, immediately softening the edge of the day or the night, although it often makes her think of the huge difference between this face the world sees and the real Rose. Terrible things, good things, have happened and yet her face hardly seems to register that inner barometer. Her face might lighten, might look happier even, at times, more sober, sadder, at others. It will age, has aged, but at no time is there real exposure of the intense depth of either immense pain or immense joy she might be feeling. It is a mystery. The small Rose whose swift moods, happinesses, despairs, had her mother saying, 'If your face gets much longer you'll trip over it,' was much more transparent. When it rained and that young Rose wanted sun or she came second instead of first in the spelling-bee, those were the tragedies of her life. And they show on her face. When did that change? When did she start hiding behind this mask?

Did they still have spelling-bees in primary schools? Probably gone out of favour long ago. Were already on their way out when she was winning them. Miss Graham believed that teaching by rote was the only way to go and was fired by a zeal to turn out pupils who could read and write and knew where to put apostrophes. Miss Graham thought that competition wasn't a bad thing. Miss Graham's face was a good example of a face that showed nothing other than a pleasant smile or cold displeasure. None of the children knew anything about Miss Graham's personal life. It would have been impossible to judge if she was happy or sad, ill or well, from looking at her face. Rose wonders if Miss Graham ever did anything illegal. Unlikely, but one can hope.

All adult faces, Rose decided, are uncommunicative. You meet someone, they say how's things, you say fine, you ask them how they are, they say fine, and you both go on your way, any inner turmoil, anxiety, pleasure, sexual contentment, well hidden. Look at Knock-Knock. Bugger Knock-Knock. Get out of my head. Take Jo. Always cleaning, washing, being nice to guests, cooking, baking, organising tours, flights, bus tickets. A word here, an interview there, letters, emails, accounts, financial statements, work spraying (unfortunate word Rose) out in all directions, it seemed. Who knew what Jo really thought of it all. If this was what she'd seen as her destiny, her life. And this business with Lizzie. Not a word to Rose about it. Why? Rose can't remember the last time Jo mentioned Malcom. Perhaps they'd fallen out as well. No. Malcolm is fond of his mother. The last time she saw him was at Thelma's funeral. He and Lizzie had been pall-bearers. Must have been hard for them, carrying her coffin. Perhaps not. Perhaps they wanted to do this one last thing for their much-loved grandmother.

None of us ever talks about death either. Had she ever said to anyone when they asked how she was, 'I'm a bit worried about death, whether I'll know, what it will be like,' although it had been on her mind for months and months. Do Jo or Wesley think about death before they sleep? The way our skeletons outlast everything else, except perhaps hair. That in the end all our dramas, crises, tragedies, come to this. Bones, skulls, are dug up all the time, revealing secrets not available anywhere else. Just this morning there was a report in the paper about the discovery of the grave of a powerful Iron Age queen who had been buried alongside her richly decorated chariot in the fourth century BC. She was in her late twenties. In the grave were the remains of a harness which, it was hoped, would shed light on the puzzling links between the Celts of East Yorkshire and tribes living in Northern France at the time. Ordinary people were placed in simple graves, sometimes with a brooch, while leaders were buried with their chariots. This chariot was decorated with coral from the Mediterranean. Teeth and bones would be analysed to discover whether this woman was descended from Gaulish immigrants. Iron Age burials were relatively rare. Most people were left outside to rot after death. But the Celts of East Yorkshire had distinctive death rituals.

Perhaps they too had a Church of the Golden Light?

Does Olga think about the implacability of time? No, Rose thinks, Olga actually embraces time because to her the past and the future are just other dimensions going on parallel with this one. So the dead are always there with the living. Rose understands this more since Ada's accident. Rose thinks Ada is somewhere close, invisible but close; she senses her presence at times, hears her voice. She supposes this is a normal phenomenon when someone has died in a road accident. No dying on the road for me, she thinks, remembering those two little boys playing some sort of game with pretend guns. They'd run out from the driveway next to the house where she'd been looking at books the owner wanted to sell. 'Bang! Bang!' yelled one. Too late. The other one had darted behind one of the phoenix palms. Just as the first one ran towards the tree the other one jumped out from behind it and yelled 'Bang!' The first boy dropped where he stood. 'No dying on the road!' called the other one urgently, 'Mum said no dying on the road!' The dead body lifted its head and slithered to the safety of the verge where it collapsed again. No dying on the road. Perhaps their mum should have had a talk to Ada.

Bridget Pearl was not satisfied with their talk. She'd be back and keep on coming back until Rose gave her the information she was looking for, whatever that was. She'd asked if she could hold the baby. 'Just for a minute,' she said, 'before I go. I offered to cook dinner for Claude and Elena so I'd better not be late.'

She cuddled George in the crook of her arm. 'Hello doll,' she said, and the baby stopped his aha-ing and dribbled happily at her. 'He's lovely,' she said when she handed him back. 'How could anyone hit him?'

'You mean if he wasn't lovely it'd be OK?'

'No!' Bridget was appalled. 'Of course not.'

'Sorry,' said Rose. And she was. Stupid thing to say. What is the matter with her today? 'Sorry.'

'You're tired,' Bridget said.

No, thinks Rose, well, I am, but it's not tiredness that's making me like this. I did something terrible. Something smack against everything I think is right. And I did it to poor Thelma's house. How could I do it? And what will happen when Jo and Wesley find out?

'Aha aha, aha.' He's awake again. She'll ignore him.

Rose in the mirror. So neat it's sickening. Neat eyes, neat nose, neat mouth. All very – neat. No idiosyncratic jaw or nose, not even large ears. Her eyes, always a pale hazel, were now even lighter. Underneath the face is a thin body. A thin, scarred body. That gash across her breast is unsightly and Rose hates the way her breast looks now, but even so, Rose likes her body much better than her face. Her body let her down, that's true, but only once, only once please. Her body is hardworking, reliable, supple, strong. She likes her hands, the skin rough between the slightly embossed veins. These hands, they've done well and they'll go on doing well. She grimaces at Rose in the mirror. Neat, she thinks, you were a neat little girl, and you're a neat woman. No passion, thinks Rose. Style maybe, but no passion. She pushes away the image of red spray-can. That wasn't passion, that was senseless, stupid, out-of-control rage. She hopes to God she's not going to make a habit of that sort of thing. Maybe it's yet another variation on the effects of the menopause. Oh come on Rose. Once. You've done something like that once. Don't make a drama out of it. It was a mistake, but it doesn't mean you're Mr Big.

An afternoon a few days after her father died. Ada – bright red beret on her dark hair, long red scarf slung around her neck, the belt of her old blue coat tied in a tight knot around her thin waist — strode through town like The Fool stepping out into the unknown. Rose scurried along at her heels like the little white dog. 'Where are we going, Ada?'

'To see someone who might get me a job.'

'Mr Big?' Rose said.

'You've been reading too much Chandler,' Ada snorted.

She walked as though on a mission, as though nothing would deflect her from her goal. People on the footpath stepped back to let her through, others looked away, embarrassed perhaps.

When Rose was older and this image popped up it always struck her how often, more often than not, it is the victim from whom we turn our eyes rather than the perpetrator. People hang around courts, houses and streets to see perpetrators, but there's not the same unloosed avidity toward victims. Perhaps they're too painful a reminder of our own vulnerability, our fragile dominion over the flesh surrounding our bones. We take that inward breath, oh no, we think, not another one, and we turn away from the bruised face, the old battered mouth; we turn off the television, unable to bear the ravaged face of the mother begging for someone, anyone, to please, to please tell her where her daughter is. Perhaps there's an old, deep, unspoken, communal guilt that these things happen at all. And, thinking of things buried deep within us, Rose thinks again of the Skeleton Woman dancing, clatter clatter clatter, rattling her bones to the music only she can hear.

The baby's aha-ing is increasing in volume. She could try some boiled water again. She offers him the bottle. He's not silly, he doesn't want boiled water, so he's not going to drink boiled water. Nothing for it. It might be Saturday night, but she will have to ring Alice and be done with it. She carries him to the phone. He stops aha-ing. She looks at him suspiciously. Maybe he's been sleeping too much. Maybe he's just wakeful? Why the hell can't babies be born talking?

This is ridiculous. He will just have to go to bed and stay there. She simply must lie down. He's perfectly safe in the carrycot. There's absolutely nothing wrong with him. Anyway he's stopped aha-ing. She stares at him suspiciously, waiting for him to start again. He doesn't.

As she drifts off she decides it's a good thing no one knows what another person is thinking. Oh you can guess, and we all get good at guessing, informed guessing, informed by our own experience. But it's just as well all our suffering lies unexposed, because we probably couldn't handle the raw and bitter truths behind all the faces we see and they couldn't handle ours. It's enough to look into our own eyes.

There's not been a sound from Knock-Knock. The silence is magic. The silence is uncanny. The silence is – worrying. She rips out of bed and moves quickly to where George is sleeping. He's still breathing. Everything's OK. She creeps away. 'Aha, aha, aha,' he says.

Rose goes back to bed but she can't get back into the drifting-off stage. She lies still and breathes deeply. In, out, in, out. Aha-aha-wah-wah. She reviews all the babycare books she has in the shop. Why the hell hadn't she read them? She thinks of all the people in the world who are asleep. All those lucky people who don't have babies. All those fortunate people who do have babies but have babies who go to bed and go to sleep. All those rational, sensible people who haven't sprayed their neighbour's house and sound system, haven't caused a problem for the person they love most in the whole world, haven't had cancer and so can't be worried about it coming back and are therefore beautifully, wonderfully, amazingly asleep.

It might be better to lie on her right side away from the carrycot.

It's not.

Why is a baby's wail such torture? Why do people bother with electric rods and dripping water when they could just stick a crying baby in the same room as the prisoner? The information they want would come pouring out in two minutes flat.

'Please George,' she pleads out loud, 'please.' It makes no difference. No wonder people have to walk out of the room, she thinks. I'd walk out of the room but I'm too bloody tired. I could crawl, I suppose. No wonder people leave babies on other people's porches. Maybe she should pack him up and deposit him on someone else's porch and come home and sink into blissful slumber.

'I'm going to go mad soon,' she decides, 'stark raving bonkers.'

She picks him up, shushes, and he stops. She puts him down again and he starts aha-ing. 'Right,' she says, 'right. As long as we're clear about this. You're a bloody wanker and all you want is attention. Just as long as you know I know.' She picks him up, and takes him back to bed. She fixes a pillow as a bolster between them, takes her arm away. He starts wailing. She puts her arm around him. He stops. 'OK,' she says, 'I give in. You win. OK? Are you listening you little creep? You win. But be warned. I'll remember this. Next time you want a smile you'll be out of luck. And for Christ's sake kid, if I roll over on top of you, for the love of God, yell.'

NINETEEN

There's a sound on the edge of her consciousness. Five o'clock. Sunday morning. This happened yesterday, she remembers, it's all that baby's fault. But he's sound asleep. At some stage during that interminable night he'd fallen asleep and she'd carefully, heart knocking so loud she was sure he must hear it, put him back in his own bed. Maybe someone has left another baby on her porch. She grabs the torch, more from habit than any need for a light because it's quite light. The wind is still yowling like a wolf as it hits the house running. All the ranunculas will be well battered by now. The noise has come from the front. It'll be one of those halfwits, brain sodden with booze, egged on by his equally intelligent mates who think it's a brilliant idea to wake her up. Yeah mate, she's probably pretty desperate living here all on her own, she'll have the bacon on, the eggs, all the trimmings in no time. Probably top them up with a good swig of sherry. Not often she gets the chance of a real man's company. You go for it mate. This cunning ploy has never worked in the past, but it's like winning Lotto. One day, they think, one day. The older hands hide by the gate giggling and cackling like a bunch of five year olds as the new one leaves at a much quicker trot than he goes in.

Rose's birthday morning is not getting off to a good start.

Her eyelids have turned into sandpaper and are only open because she can't see to walk otherwise. Painfully, she squints through the sitting-room window. She's wrong about the alkie. There is something there, something dark on the front porch, right up against the door, but it's not one of them. For Christ's sake, she was only joking about another baby! Carefully Rose pulls the curtain wider. Looks like a bundle of clothes. But a bundle of clothes doesn't breathe. A bundle of clothes might pong, but it doesn't breathe.

She unlocks the door, opens it quickly, gives the bundle a poke with her finger then shuts the door and locks it. Silly thing to do. But she's established it is human. A human body. Stupid, Rose. Never give anyone a chance to grab your arm and pull you over. She was lucky. The bundle just gathers into itself like a crab, but instead of scuttling away, it becomes quite still. The breathing seems to stop. Must be an alkie.

Rose goes to the window again, takes a look out towards the front gate. No one. Or if there is, they're well hidden. Then she sees drops of blood on the path. Damn. As well as idiots looking for the kind of comfort they didn't get from their mother, Rose also gets a few who think, because she is female, that she is some kind of Florence Nightingale panting to fix people up. As a child Rose was never attracted to Miss Graham's theory that every kind action amasses one more star in the crown you get to wear when you stand in front of the Pearly Gates. Leaving aside the star in the crown and the Pearly Gates allusions (which made Ada spit tacks and then laugh like a hyena), even then Rose had not thought it was a fair deal. It was like you had put the starry crown on lay-by and you were going to be paying it off forever. With no guarantee. The small Rose wanted her paybacks to come soon as possible after the good turn, and the grown-up Rose is not much different.

Rose risks another peep through the window. The mound is still there. Breathing again. Just. Bugger. She approaches the door very quietly, turns the key as softly as she can, eases the door just open. The bundle – which is enclosed in a blanket she now sees, not clothes – still doesn't move. This time Rose has armed herself with an umbrella. 'Off you go,' she orders, giving the heap a sharp poke, 'off you go!'

The mound moans. A woman? Surely that's a woman's voice. Rose sees a shudder ripple through the body and a head appears, like a turtle coming out of its shell. Shaking. Mumbling. Dark hair.

'Who the hell are you? What are you doing here?' Rose demands. The mound turns its head. 'Oh Jesus,' says Rose. Lizzie? There is a huge swelling over one eye, which is barely open, and somewhere under the purply mess, which was once a cheek, is the other eye. It's Jo's daughter all right. There's a gash from the nose to the side of her mouth, which is bleeding. The fingers which hold the grey blanket are swollen and gouged as though someone has trodden on them and pressed hard.

'Jesus!' Rose hasn't got time to be sick. Someone could be watching. Lizzie's got herself this far so it must be OK to move her. Rose leans down and puts her hands under the armpits and pulls. She moans but when Rose stops, motions her to carry on. She is naked underneath the blanket and whoever it is who's done her face and fingers has had a good time jumping up and down on her chest as well. There is a strong smell of booze, as though something has been spilled either on the blanket or on her.

Rose stares at the face. Surely she's made a mistake. But it is Lizzie. Underneath all this mess it's definitely Lizzie.

Rose takes a deep breath and hauls. There's probably a trail a mile wide to the front door but no good worrying about that right at this minute. Lizzie's as cold as a frog's so Rose, with a heave that nearly breaks her back, manages to get her to her feet, and half-walking, half-carrying her, makes for the Morris chair. Both of them are breathing hoarsely, like someone with pleurisy. Rose awkwardly slides Lizzie onto the chair. 'Don't fall off,' she says sharply and turns the heater on. She goes smartly through to the bathroom to run the bath. Warm her up, wash some of the mess off, see what the damage is. No. She swings back to the kitchen. Better ring someone. Ring Olga, she thinks, ring Olga first. No, ring Alice first.

When she gets close the pulverised mouth tries to speak. Tears and blood run down Lizzie's face. She shivers and breathes in quick hard gasps.

'You're all right now,' Rose says, 'don't worry Lizzie, you're all right now. I'll look after you.' Don't know how but I will.

The face nods, cries some more. Her sobs are hard to listen to. 'Shit!' Rose races back and locks the front door. She leans against it for a second. 'Happy birthday,' she tells herself and is not surprised to feel tears on her face. She goes to the phone, rings Alice, and then Olga. 'Right,' says Alice, after she hears the story, 'I'll be there very shortly.' Olga draws a sharp breath. 'I'm on my way,' she says.

Lizzie feels chilled to the bone. Rose gets the heater from her sewing room and turns it on full bore. The bath can wait till Alice arrives. If Alice says the police will have to be notified, Lizzie will need to be seen by them as she is now. Rose knows that much. She will need x-rays, maybe hospitalisation. This is way out of Rose's league.

'Oh fuck,' thinks Rose, 'George.' She runs to the bedroom. Grabs the carrycot and hurries back to the kitchen. The battered face looks down at him. The mouth says something which could be, 'Thanks.' Rose feels the tears on her face again. 'No,' she says to Lizzie, 'don't.' She drags the black chair over and puts the carrycot on it.

Alice and Olga come into the kitchen. Alice goes straight to

Lizzie. After a hard stare and a careful lifting of the blanket, 'Ring the ambulance,' she orders Olga, 'and the police. Tell them to meet us at the hospital.'

George starts to cry. Rose lifts him out. 'Your timing is stink,' she whispers. 'I'll get his bottle,' she says, and as she goes to the bench the kitchen is full of people. Jo and Wesley and two strangers who she realises a moment later are not strangers, they're Mr and Mrs Hipp.

Lizzie cries out. The sounds are guttural and impossible to understand, but the meaning is clear. Rose hugs George to herself, defensively. 'No,' she says, 'don't worry Lizzie, the baby stays here.'

'That is quite enough from you,' Jo says. 'We're his grand-parents, we have a right.'

Lizzie shakes her head violently and makes the same awful noises.

'The police will meet us at the hospital,' Olga says.

'No,' Jo cries loudly, 'no. We'll look after her. And the baby. We don't want the police involved.'

Mrs Hipp looks as though she's going to faint, Mr Hipp is deathly pale. Wesley looks as though he's about to be sick.

Jo goes to Lizzie. 'I'm sorry,' she says, 'I'm sorry. I'll make it up to you. I thought it was the depression. Truly. I thought it was the depression. Please Lizzie, please don't let them get the police. We've talked to Royston. We'll sort it out. Let's just keep this in the family.'

'Stand back Jo,' says Alice, 'are you saying Lizzie told you what was going on and you didn't believe her?'

'Don't look at me like that! You know Lizzie – she's always inclined to exaggerate – always made a drama out of every little thing – I just thought – well – I just thought she was doing it again.' Jo looks ill and after that first shocked incredulous stare, she's not looking at Lizzie.

'Look at her,' Alice sounds stern, 'look at your daughter, Jo. Does this look as though she's making a drama out of nothing?'

'No!' says Jo, 'of course not, but – I just thought it was another one of Lizzie's – oh,' Jo cries, 'if you must know, she said she was frightened of Royston, frightened. She thought he might have a violent streak. And that was it! Just that she was frightened. I really thought she was exaggerating. Lizzie does exaggerate. Please, please don't get the police.'

'You should see my son,' Ellie Hipp says, 'he's heartbroken. He admits he lost his temper. He's never done this sort of thing before. Never.'

'I know,' Jo says, not listening to Ellie, still following her own line of reasoning, 'I just know from experience – Lizzie can be very – irritating – I just thought she was angry with Royston and she –' Jo shakes her head.

'Royston admits he got really angry,' Mrs Hipp says, 'he says he got angry because the baby had gone and she wouldn't tell him where. He panicked. Things just went black, he says. He wasn't responsible for his actions. She wouldn't tell him what she'd done with the baby. Please, Lizzie, for the baby's sake, just see him. Just see him. Before you call the police. That's all we ask. He's truly, truly sorry.'

'They always are,' Olga says, 'when they get found out.'

'Royston's not like that!' his mother says fiercely, 'my son's not like that! He's not one of these monsters! He just got angry. Tell them Ellie, tell them, we're a respectable God-fearing family, it's just – the baby – Lizzie's been sick – he's been working all hours – it's all been too much for him – for both of them. He must have a second chance! He deserves a second chance!'

'He'll get a second chance,' Alice says, 'but not by hiding what he's done. Believe me, he must face up to it if he wants to make things right.'

'You're all loving this aren't you,' Jo says, her face very dark, 'you're just like the rest of them in this town, always jeered at our beliefs. Now you can dance on them to your heart's content. I hope you're very happy!'

Alice stands up. 'That's enough Jo,' she says, 'that's quite enough. You're all forgetting the baby. This baby was hit hard. This small defenceless baby, your grandchild, was hit so hard he was blue from the shoulder to the waist. You saw him yourself Jo. There is no excuse. Royston was obviously "losing his temper" well before the baby went missing, so he can't use that as an excuse. You will have to accept that. I'm sorry Mr and Mrs Hipp,' she says, and she really sounds as though she is, 'it must be terribly painful. But you must see that it can't be hidden away. Not for anyone. Not for Lizzie, not for the baby, not for you, and especially not for Royston.'

'No,' Mrs Hipp moans, 'no, no!'

'Very well,' Jo says, 'very well! If our name is going to be blazoned across the newspapers we're not going to be the only ones! If my grandson stays here I'll go to the papers myself. I'll tell them my daughter is suffering from severe depression and doesn't know what she's doing. I'll tell them my grandson is being kept here against my will, in the care of a woman accused of sexual misconduct with one of her pupils!'

Rose thought she was in a rage yesterday. Now she knows compared to how she feels at this moment that that was just an outburst of mild irritation. She feels her whole body shaking. 'Do it,' she shouts, 'do it! Fucking do it! See if I care!'

This time it is her voice, not her mother's. It's her own voice. Olga moves to stand by Rose.

'It's not right,' Jo says, 'it's not right, it's not people like us,' she looks directly at Olga, 'it's not, is it? We're not like that. These things you see in the paper. It's not like us. You, of all people, know that.'

Olga doesn't duck. 'It's true,' she says, 'it's true there are more of these cases amongst my people. That what you want me to say Jo?'

'We're not like that. The Hipps, I've known them for years and years, they're not like that. This is – this is – we can't judge Royston in the same way as those others. He's just not like that.'

'You mean he's not brown so he can't possibly beat up his wife and child?'

Jo doesn't answer. But it's what she means. They can all see that. Royston, in Jo's mind, is a special case.

Olga says, 'Doesn't matter what colour you are Jo, no mother wants her kid's name in the papers.' Olga's voice is tired, as though the effort to speak is too hard.

'Olga, please, please persuade them to give Royston a chance and please, please make Rose give us the baby.'

'Just go,' Olga says to Jo, 'just go.'

From outside they hear the ambulance pull into the drive. Jo gives a loud moaning cry and stumbles from the room. Mr and Mrs Hipp, with one last distraught glance at Lizzie, follow her. Wesley runs outside and over the sounds of him retching violently they hear running footsteps and then a knock at the door.

'I'll go with her,' Rose says as Olga goes to let them in.

'Rose,' says Olga, 'do you think you'd better get dressed first.'

Rose looks down at her old extra large T-shirt with the words Who Killed Minnie Dean? printed across it.

'I'll tell them you'll be out in five,' Olga says.

TWENTY

Rose watches Lizzie's hands as the nurses bathe her. She clenches and unclenches her fingers and occasionally Rose hears a sigh. Rose sits on a chair holding George, whom she must get used to calling Simon. Or Simmie.

Alice has to go to another emergency. Someone has surprised a swarm of wasps and run inside with the wasps close behind. The whole household – mother, father, three children – has been stung, one child badly, and is now with a neighbour while the pest destruction officer deals with the wasps inside their house.

Rose, now dressed in jeans and a blue shirt, held Lizzie's hand in the ambulance while Olga carried the baby. Olga has now taken a taxi back to Rose's house to pick up her own car so she can come back and collect Rose and George/Simmie. Lizzie has a couple of broken ribs, severe bruising everywhere, but it's her eyes, the right one particularly, that cause concern. Nothing can be properly diagnosed until the swelling goes down, but the worry is that something at the back of the right eye has been so badly damaged, the sight will be impaired. The left one, they think but don't know for sure, is not as bad, but bad enough. Her nose and teeth, miraculously, are OK. All the damage is, they say, superficial, which means it's bloody sore, looks awful, a couple of stitches in the upper lip, but will heal in a couple of weeks. Her left ear is ripped and has stitches in it. Lizzie is given pain relief, but nothing can dull the agony inside her.

The two police officers are exemplary. Kind, careful, but determined to get every detail Lizzie can tell them in that hoarse, gravelly, pain-racked voice which, until they get used to it, is very hard to understand. They take more photos, look at the baby's chest and arm, take photos of that, say they'll be in touch, that Lizzie should concentrate on getting better, that they'll deal with Mr Royston Hipp, who is at present at the station helping them with their enquiries. It's likely he'll be there some time and he will be warned to stay away from her and the baby, so Lizzie mustn't worry about him turning up at the hospital. Tomorrow, no doubt, Lizzie's solicitor will make application for a restraining order and the police will support that.

They turn to Rose. It's a shame Rose didn't get in touch with them on Friday when she found the baby on her back porch. If she'd contacted them they might have been able to prevent Lizzie's injuries. Rose agrees with them. The reservations, fears, anxieties – let's face it Rose, all on your own behalf, not the baby's – have all gone, scarpered, disappeared, just when she needs them to bolster her conviction that she'd done the right thing. 'Hindsight is a scary thing,' she says. The officers nod as though they understand. They are kind, in an impartial, detached way, they write down what she says. They keep their faces free of expression so she doesn't really know what they think of her. Not that it matters. She thinks badly enough of herself for the three of them.

They finish their questions, the one taking notes closes his notebook. They have a word with a nurse, then leave, this young man and young woman in uniform. Rose thinks they probably see more horror in one night than she will in a lifetime. At first glance they look like teenagers, but their eyes give them away.

The nurses finish and between them move Lizzie to a clean bed in a single room. Rose goes with them, not really knowing what else to do. Will Lizzie be OK when Rose takes the baby away? Will she understand this second separation is temporary? If it looks as though she's upset, Rose will stay. She will sit in the chair all night and the nurses will just have to put up with it. George/Simmie has had a couple of crying spells, doesn't like the strangeness perhaps, but he's had a bottle, been changed, seems more settled. He's not really sure about Lizzie and cries whenever he's near her. Who can blame him? She probably doesn't smell at all like the mother who left him on Rose's back porch not quite two days ago.

'Rose?' Lizzie's rough voice has become a bit clearer. The pain relievers no doubt. It startles Rose. She sits up straight.

'Yes Lizzie, I'm here. We're both here. Simmie and me.'

'You go,' Lizzie says, 'you take him and go. I'll sleep now. Come back later. He shouldn't be here.'

'He's all right,' Rose says, 'he's all right. Look, he's sound asleep.' She shows Lizzie the baby and Lizzie lifts her poor, hurt face and Rose sees a tremor. An effort at a smile perhaps? Lizzie goes to shake her head and winces. 'OK,' Rose says, 'OK. We'll just sit here and wait for Olga to find us, and then we'll go. You don't have to worry about your boy. No one will hurt him while he's with me.'

Lizzie lies back and in a little while she sleeps. A nurse pops in, checks, smiles at Rose.

'Sleep will do her the world of good,' she whispers, and goes. A woman in a blue dressing gown, holding onto her stomach, walks slowly along the corridor towing a chrome stand with a metal box and trailing wires. She and Rose exchange smiles.

Oh that first trip to the toilet after the op. She'd had a haemo-vac attached to catch the fluids draining off both wounds.

Rose remembers sitting on the toilet, trying to manage the long trailing tube and wipe her bum at the same time, shaking her head in disbelief that she was actually there, in that hospital toilet, having had an operation for breast cancer.

'How long did it take you to believe it?' Sibyl had asked later.

'I didn't,' Rose said, 'still don't.'

'Neither do I,' said Louise.

'Me neither,' said Sibyl.

Sibyl and Louise must believe it now.

Rose sees a man on a trolley being wheeled past. 'The bloody cat,' he is saying, 'I should have left the little rat's-arse up the tree.'

Rose wonders where the hell Olga is, what's holding her up. It's a relief to close her eyes though, shut out this hospital room, the green curtains at the window, the cream locker, a drawer and cupboard by the bed, the spare pillows piled on a chair on the other side of the bed, to close her mind to the sounds outside the room, the small noises Lizzie makes as she sleeps. Rose understands exactly how Jo and the Hipps feel. Who would, could, understand better? She'd skulked home for exactly the same reasons four years ago. Well it would all come out now. And she would have to deal with it. As would the girl Phoebe, her father, and everyone else, Marcy included. Rose had told Ada and Claude about the parents' urgent desire that their daughter not be put through the hoops of the media and court circus. 'I wasn't worried so much about Phoebe,' Rose told them.

'No?'

'No. I could see how it happened. She knew I was going to talk to her parents. She'd been impossible since I announced the cast. She'd badly wanted Juliet. I think now she'd told everyone she was a sitter to get it. She was the principal's daughter after all. She as good as said it.'

'In front of witnesses?' asked Claude.

'Of course not,' Ada answered for her, 'do they ever? How often,' she turned on Rose, 'have you been told not to be on your own with a pupil?'

'It's no good, Ada,' Rose said, 'they were absolutely determined not to believe me. I wasn't sure anyone believed me. I thought perhaps Marcy was just using her mother as an excuse, that perhaps Marcy thought that I really had made some sort of advance to the girl. We hadn't been getting on that well. Anyway, the thought of cameras, lights, journalists asking questions – you've both seen them – they'd probably have followed me here, done the whole dance. I knew I'd never get another job in the education system whether I proved Phoebe was lying or not. I suppose I was in shock.'

'You were a willing conspirator in your own downfall,' Ada said.

'If you say so,' Rose said, although she knew it was Ada's anxiety that made her sound so sharp.

Rose worked out the statutory month, went into school every day to an environment where everyone knew the real reason she'd resigned, where half the staff believed the girl on no other basis than that Rose was what she was, and the other half didn't believe the girl but understood why Rose had made that particular decision. 'We're all paranoid about the media,' one of them told Rose, 'it comes with the territory now.'

'Why didn't you go to the union, you should have gone to the union,' Claude said.

'I didn't need the union, I needed a fairy godmother.' A poor joke was better than nothing.

Ada and Claude didn't even smile. 'Why didn't you call us?' they asked, 'we'd have come like a shot.'

Which was exactly why Rose didn't ring them.

'Phoebe's been through huge anxiety,' her father said, 'it's already cost her a lot to even tell us. She didn't want to. But we saw she was upset, and we persisted.'

'She's lying,' Rose said.

Denis Gerrison went on as though Rose hadn't spoken, hadn't said this over and over. Previously Rose thought the principal was a fair man although she sensed he was uncomfortable with her once he'd found out about Marcy. But he'd been pleased with her work, gratified that her school productions were widely praised by parents and public, appreciative of all the extra time she'd put in. Now he looked at her as though she was the pervert his daughter made her out to be, that the lie simply confirmed what he'd privately thought.

Mrs Gerrison said Rose had done enough damage without compounding it by making the whole thing public. 'I appeal to you,' she said, 'if you have an ounce of common decency left, surely you can't want that.'

'She's lying, Phoebe's *lying*,' she repeated.

'Miss Anthony, I know my own daughter. Believe me, I know when she's genuinely upset or not.'

Claude had been right. She should have had some sort of advocate. Too late now for even a fairy godmother. Leave it to the Skeleton Woman, Rose. She'll do it. Eventually.

Boom boom, thinks Rose. Poor Maisy liked Fairy Tales. You only had to say Once Upon A Time and she would quieten, would stop shouting, and come close and hug you, her eyes peaceful and anticipatory. Once upon a time, Rose thinks, there was a girl called Maisy, a Down's syndrome girl, who came to live with a girl called Rose and her mother called Ada. For two years Maisy was happy. She loved Ada intensely. Almost as much as she loved jokes, loved making Rose and Ada laugh.

One day Maisy caught a cold that turned to bronchitis and then pleurisy so, so quickly. Rose and Ada read to her all the time. Maisy would only stay in bed if they read to her. She listened intently to the first few words then seemed to go off into a daze. But if you tried to skip, or if you went too fast, her eyes would open and she'd say hoarsely, 'Start again.'

Maisy liked Rose a lot, but she adored Ada. She put up with Rose because Ada said she must be nice to Rose and she must stay in bed whether Ada was there or not. The doctor had given strict instructions. Maisy must stay in bed, but at first Maisy would only stay in bed if Ada was sitting beside her. Thelma and Jo took a turn. Even Peter Paul Pearl and Claude took a turn. They were all fond of Maisy in a funny sort of way, even Claude. But it was Ada Maisy wanted. When Ada sat by her bed she was quiet. She looked up at Ada out of her small blue eyes and was happy. Her nose ran constantly and she made no attempt to wipe it unless Ada was there. When Rose was at Maisy's bedside and she had to wipe Maisy's nose she did it, heaving all the time. Maisy thought this was very funny so that was good.

In just two short weeks she got weaker and weaker. You could hear her stertorous breathing all over the house. Ada tried everything she could think of. Chest rubs, lavender inhalations, hot lemon drinks, even a drop of brandy, but nothing eased that hard breathing. Even the tablets the doctor prescribed, that Maisy would only take if Ada was holding the glass of water, did no good. She was overtaken by fits of coughing that left her spent and breathless, and Ada and Rose had to hold her up until the paroxysms passed. Rose was scared Maisy would die during one of these seizures, but was even more terrified she would die while Rose was there on her own, or just with Jo. But Maisy died peacefully one night listening to Ada read Cinderella. Ada had just got to the part where the prince was fitting the glass slipper onto Cinderella's foot when the hoarse breathing stopped. In the kitchen, Rose was drying the dishes and suddenly became aware that it was very quiet. She listened. Nothing. No terrifyingly laboured harshness, no sound of the struggle not to cough, nothing. When Ada came through into the kitchen Rose was crying into the tea towel. Ada put her arms around Rose and held her. 'I know, I know. Maisy only had one thing to offer and that was absolutely unconditional. God knows she's a lesson to all of us, me especially.'

Frankie Beacon didn't attend his daughter's funeral service but at the grave where she was buried beside her mother, in the pouring rain, he turned up in grubby shorts and singlet, drunk. He sobbed and cried loudly all through the short service. 'Oh,' he wailed, 'oh Hazel, why did you leave me? Why didn't God take me too?'

Rose and Jo dared not catch each other's eyes. Both imagined themselves mimicking Mr Beacon. 'Oh Hazel, why did you leave me? Why didn't God take me too?' Rose's shoulders trembled, and Jo turned away. Rose gave a little gasp and Ada glared at her, although a moment before she'd rolled her eyes at Claude and Peter as if to say she wouldn't mind helping God out.

Even Sam Porohiwi got sick of Frankie in the end and marched firmly over to him. Rose hoped he was telling him it was a bit late now to be crying over the daughter he'd neglected when she was alive and that if he couldn't pull himself together he'd better leave. That's what Rose would have told him. But Mr Porohiwi was a minister so he probably had a different message for Frankie. Ada and Thelma had organised afternoon tea and quite a few people came. Some of the kids from school, a couple of teachers, Peter Paul Pearl of course, Thelma and Jo, Claude, even the doctor popped in briefly.

You'd wonder, thinks Rose as she sits on that hard chair in the hospital room, why Maisy was allowed to live such a short and, from the time her mother died until she came to live with Ada, unhappy life. What was the point?

Through the window she sees trees tossing violently and heavy rain beats like big drumsticks against the windows. Beyond the trees is a tall chimney, grey and solid against the dark sky. It stands firm against the bruising blast of the wind.

The way this morning's gone Olga's probably had a puncture. Rose feels uncertain about Olga, as though the balance of something has shifted. She feels Marcy trying to get into her mind, but deliberately shuts her off. Too late, she thinks, too bloody late. Rose wants to talk to Olga. If Olga still wants to talk to her. Olga has a hard row to hoe and Rose has made it harder. Not because she didn't want to do what Olga wanted but because she did, and it was too scary. We are all aliens, thinks Rose. You're being melodramatic Rose. It's true though, melodramatic or not. Why didn't I see that before?

It's too hard, everything's too hard. If this was a Fairy Tale it would definitely be a good time for a Fairy Godmother to unpack her wand and start waving it about. Rose just wants to go home with Olga, close the door, and forget everything. Olga, she thinks, where the hell are you?

She doesn't want any more. She can't cope with any more. She's had it up to here. She doesn't want the business with Lizzie, the mess with Royston, she especially doesn't want right at this moment to be reminded about a woman who'd tied an electric cord around her daughter's neck and tried to hang her because the girl had told her mother a lie. She was only stopped by a neighbour who heard the girl's screams. Or the man who beat his son with a piece of four by two because the boy had lied and whom a jury decided was innocent of assault.

Something is happening to her brain. It only wants to bring up unpleasant, inconvenient and brutal episodes that she can't even remember reading or hearing. Maybe she should stop reading papers, listening to the radio, or watching television (and withdraw into a cocoon where she works in the shop, looks after the house and garden, sools the black cat away from the pantry window sill) and she wouldn't even know when planes smash into black towers. She wouldn't know there were no survivors so far and would not have the firemen's faces imprinted on her brain. She would work away happily on needlework projects, and Sib and Louise would not be told their bad news, and Rose would not even have had cancer so she would be free of this bloody never-ending fear every time she feels a bit tired.

Thank you very much Brain, Rose thinks, you can't let me forget for one single instant can you.

When Olga does appear, Claude is with her. Rose is leaning back with her eyes closed. Maybe this whole thing – the baby, Lizzie, Jo and Wesley, the Hipps – is a dream from which she'll waken soon. 'Rose,' Olga touches her gently, 'Rose.'

Rose opens her eyes and smiles at Olga, sees Claude and smiles at him. He looks as though he will burst with something. Anger? 'Come on George – ah – Simmie,' she says to the baby. 'We're going home.'

Olga has a quick look at Lizzie, Claude grabs the bag with the baby's gear in it. Olga looks hassled. Why is Claude angry? Maybe Olga actually did have a flat tyre. But why would that make Claude angry? Have he and Olga had an argument? When Rose is seated in Olga's car, and George/Simmie is safely strapped in his baby seat, they tell her.

'Your house has been sprayed. Done over. Hell of a mess.'

'Was it red paint?'

Olga nods.

'Knock-Knock?'

'Has to be,' Claude says, 'but he's gone, vamoosed, vanished. I rang that bugger Wesley. Gave him a piece of my mind. Told him it's his responsibility. You're coming home with me,' Claude says to Rose. 'Elena says you've had enough for one day.'

'I want to see the house,' Rose says.

'Told you,' Olga says to Claude.

Claude shakes his head but he doesn't try to dissuade her. Olga starts the car and drives slowly away from the hospital.

TWENTY-ONE

There is red paint everywhere. Over the kitchen walls. Criss-crossed over the table, the macrocarpa bowl, the lemons, the William Morris chair, the black chair, the cushions, the bench, the floor. No room has been spared. In the sitting room Ada's wall hangings, including the one of the Hutt Valley, are covered in red paint and the furniture, curtains, carpet, all have wild red streaks over them. In the sewing room, the fabrics, threads – everything – have been mixed up with paint and left in a huge glutch on the floor. There is red paint on the windows, the walls, the doors, on the fabric work-wall where *The Skeleton Woman* used to hang. Rose walks silently through the entire house. There is nothing that hasn't been sprayed. Her bedroom, her wall hanging which Olga admired so much, the books by the bed, the dressing table, mirror, the doors and contents of her wardrobe. All have been lashed with red. The bathroom and toilet, the laundry, even the pegs, have been doused. It will take an army to clean whatever is salvageable, most is not. She goes into Ada's bedroom. The damage is complete. Pillows, duvet, the clothes, shoes in the wardrobe, the dressing-table drawers have been pulled open and red sprayed inside. Rose feels deathly tired. 'Claude,' she says.

'Rosie?'

'Ada's trunk,' she says. 'I promised Sibyl she could have a trunk of Ada's. She wants to make a memory box and an ordinary box is too small. She wants a trunk because she has a lot of memories.' Her voice wobbles, but she takes a deep breath.

Claude looks around the room. No trunk is visible. He walks carefully to the bed and, slithering his hands under the duvet so he can turn it over and avoid getting paint on himself, he crouches down and peers underneath the bed. He takes a quick, sharp breath. 'It's here Rosie.'

She hugs Simmie to her while Claude, after raising an eyebrow at Rose and getting a nod of agreement, spreads the duvet on the floor, unsprayed side up. Carefully he drags the trunk out, lifting it slightly to slide it onto the duvet. The trunk is untouched with red. Olga puts a hand on each corner of the duvet and pulls and Claude holds the other two corners steady. They move slowly through the house and out onto the back porch. There, Claude gives the trunk a closer inspection, finds it as clean as he thought, and with his legs slightly bent and bum stuck out in the approved monkey position he lifts the trunk, Olga opens the boot and there it is, safe. Ada's trunk is safe. Something, Rose thinks, something of Ada's has been salvaged. The trunk is Sibyl's, but whatever's inside was Ada's and is now Rose's.

Olga locks the door behind them. Rose thinks of stable doors but doesn't say so. Standing on the back porch, taking off her gumboots – now blotched and smeared with red paint from the floors – she shudders. 'Stupid,' she says, 'stupid.'

Elena has the front door open and as soon as she hears the car she limps out. Elena was once a star as well as a staunch behind-the-scenes worker at Hutt Repertory Theatre. In all the programmes up until three years ago her name either appeared in the cast list or among the production team. She learned to tap-dance so she could play Maxine in *Stepping Out*. Now she had difficulty moving without a walking stick. Her friends from Hutt Repertory made sure she got to see any performance that she was well enough to attend. There were always seats kept for

Elena and Claude and the committee had even purchased an ergonomically approved chair especially for her. She is still a strikingly good-looking woman although her face is fatter from the medication, her once-square shoulders stooped and those beautiful hands knotted and twisted out of shape.

Claude built their house in the late sixties. His mates from the Carpenter's Union helped. It took him two years, but by the time he finished and he and Elena moved in it had only a small mortgage on it, long since paid off. It's a two-storey house, wooden, large. It stands on a half-acre section of trees and gardens. It has a picket fence which Claude paints every summer. He likes picket fences and is prepared to do this regular maintenance for the pleasure of having one. Claude said the Hutt Valley was the worst place in New Zealand for pretentious fences, huge brick or concrete monstrosities that wouldn't be out of place in front of a baronial hall. 'I'll tell you how you know you're in the Hutt,' Claude said. 'If you can't drive for more than half a kilometre without having to negotiate a roundabout, if every second street is called a Grove, and if all you can see are high, thick fences, you're in the Hutt.' He always added, because he really liked living there, 'We have great trees though. The best pohutukawa in the country. And great gardens because the best gardeners in the country live in the Hutt.'

Recently Claude hired an architect to draw up plans to modify the house and make it easier for Elena. Rose suspected Elena would like something smaller, one storey, with not so much garden for Claude to worry about. Rose wondered sometimes about the brothers. Sim and Ada only had the one child, Claude and Elena have none. Maybe the brothers had low sperm counts, she thought, having read the phrase somewhere.

There's someone behind Elena, but Rose doesn't see who it is because Elena holds out her poor hands to Rose and says, 'Oh my dear, my dear.' And it's there, in the arms of a woman she's never really liked and who's never really liked her, that Rose cries for her house, for the old ordinary oak table, the chair so carefully recovered, the macrocarpa bowl, even the lemons. She cries for Simmie, for Lizzie and even for Royston. She cries for Jo and Wesley, for the Hipps. She cries for Louise. She cries for Sibyl and Kitty and what they have to face over the next months. She cries for Maisy. She cries for Ada. She cries for all those poor kids she didn't want to think about earlier. She cries for herself.

Olga and the other woman, Bridget of course, take the baby, and while she sobs and Elena holds her, Rose hears the comforting sound of someone else preparing a bottle of food, of the baby being changed and washed, the sound of him drinking. She and Elena are somehow on the couch and Rose lies in Elena's arms and cries and cries and cries.

'There, there,' says Elena over and over, 'there, there.'

'I must be hurting you,' Rose sobs.

'I took some pain relievers,' Elena says, 'they should last another two hours. So go for it.'

Finally Rose blows her nose, becomes aware that Claude is standing, looking out his front windows, muttering quietly to himself and blowing his nose. She sees Puti. With a tray. Puti? When did she arrive? Olga must have rung her. Well of course Olga would have rung her oldest sister. But why would Puti come round here? Puti places a tray of tea and toast on the coffee table in front of Rose and Elena. She puts a hand on Rose's shoulders. 'Ka aroha rā Rose, I feel for you,' she says. Olga, where is Olga?

Bridget sits down opposite them with the baby and another plate of toast which she eats while she feeds him. 'My sister's twins always got hungry together so I was roped in. I don't know why, but feeding babies always makes me feel hungry too.' Puti pours tea for Rose, Elena and Claude, and makes coffee for Bridget.

'Where's Olga?' Rose asks.

'Calling in the troops,' Puti says.

What the hell does that mean?

Rose is starving. Her house and all her belongings are wrecked, Lizzie is badly hurt and in hospital, Jo is going to the papers with the story Rose has done her best to hide from for four years, Sibyl and Louise are facing who knows what, Olga has vanished who knows where, and Rose wolfs down toast as though everything in her world is OK. She smells more toast being made and thinks, good.

'Fucking hell,' says Claude, and everyone looks at him, shocked. Claude never uses anything worse than bugger in front of women. Elena rolls her eyes at Rose. 'It's that sort of day,' she says, and Rose gives a small giggle.

'Wesley,' Claude says, and goes to the front door.

Rose looks across at Puti who places a plate of fresh toast on the table. 'Really,' she insists, 'really. I want to know. Where's Olga?'

Puti looks at her consideringly. Makes up her mind. 'You know Rocket,' she says, 'she's looking for Knock-Knock.'

'Oh no.' Fear covers her like a blanket.

'She'll be OK,' Puti says, 'she's not on her own. Marama is there, and Leo, and probably Makere. Don't worry. They won't let her do anything she shouldn't.'

'I wasn't thinking of her doing anything,' Rose says, 'I was thinking more of Knock-Knock.'

'Don't worry,' Puti says.

Rose looks at her.

'Yes, well,' Puti says, only half-joking, 'she's been spoilt that's her trouble. She thinks she can fix everything. But will she be told? No. Well, not by her sisters anyway. Maybe you'll have better luck.'

Claude comes in. He's frowning. 'Malcolm's with him. Think you should see them,' he says.

Rose takes a sip of tea. 'All right,' she says.

Wesley looks as though he's facing a firing squad. He's not wearing his shorts today. He's in fawn trousers, check jacket, pale shirt and a tie with green parrots on it. Malcolm doesn't look much happier than his father, perhaps a little more composed. Malcolm's jersey, an Arran pattern in bone-coloured wool, is beautiful. Rose loves Arran. One day she will go to the Shetlands and see the place where it still flourishes. Finola's work, no doubt. He wears it over a check shirt and jeans. Rose introduces them to Puti. 'Olga's sister,' she says to Wesley. Malcolm says, 'Hello Puti.' So he knows her. Rose wonders where their paths have crossed. Probably when you're a ministerial advisor you talk to people in Puti's job. He sits down on the chair next to Wesley. He and Wesley refuse tea.

'Rose.' Wesley stands up. Malcolm nudges him on the back of the leg and he looks round. 'Oh, oh OK.' He sits down again. 'Sorry,' he says. 'And sorry for barging in. Had to see you. I'm so sorry about the house. You were quite right. Those young men were trouble. I should have listened. I know a firm that cleans up this kind of mess. Would you like me to get in touch with them? They've got an after-hours number.'

Rose says, 'Have you seen it?'

Wesley nods.

Rose says, 'I don't think there's a hope in hell it can be cleaned.' Her voice shakes, but she controls it. 'I need to have another look at the place anyway. I have to make up my mind what to do.'

'They can do wonders,' Wesley says. At least he hasn't reminded her that the church wants to buy it. Maybe they don't now. 'We can do a cleansing ritual if you'd like that.'

Claude snorts. Malcolm looks out the window disassociating himself from his father and from the Church of the Golden Light. It occurs to Rose that Malcolm would have to have passed a security check to get his job. She wonders what they made of his parent's church affiliations. Must have provided a bit of light relief from their usual delvings into applicant's backgrounds. Perhaps a Church of the Golden Light cleansing ritual wouldn't be too bad a thing? My brain's finally crumbling, thinks Rose. She says nothing.

Wesley says, 'Jo was extremely upset this morning. When we got home I called the doctor and he's prescribed some pills. I rang Malcolm and fortunately it was one of his rare weekends off.'

'I would have come anyway,' Malcolm says. His voice is strong, slightly defensive.

'At the moment she's sleeping.' Wesley sighs. 'Finola's there with her. The Hipps are there too. Somehow none of us want to be alone at the moment.' Wesley shakes his head and takes a deep breath, gets out his hanky and blows his nose.

'There will be no going to the media,' Malcolm says in a very firm voice. Wesley looks gratefully at his son.

'I'm not defending Mum, but in some respects I can see how it happened,' Malcolm says. 'Lizzie does enjoy a bit of drama and, given their two personalities and their history, I can see why Mum thought what she did. But you can forget the media.'

'What I can't understand is why she didn't tell me.' Wesley is genuinely puzzled. 'I'd have had a word with Royston. And with his father and mother. I'd have got Malcolm to help. Because that's what Royston needs. Help. That's all there is to it. They'll all have to face that. If Jo had just told us what Lizzie said we might have been able to stop it before it got to this stage.'

'That's what the police said to me,' Rose says, 'and they're right. If I'd got in touch with them on Friday the outcome might have been different.'

Wesley looks at her and tries to smile, and Rose sees he's a human being like the rest of us, that he's feeling terrible, but at least he's trying to do something about it. 'I understand what Ellie Hipp's saying,' he says, 'but if it rebounds on the church then so be it. Royston's not the first and he won't be the last to call himself a Christian and behave like this.' Wesley blows his nose again.

'It's a mess, the whole thing,' Malcolm says, 'but sweeping it under the carpet's not going to do anyone any good. Finola rang her sister, who works for Child, Youth and Family, and she suggested a family conference.' Malcolm looks just faintly revolted at the thought. Puti grins. 'Sorry Puti,' he says, 'I'm not a great believer in that sort of thing, but seeing we asked for advice I suppose we'd better take it. And I can't think of anything else. Of course I don't know if Lizzie will agree. I popped into the hospital but she was asleep. I'll go back later, but I won't ask her today anyway. She needs to get better first and we need to find out what's been done for this depression she's been having. I'll have a talk to Lizzie's doctor.'

Wesley looks at his son with something like an awed respect. 'He went and saw Royston,' he says.

'An officer stayed in the room,' Malcolm says, 'but there was no difficulty about seeing him. He'll probably be out on bail tomorrow. His father says he'll put up the money and that Royston can go home with them for the time being.' Now it's Malcolm's turn to shake his head. 'God knows what can be done about Royston. Finola's sister said something about an anger-management course.' Malcolm's lips curl as he says the words. 'Not that Royston's our business. Our business is Lizzie.'

'I think Royston is all of our business,' Puti says quite firmly.

Malcolm looks very surprised. Perhaps, thinks Rose, he's not used to being contradicted. He tightens his lips. 'You may well be right,' he says, obviously not believing a word of it, but not wanting to cause any dissension.

'Oh I am,' Puti says.

Malcolm says nothing.

Wesley takes another deep breath. 'Puti's right,' he agrees, then spoils it. 'We are our brothers' keepers after all.'

There is silence while the room seethes with unspoken retorts. Then Claude says, 'And how far are we supposed to go, Wesley?'

'As far as we have to,' Wesley says. He looks at Claude. 'Solidarity Claude. We have to help each other, whether we like each other or not. Especially if we don't. That's what it's all about. Solidarity,' he repeats.

Claude actually looks quite shocked. Wesley's used the one word that would make Claude understand. He has to have used it on purpose. But Claude's not going to give in too easily.

'Solidarity,' he says, 'who with?'

Wesley looks at Claude as though he's not very bright. 'All of us,' he says, 'all of us.' He should have left it there, but of course, being Wesley, he can't. 'No man is an island,' he quotes.

There is another silence while everyone resolutely stops themselves from saying one single word. It's Wesley's fate, thinks Rose, to say the things we all know are true, but to say them in such a way you want to either argue with them or go out and do the opposite.

'Well,' Wesley says after a while, 'I just want to say if there's anything I or the Church of the Golden Light can do, please, please just say.'

Rose has never admired Wesley for anything other than his ability to work, but now she sees someone different. Any doubts she may have harboured about his state of mind are just shallow readings of him. She sees that he's a truly devout man with an unfortunate manner. He is genuinely distressed, intent on making it clear that he'll do what he can. That he doesn't have a choice and neither do any of them.

Malcolm and Wesley stand. Malcolm looks at Rose. 'I'll keep in touch,' he says. 'If Lizzie agrees to a family conference, you might like to come too. Bring the baby.'

Rose knows Malcolm's revulsion is being mirrored in her own eyes but she says, 'Yes of course I'll bring him.' Solidarity, Rose.

'And,' Malcolm gets out his wallet, 'Finola and I would like to provide – we thought – you must have had extra expense –' Malcolm's voice trails away on '– anything he needs.'

Rose smiles. 'I'll be OK,' she says, 'but thanks.' She becomes aware that Puti is frowning at her. 'Of course,' she improvises rapidly, 'I wouldn't mind a proper bed for him. Perhaps you could bring the one from Lizzie's and any clothes or bedding you can find. And Lizzie will want clothes.'

'I'll get a key from her. Or Royston,' Malcolm says. He puts his wallet away, but he looks as though he feels better.

'And please, Rose,' says Wesley, 'when you see Lizzie, will you ask her – if I – if she'll see me? It might come better from you.'

Rose nods. 'I'll ask her.'

'There are things,' he says, 'things I'm not at liberty to say, secrets which are not mine to divulge –' He pauses portentously and Rose, a second after telling herself she's misjudged Wesley, feels the old irritation rising inexorably like sap in the spring. 'When Jo's better perhaps,' he adds mysteriously. She wants to hit him. Oh God, she thinks. No, I don't mean that.

Wesley looks across at Simmie, in Bridget's arms. 'May I?'

He looks down at his grandson, then gets down on his haunches and stares at the little face. 'Hello wee fella,' he says, and Rose immediately swings back to liking him.

'Hello Simon,' Malcolm says. The baby's eyes look at his grandfather and then at his uncle, over the bottle of milk. Wesley smiles at him, stands up. 'Please tell Lizzie I'm, we're both, thinking of her.' He looks at Rose pleadingly, 'And when she's ready, and only then, I'll come and see her. You'll let me know about cleaning the house?'

'I will.'

Rose thinks of the Hipps. How she would feel if that baby in Bridget's arms grows up and beats up his baby and his wife? Which, if all she's heard and read is true, is not exactly un-known. Nurture, she thinks, nurture. Have to bank on nurture. What else have we got?

TWENTY-TWO

It's Ada's voice, it really is Ada's voice. It's coming out of the tape she made especially for Rose. It's Ada all right. She's explained the tape is not a copy of the one she made with Sam Porohiwi, that she did this one for Rose alone. 'But I know you,' Ada says, and there's such a wealth of love and concern and understanding in that taped voice that tears threaten again. 'You won't want to listen to it but whenever you first hear this tape, whatever the situation, it will be exactly the right time. I've got something to tell you, something I should have told you years ago. Something I'm too much of a coward to tell you now while I'm still with you in person. The best thing and the worst thing I ever did.'

Rose is on her own, in Claude and Elena's sitting room. Ada's trunk is on the floor, its silvery tin top with the wavy wooden braces flipped open to expose papers, more tapes, other stuff that Rose has still to sort through. Now Rose stops the tape. 'Claude,' she calls, 'Claude.' He comes on the run.

'Sit with me,' Rose says. 'I can't do this on my own.'

Claude touches her on the shoulder and sits down on the other bed. 'OK Rosie,' he says, 'OK. We'll do it together.'

Rose turns the tape back on.

Ada says, 'I have to go back to when I married Sim. I fell in love. I didn't see till after that I fell in love seriously and he didn't. He loved me in the way you might love a puppy or a small child. I wanted marriage and he gave it to me. Sim only ever loved one person and no, that wasn't himself. It was

Thelma. She loved him too. Their love was the sort of thing you read about but never quite believe. The sort of love the poets write about. Obsessive, addictive, unstoppable. I realise that now, didn't at the time. But Thelma was married. Her husband had been badly disabled by an accident on the wharf, which is how Sim got to know her because he was on the welfare committee. They'd known each for two years or so when I came along. He'd wanted her to leave her husband, but she made it clear divorce was out of the question. Thelma was terribly torn, but she wouldn't leave her husband when nothing that had happened was his fault. Sim was very angry and refused to see her until she changed her mind. I think he thought this would change her mind. But it didn't. And then I came along. I think, at least for a while, he genuinely thought marrying me would make him forget her. I don't think even he realised just how strong their feelings were.

'Anyway, we married and were happy for a while. Yes, we were. Then, inevitably, he went and saw Thelma, couldn't stay away really, and the whole thing started up again. I had two miscarriages and I was so miserable, and then I noticed he was often home later than Claude, and that he was out a lot. He always had an excuse. He was at one of those interminable welfare committee meetings, or taking his turn at one of the clubs, or at the pub. In those days, Rose, there were all sorts of clubs, just about every port had its brass band, many even had drama groups, all of them had sports teams. Those were the days eh? For a while I went along with that.

'Then I found out. In the oldest way. Perfume on his clothes, lipstick on his collar. The Skeleton Woman had, no doubt, decided it was time for me to open my eyes, time to grow up. I was hurt, so hurt, and as if that wasn't enough he told me Thelma was pregnant. With twins, and that they weren't her husband's. He said her husband thought the babies were his and was ecstatic. He'd always wanted kids and thought his accident might have put paid to that dream. He'd just never believed one would come along. I'd just been told I would never carry a baby to full term. What a mess. I was so angry, so angry. Sim and Thelma would pay, I decided. He'd married me under false pretences and he would pay. There was a lot more of my father in me than I'd realised. So I told Sim I would keep my mouth shut, I wouldn't tell her husband, if Thelma gave me one of the babies. Course she said no at first. So I said I'd be over to tell her husband the full story that night. She said go ahead then. There were some things she wouldn't do even for Sim. If she and Sim had to become public knowledge, then so be it. Sim talked her round. He said no sons of his were going to start off like that. I think also he had a bit of a worry about Claude, what he'd say, how he'd react. Claude was his Achilles heel. He didn't want Claude to know. I didn't think Thelma would wear it, even then, but she finally said yes. Maybe she felt guilty about me. She told me later she hoped her husband would die before she had the babies and she could tell me to forget it.

'She had the babies and they were girls. I would have laughed if I hadn't been so busy. Thelma was young and strong and had a relatively easy labour, but I'd never seen a baby born before, let alone two. I remember thinking good, at least one of Sim's dreams had gone askew. Daughters, what a laugh.

'I'd organised that when Thelma went into labour she'd send a message and Sim and I would go around, ostensibly for me to help. The plan was we wouldn't let anyone know, not even her husband, until she'd had both babies. I was there in the room when they were born. Sim couldn't face it and the husband was too worried. He was convinced the babies would be born deformed we found out later. The twins weren't identical, and one of them was born just before midnight and the other one just after so they even had different birthdays. We only called the midwife after Thelma had the second one. If she knew it wasn't a single birth she kept her mouth shut. As far as the husband knew the doctor must have been mistaken and she'd had just the one perfectly healthy little girl. Thelma nursed both babies for the first fortnight. She insisted. Said they must both have a good start. I was so happy I didn't care. I had my baby. I had made Thelma suffer. And if she was unhappy so was Sim.

'I came back home with my baby and left Thelma with hers. No one asked any questions, why would they? I'd carefully got myself fatter as time went on, prided myself I looked pregnant. The story was I'd gone to help Thelma, gone into labour myself and we'd had babies a day apart. You might think you couldn't get away with it today but you'd be wrong.

'Three months later Thelma's husband died. To my fury she then insisted on buying the house next door. If I objected she'd call the whole deal off. She said the kids must get to know each other. Sim agreed. I made it as difficult as possible. I had nothing to do with her and I didn't allow you to play with Jo, but you used to talk to her through the fence and sometimes I saw Thelma watching and I would think good, I hope you're suffering.

'Once you went to school I couldn't do much about it and you and Jo became really good friends. You didn't look alike. You took after Sim and Jo took after Thelma.

'Sim and I slept in separate rooms. The story was that I had trouble sleeping and my tossing and turning disturbed him. Oh sometimes he tried to get things on a better footing, but I wasn't having any. He had this other life with Thelma. I didn't want to be the spare part. I thought Claude must know. I thought he wasn't saying anything because he wanted to spare my feelings. After Sim died I realised Claude knew nothing. But the Skeleton Woman had one last card for me. On the night that Maisy Beacon belted Harry Oliver with my shovel, I had to ask

Thelma for help. Even though I hated her I knew she was the only one I could trust. Because Maisy had killed Harry and neither of us could see that poor girl dragged through the courts or incarcerated in one of those homes just because a drunken yobbo had tried it on with her. And I couldn't help thinking Rose, what if it had been you. Also it seemed like a just penance.

'We dragged his body off our section and put it in a place where we hoped it would never be found. They were putting new pipes along Regent Crescent at the time and there were huge open ditches all over waiting for the pipes to be put in. We found a place where they'd put some of the pipes in but hadn't closed them over. Somehow Thelma and I moved a big pipe. Then we dug the ditch a bit deeper, put Harry there, and put the pipe on top. We put as much soil and shingle down the sides as we could. It was the best we could do.

'On the way back, Thelma started talking. I'd been feeling very sorry for myself, drinking myself silly, and suddenly I was listening to her tell me what a bloody fool I was making of myself. She said if I didn't pull myself together she'd take you back. She said she didn't want to, that it would be devastating for you, and for Jo, but she would do it. She'd had to bear all the hard looks, all the sniggering asides, all the gossip, as well as the grief and loss of the one she loved best in the whole world, but she was buggered if she was going to stand by and see me ruin her daughter's life as well. She said we'd both suffered and now it was time to give it away. "We might never become close friends but we can be friendly neighbours," was how she put it. She turned out to be a very good friend, the best I've ever had. Neither of us wanted you girls to know. Both too ashamed, I think. When I look back now and think of what I did it seems like another person did it. Not me, but someone else. Someone quite different. Which, in a way, it was.

'Thelma and I both held our breath until the pipes in that particular part were filled. Those few days were tough. I'd never have got through it without Thelma. And Maisy had a good two and a half years with us. The doctor told me she'd never make old bones but I thought if I looked after her, she'd have a bit longer than she did. Poor Maisy. Makes you wonder doesn't it.

'I know what I did was wrong, but try as I might, I can't be sorry. Not when it brought me you, Rose. I loved you the first moment I saw you and I love you still. I regret not having the guts to tell you, but, otherwise, I'm selfish enough to say I regret nothing and that if I was faced with the same situation I'd do it all again. I know you'll be upset and not just because the friendship you had with Jo is no longer there. As far as that's concerned I just want to say that if Thelma and I could do it, there's no reason why you two can't do the same. But I'm old enough to know there's nothing I can do about it. It's up to you two. I think you'll be upset Rose and I know when you hear this tape I'll be dead so you won't be able to tell me off. I'm not sorry, so no good pretending I am.

'I'd like Claude to know that I forgave Sim long ago. How could I not when, if it wasn't for him, I'd never have had my daughter. And I was lucky. I got a second go at it. I met Peter. But that's another story. I hope you'll both forgive me for keeping the secret, but I know you'll understand why. I'm going to stop talking for a while now. Been a bit of a marathon. Don't be too upset Rose.'

The tape clicks off. Rose and Claude stare into space.

Then Rose says to Claude, 'I'm not as surprised as I should be.'

Claude looks at Rose.

Rose says, 'It's like there's been a jigsaw in front of me with a piece missing, but I was so used to seeing it I didn't even realise it was incomplete. Until now. So many things fall into place. I've never known why I persevered with Jo. Now I do. And I always thought Thelma had a real soft spot for me. Simple really.'

'Anything else in the trunk?'

'Some photos, clippings. The best thing as far as Bridget's concerned is Peter's unfinished novel.'

Claude laughs. 'So that's what she's got. She's absolutely glued to it. Be lucky if she surfaces for meals.'

'She says it's about a woman who loves a man so much she gives up one of her babies.'

Claude stares at Rose.

'It's called *The Cross of Stars*.'

'Oh,' says Claude. He frowns, 'And what does that mean for God's sake?'

'You'll have to ask Bridget. I'm going to go and see Jo.'

TWENTY-THREE

Monday morning. Rose sits on one side of Lizzie's bed, Jo on the other, while a woman bustles in and out with cups of tea from the trolley in the passage. Jo has asked to be present and Rose, with Alice's approval, has agreed, but on two conditions. That Lizzie agrees and that Jo remains silent. Rose is certain Lizzie will jib at Jo's presence, but she just looks at her mother expressionlessly when she asks if she can sit with her and then shrugs as though it doesn't really matter.

Rose is uneasy. She thinks this would be better done by one of the experts. But –

'She trusts you Rose.'

'She left her baby with you Rose.'

'It might come better from you Miss Anthony.'

'We'd like to try it this way first.'

'We'll be in the ward office if you need us.'

And the clincher. 'It'll work out better for the baby if we do it this way.'

So here she is. She wishes she was somewhere else. She wishes she was dusting the shelves in the shop and not Carlos, dallying over any book he fancies, putting one or two aside in lieu of wages. She'd hardly got the request out before he agreed. 'A day or two, I'm yours,' he said, 'keeps me out of mischief while I'm waiting for the phone to ring.' Which is an exaggeration because he has as much work as he wants. Lucky Carlos, to be able to pick and choose. His parents left him their house which has a flat attached so he has no mortgage, a small income from the flat, and painting signs four days a week brings in as much as he wants. 'I never want to be a millionaire,' he told Rose once, 'just earn enough to sit in the sun and read whenever I feel like it.' He has no partner, male or female. 'There's something left out of me. I'm not ambitious and I think I'm asexual,' he confided to Rose. 'Actually, I prefer books.'

Morning tea is served. The tea is weak but deliciously hot. 'Biscuits?' the woman asks. They decline.

'Nana,' Lizzie says when the woman has gone, shutting the door behind her, 'it was Nana. She told me and she told Malcolm. We both thought it was crazy, you and Mum not knowing, but she made us promise we would never tell. She wanted someone to know before she died. She really loved Sim, as she called him. She really did. Even when she was dying she thought of him. She said she'd promised Ada never to tell.' Lizzie gulps her tea, swallows, then says, 'I let her down. I told you,' she says to Jo, 'I went and told you.' There is dislike and resentment in her voice, as though her breaking the confidence Thelma reposed in her has nothing to do with her and everything to do with Jo. Jo is silent. So far she's keeping her promise but Rose is on tenterhooks. Lizzie drinks her tea slowly, her hands around the cup as though she's cold.

Yesterday. Rose refused all the offers from Claude, Puti, Bridget, even Elena, to accompany her. Olga hadn't returned and wasn't at the café because Rose rang. Rose thought this meeting with Jo would definitely be unpleasant, probably painful, but she knew she had to do it on her own. The door opened. Jo took one look at Rose. 'Lizzie told you.' Her voice was bitter but there was a deep vein of something else moving slowly underneath the bitterness. Relief?

'Lizzie? No, Ada did.'

Jo frowned, said carefully, 'Ada told you? When?'

'She made a tape. Can I come in Jo?'

Jo turned and walked down the hall and Rose followed. Jo led the way into the sitting room. It was like walking into a furniture-shop window. Looking around, Rose found it hard to believe she and Jo were really sisters. Don't be such a pain Rose, not everyone wanted to spend hours placing a chair or a cushion.

The couch, patterned with roses, stood along one wall, chairs that match each side of the fireplace. There was a polished rimu coffee table in front of the couch. No clutter, no books, not even a cushion. There was a fire going in the grate but the room felt cold. Along the outside wall was a row of large windows overlooking the gardens and wide lawn. Jo indicated a chair by the windows and she stood looking out. There was a little pale sunlit patch on the floor and Rose thankfully placed her feet in the middle of it.

Jo said, 'I know you didn't touch that girl.'

Rose nodded. 'I know you do.'

Jo kept looking out the window as though it was preferable to looking at Rose. 'I've always envied you,' she said after a long pause.

'Why?'

'Why do you think?' A flash of temper there. 'It wasn't very enjoyable being the daughter of the woman whose bed another woman's husband died in.'

'People soon found something else to talk about.'

'Oh no. They never forgot. Some of them still look at me, waiting for me to do the same. That's why Lizzie was such a worry. She was so like Mum. It seemed too good to be true when she married Royston.'

Rose looked away, at the opposite wall. She felt her eyes stop, swivel back, then prickle. One of Ada's wall hangings. Of course. Jo inherited that from Thelma. Rose remembered Ada sewing it. *Resolution*, she called it. Its background was red, Thelma's favourite colour. In one corner was a large black circle and running out from that a series of fine jagged or curving lines, all in different primary colours. They were either bursting in, or bursting out of the black and came to an end in a wide yellow circular line. Outside the yellow line were stylised flowers, roses, irises, tulips all mingling with the spring narcissuses Thelma loved. The words 'For Thelma, 1986' were stitched along the bottom. It should look totally out of place on this wall. Somehow it doesn't.

'I'd forgotten,' Rose said, 'that you had that hanging.' She remembered she had none of Ada's work herself now. Because of your own stupidity Rose. 'She made it for Thelma's sixtieth,' Rose said, as though Jo didn't know.

Jo's mouth worked irritably. 'Don't you mean your mother's sixtieth?'

Rose thought how to say what she wanted to say and then said it. 'My mother's name was Ada,' she said. 'Yes, I know, I know. But there's a lot more to mothering than giving birth. I know it wasn't Thelma's choice, but she did agree.'

'Because she loved Sim Anthony more than she loved us.' The bitterness again.

'Yes.' There's nothing else to say. It was true.

Jo sighed, a long sigh. 'I knew as soon as you found out what Lizzie named the baby it was only a matter of time.' She gave a dry little snort. 'Your precious Skeleton Woman at work, I suppose.'

'Probably.'

'This mess. It's all my fault.'

'Parts of it, parts of it Jo, but only parts. Lizzie's got to take some responsibility. Royston too. And me, for that matter.'

'What's going to happen Rose?'

Rose had expected a big dramatic scene and was surprised at the comparative ease of this meeting. Perhaps it is only the small things we jump up and down about; perhaps the big things are more easily accepted simply because they are so huge.

Lizzie puts her cup back on the locker and looks away from her mother towards Rose. 'It was when I first knew I was pregnant. I was really excited and happy and it just spilled out. I said I wondered if it would be twins. Mum said, "Do be sensible Lizzie,"' Lizzie mimics Jo, 'in that know-it-all way that always riles me. She said "Just because you think you'd fancy twins doesn't mean you'll have them. Twins run in families and there are none either in the Hipp family or in ours."' And I said, "Oh yes there are." And then she kept on to know what I meant until in the end,' Lizzie looks at Jo as though she hates her, 'I told you! I broke my promise to Nana and I told you. I just wanted to shut you up.' Lizzie slaps her hand against the bedspread in time with the words. 'I – just – wanted – to – shut – you – up.'

Don't say a word, Jo, don't say a word, Rose pleads silently. After a while Lizzie says, 'Malcolm was really wild. A confidence is a confidence and I should be ashamed of myself. Malcolm's always been like that and I don't usually take any notice, but this time he was right. I couldn't get it out of my mind. Nana had trusted me and I'd let her down.'

Jo puts her hand out but Rose frowns and she pulls it back. She's as pale as her daughter is flushed.

'That's why I didn't want to see you. I couldn't. Every time I saw you it reminded me that I'd let Nana down. And you were – funny – anyway. I know Dad was worried.'

Jo nods, but doesn't speak. Good one Jo, keep it up.

Lizzie sighs. 'It was all my fault. I knew it was. Malcolm was disgusted so I stopped seeing him. Finola's nice but – I felt terrible.'

'I should have known the minute I heard the boy's name.' Rose voice comes out as though there are cracks in it but Lizzie doesn't notice.

'The Hipps are great on family names. They wanted Elmore. But I stuck out for Simon. So he's Simon Elmore Hipp. They all wanted to know why. I just said I liked it. I knew it would make Mum and Malcolm really steam.' A reminiscent pleasure colours Lizzie's voice. She had delighted in upsetting her mother and brother. Maybe she saw it as paying them back for the months of self-disgust and anxiety she'd suffered after spilling the beans to Jo.

Physically, Lizzie's looking better, her mouth is clearly not so sore, she can drink the hot tea and her words come out without effort. She's tired though and her eyes are wary, guarded, but that's understandable. Revenge always comes back and bites you on the bum, as Rose knows only too well. From the outside it's easy to see that it's not worth it, but from the inside it always seems that it's the only gratification on offer.

'You've seen Malcolm?'

Lizzie nods. She doesn't say any more, just looks out the window at the trees. The wind has dropped. Hopefully the gales are on the way out. At least the washing dries quickly now the rain has stopped. 'Is there anything more satisfying than a line full of dry washing when you've got a baby in the house?' Elena asked that morning.

Rose thinks of Olga as she and Lizzie stare out the window and Jo stares at Lizzie. They all sit like people waiting for something. It seems like a century ago Olga suggested Rose sell her place and go and live with her. When she rang, finally, to say she was home but wouldn't come round to Claude's because she had to do the GST returns, organise the banking and make sure the orders had been done, Rose felt bereft.

Olga's had second thoughts, Rose is sure of it. Rose is not keen on the idea that Olga had accepted her refusal so enthusiastically, but it keeps hanging around in her brain and catches her when she's not expecting it. If her brain's not dredging up unpleasant thoughts about Olga it's busily searching through its files so it can bring up things like the little girl who'd been kept prisoner in a wardrobe for months. Hardly any food or water, just shut in the darkness. She was found nearly dead and is now in hospital. Her mother is being psychiatrically assessed. Surely someone, someone must have known there was a child, must have wondered why they didn't see her around. Surely she was missed at school. Once, Rose had relegated these cruelties to Dickens or Bronte or third-world countries, but that was because she was firmly into keeping her eyes shut to what she read in the papers and what she saw on television. You were a bloody wimp Rose. Look at the last time you were at the hairdressers. He was just back from India and he told you, he actually told you quite matter-of-factly, that some very poor Indian parents deliberately maim, injure and disable their children simply to make them better prospects for begging. He said you see them everywhere on the streets and people walk by, immune to their suffering. Your brain remembered, but it didn't make a bloody atom of difference to you. You skated on very happily, Rose Anthony. That's all very well, thinks Rose, but what difference can one person possibly make? Well first of all Rose, you can get this train on the tracks. You know what you have to do, so do it.

'Lizzie,' she says. There must be some signal in her voice because Jo sits up even straighter in the hospital chair. She's like a runner waiting for the starter's pistol. Now they're away. 'Lizzie, a police officer came to see me this morning. Royston is sticking to his story, swears he didn't hit the baby. He admits hitting you and, now that he's calmed down, knows he needs to do something about his temper. He says that when you wouldn't tell him where the baby was he thought you'd done something dreadful and that's why he panicked, why he lost his temper. He's unshaken about harming the baby. He's never wavered about that.' Rose takes a quick slurp of tea, thinks, get on with it Rose. 'I went and saw him myself just to, I don't know, see for myself I suppose.'

Royston hadn't wanted to look at Rose. When they brought him in and he sat down opposite he kept his head bent and sat silent. He looked unkempt, somehow, although he'd obviously showered and shaved. His face wasn't sullen, as far as Rose could judge, but it was resistant. He kept blowing his nose, which was very red, and his eyes, when he lifted them, looked sore. 'Hay-fever,' he said, when she asked him for something to say. This is Simmie's father, she repeated to herself, Simmie's father, so something had to be done.

'We met at the wedding, Royston,' she said finally, 'I'm Rose. I always thought I was Ada Anthony's daughter, but I've recently discovered I was really Thelma's – hers and my father's. Jo's my sister. Did you know that?'

He shook his head, but he seemed to relax. He darted a quick look at her and she smiled, she hoped in a friendly fashion.

'This is a mess Royston,' she said. 'I know you've told your story to any number of people, but I'd like to hear it please. If you will.'

'Remember,' Alice had told her, 'he won't look angry or violent, he'll probably look young and scared so just remember what he did. What he must have looked like on Saturday night. Both of them are Royston. He's given room to the violent part of himself once; he'll do it again unless he learns not to. He won't want to reveal what you want him to tell you. It's one thing to say it to police officers or a lawyer, but quite another to face you. He knows you're the one his wife left their baby with, the one who saw the bruising on his son's body, the one to whom Lizzie went for refuge. He won't want to face you and say yes, I did that. So he'll do anything to avoid it even if it means shifting the blame on to someone else. Don't believe him just because he looks sorry and ashamed, only believe him if you can tick off everything else and that's all you've got left. Like they say in the best murder mysteries, you eliminate all the suspects and what you've got left must be the murderer.'

Royston was unshakeable. Yes, he'd hit Lizzie, yes he lost his temper, yes he went mad. He said it over and over, yes, he did all that, but he did not hit the baby. It was because the baby was missing that he lost it so completely. He didn't make excuses, he knew he would have to do some things he wouldn't want to do, that all the newspapers would carry the story, that everyone at work would know, his brothers and sisters would know, the people he went to school with would know, everyone in the Church of the Golden Light would know. He would have to appear in court and plead guilty to assaulting his wife and accept whatever sentence the judge handed down. All this he knew. But he was adamant. He did not touch his son and nothing Rose or the officers or his parents or the welfare officer said made him retract this one fact.

'Thank you Royston,' Rose said at last, feeling as though she'd run a marathon. She'd only been there an hour, but it felt like days.

He lifted his head, blew his nose, and said, 'You believe me?'

'Yes,' she said, and thought this is probably wrong, I've done it all wrong, but she believed him so she might as well say. She didn't like him much, even if he was Elmore Hipp's great-grandson, but she believed him on this one fact.

He blew his nose again and she suspected that this time it wasn't just because of the hayfever, but she remembered Alice's advice and just smiled and said goodbye.

Looking directly into Lizzie's face Rose says clearly, 'Lizzie, did Royston hit the baby?' There. It's out. Lizzie is so pale Rose thinks she will faint. Jo sits like stone. Rose sees very clearly that what the police suspect is true. 'Lizzie,' she says, 'oh Lizzie.'

'It was an accident,' Lizzie says, 'it was an accident. You have to believe me Rose, it was an accident.'

Jo's hand goes up to her mouth and presses against her lips. Anything she wants to say, might have said, is effectively stopped. Rose doesn't, can't speak. But she must. 'Keep it short,' Alice says, 'ask exactly what you want to know. No more, no less. Then shut up.'

'What happened, Lizzie?'

Lizzie's face goes through a series of contortions as she struggles against the tears. Her eyes are seeing herself over the past few months. 'I was feeling rotten,' she whispers, 'I'd been feeling awful for days, weeks, probably since I got pregnant. It was that business with Mum and Malcolm. I couldn't get it out of my head. I thought it would be all right when the baby was born, but it was worse. I couldn't understand why I was making such a thing of having a baby. Other girls my age have babies, and they manage. Why couldn't I? Royston said I should pull myself together. He said his mother had six children and she just got on with it. The doctor said I had a touch of post-natal depression but it would go away in time.' Lizzie stops.

Don't say a word, Rose, not one word.

There is a long silence. Outside she hears someone asking if someone else has taken their tablets. The silence continues.

Rose thinks it's not going to work, it's not going to work, I shouldn't have let Jo come, I shouldn't have come myself, I should have left it to the experts, it's not bloody working. What the hell am I going to do now.

Then it happens. A tap is turned on somewhere. Lizzie says quickly, 'Simmie had been crying all day. I think he sensed I was losing it. People say babies sense things. Whole hours went by and I didn't know where they'd gone. I came to at one stage and he was screaming and I was shouting at him. I was horrified,' Lizzie's got a faraway look in her eyes, 'and scared. So scared. Everything was out of control. I made up my mind I should tell Mum.' Lizzie seems to have forgotten Jo is sitting beside her. 'I didn't want to. I hadn't seen her since I told her what Nana said. But I knew I had to do something. I should have known better.' Lizzie's voice is bitter with remembered pain. 'Mum said I was exaggerating. She said I'd made enough trouble without dragging Royston into it. Somehow she got it into her head I was scared of Royston, that I was complaining about him – well I was, but about his lack of sympathy not because he'd hit me. I was the one I was scared of. I did try to tell Mum, but she didn't want to know.'

Rose doesn't dare look at Jo. 'What about Malcolm?'

'Mr Perfect? Mum's favourite child? Great job, lovely Finola, always done everything right? You must be joking. He paid a duty visit after Simmie was born and he could hardly wait to get away. I couldn't say anything to him, I just couldn't. Everything was boiling away inside me and I remembered all the times he'd done well and I hadn't. I was so tired. I couldn't believe there was so much to do. I was staggered at how much there is to do when you've got a baby. I'd just get one thing done and there'd be something else. I never seemed to get to the end of it. He was fretful at nights so I wasn't sleeping. Royston slept in another room so he wouldn't be disturbed. He said he had to work long hours and needed his sleep. He bought me some vitamins and I took them just to keep him quiet. And,' Lizzie swallowed hard and made herself continue, 'it's awful, I'm sorry Rose, but I started bleeding when I did poos and there was blood on my pants and I thought I had cancer or something. I was frantic, worrying who would look after the baby. I didn't want Mum to have him.' It's bizarre, but Lizzie smiles. 'It's piles Rose! The nurses here tell me it's piles! They say lots of women get them during pregnancy and after giving birth. I didn't know that. Funny how no one tells you these things, such basic things. Have you noticed how no one talks about piles?'

'She won't mean to,' Alice had said, 'but she might go off the track. It'll be such a relief for her to talk. Just let her go and when you judge it's right, bring her back on track. Quietly. But to the point.'

'How did Simmie get hurt?'

Lizzie shakes her head and her eyes are fearful. Rose reaches out and holds Lizzie's hand. She waits. 'He'd been crying off and on all day. I was so desperate. I was screaming at him to stop and then I had a horrible thought. Perhaps he was hungry. You see, I couldn't remember whether I'd actually fed him at all that day. What if I was actually starving my baby? I ran with him to the fridge to get the formula – I'd lost my own milk quite early, another thing Royston complained about – and oh, I don't, I truly don't really remember exactly, but I opened the fridge door too quickly and too suddenly and the corner of it hit him on the arm and the top of his shoulder. Oh God, I'll never forget his scream. You know something?' Lizzie leans towards Rose and Rose bends towards Lizzie. Lizzie whispers, 'Rose, I don't know if I'm telling you the truth or not. I think I banged him accidentally with the fridge door, but maybe I'm just saying that?' Rose gathers Lizzie into her arms and holds her. 'There, there,' Rose says, 'there, there.' Over Lizzie's shoulder she sees Jo has her eyes shut and there are tears sliding down her face.

Lizzie says into Rose's shoulder, 'Simmie screamed and screamed. I knew I had to get him away from me. That I was dangerous. That I couldn't be trusted not to hurt my own baby, my own baby. So I found an empty tomato box of Dad's, packed Simmie in it just as he was, and got a plastic bag, pierced some holes in it and fastened it to the box. I think I remembered to pack some nappies and bottles and the stuff to make the formula, but I was in such a stew I can't be sure. Anyway I was all set to take him to Nana and then I remembered. Nana was dead. I'm really going crazy I thought, I helped to carry her coffin out. For a while I didn't know what to do. Then I re-membered you. Nana said once that you were reliable and you didn't make a song and dance about things, you just got on with them. I felt such relief you wouldn't believe it. So I found a piece of card and wrote "For Rose Anthony" on it, and then I – I just put him in the car and drove him to your place. I kept repeating to myself, Rose is reliable and she doesn't make a song and dance about things, that's what Nana said, so I thought a baby's crying wouldn't worry you. And when I've had a sleep I'll come and get him. I felt so calm. I knew, I just knew you'd look after him. It wasn't until later that I thought, well of course you'd look after him. You're his great-aunt. Of course you'd look after him.'

'And you were right,' Rose musters up as much approval as she can. 'Of course you were. But tell me Lizzie. How was it Royston didn't know until Saturday night?'

Lizzie sinks into the pillows. She looks down at her fingers as they pick at the sheet. 'He was working late on Friday. They had a few people off sick and when the supermarket was closed he had to help fill the shelves. When he asked about Simmie I said he'd been crying a lot and I didn't want him disturbed. Royston had to get up early next morning and he was tired so he accepted that. He was late again on Saturday but this time he insisted on seeing Simmie. And of course he wasn't there.'

'Why wouldn't you tell him where he was?'

'He hurt my feelings,' Lizzie says, 'so why shouldn't I hurt his? Actually I quite liked seeing him upset. I thought it served him right. And it did. He had no right to say the things he did. About his mother and that. I thought I'd let it hurt him for a while. See how he liked it. I left it too long. Once he started hitting me I thought he was going to kill me and I thought if I told him what I'd done he would. Then all of a sudden he stopped and he started crying. I just grabbed a blanket and the car keys and – I didn't know where else to go – so I came to you. I'm sorry Rose, I'm sorry.'

'No need,' Rose says, 'no need. You did exactly the right thing to come to me. Exactly.'

'Did I?' Lizzie bursts into tears.

'Yes,' Rose says over and over, 'you did the right thing. Exactly the right thing.'

'Do you think Simmie will ever forgive me?'

'Of course he will,' Rose says, although she has absolutely no idea.

Rose says later, 'How do we know whether Royston would have gone berserk if Lizzie hadn't refused to tell him where the baby was or whether he was a time bomb waiting for the right trigger and he would have blown up at some stage if she frightened or annoyed him enough.'

'Which comes first,' Alice says, 'which comes first. The old, old dilemma.'

TWENTY-FOUR

Monday evening. Outside, the wind is howling its last gasps. Little by little, light and warmth are returning. Every now and then the wind resists the change and works itself up into a fury slamming against house walls and swelling suddenly against cars on the motorway, but these outbursts are short-lived and everyone knows spring is really here this time. Heads are lifted higher, faces wear smiles, florists sell as many ranunculas and anemones as they can buy and there is a ripple of interest in the shops that sell labels like Jane Daniels, Trish Gregory, Ashley Fogel. In New York the firemen are still searching.

Every light is on in Olga's Café. There are balloons, streamers, and glasses of bubbly. There is a big banner which says "Happy Birthday Rose" strung right across the room and the tables underneath it have all been pulled together to make one long table. You couldn't get a bigger contrast from the afternoon.

The Hutt Hospital waiting area was long, narrow, but not dreary any more. The walls were freshly painted in a rich cream with a sea-green trim and there were new curtains in the same colour on the windows lining the outside wall. The floor length was divided into areas where people who had diabetes, cancer, or heart conditions sat and waited to be called. Since Rose was here three months ago the old chairs have been replaced with really comfortable new chairs in the same sea-green. It should be too much green but it's not. At the far end there was an area where boxes of brightly coloured toys waited for the next child to unpack. Rose had read somewhere that toys were the biggest carriers of infection to kids, but what were you supposed to do? Ban them? Along the wall, opposite the windows, there were pamphlets, brochures, posters, all to do with the particular disease represented in the area opposite them. In the cancer area, the posters featured lots of advice and suggestions on how to cope when you were told you have cancer. They tell you what the Cancer Society offers, they advertise workshops on a variety of topics. There was also a noticeboard on the wall with the names of the doctors on duty that afternoon.

At the reception area just inside the doors a couple of smiling women sat behind computers and when you presented your card they invited you to go to your particular area and sit down. Rose and Olga walked to the middle section and sat on two of the new chairs. She noticed that lots of the posters and brochures still feature smiling women. Rose had often thought she would prefer a brochure with a woman looking serious and a message saying the whole process is scary, unpleasant, scarring in every way, but it has to be done and that's that.

The doctor who'd given Rose the fine needle aspiration had said, 'Barring accidents, you'll recover physically within a year; emotionally it will take a whole lot longer.'

Olga nudged her. Rose saw two men, one handcuffed to the other. One of them wore the blue shirt, navy trousers of the prison service, the other wore jeans and T-shirt. He stared challengingly at the eyes which fastened on him from all parts of the room. A nurse came out from an internal corridor. She smiled at the men and they moved off into the heart condition area.

'Shit,' muttered Olga, 'be a bugger if he has a heart attack while he's handcuffed to the guard. For the guard I mean.'

Rose grinned. A nurse appeared from the cancer clinic section and held out her hand for their cards. 'Thank you Mrs Anthony,' she said.

'It's not Mrs.' Rose corrects this same nurse every time, but the nurse either can't or won't alter her greeting. If you're female you're Mrs, if you're male, you're Mr. None of this Ms stuff. Rose would prefer them to use her first name, and some do, but not this one.

'We need to talk,' Olga said softly. She'd arrived at The Book Stops Here a good half hour before the appointment although the hospital was only a few minutes' drive away. Carlos was early as well though so there wasn't much chance to say more than hello.

'They rolled up the big guns on me last night Rose.'

Rose couldn't imagine what she meant.

'Puti, Marama and Makere got on to me. About you.'

'What about me?' Rose's voice came out louder than she meant it to. She coughed, oh bugger they'll think I've got lung cancer, smiled casually at the other women and the lone man who were sitting in the cancer area.

'They said I'm not treating you right. They say I should ask you to come and live with me and stop this one-night-a-week business. They say it's not fair on you.'

Rose couldn't help it, she burst out laughing, then thought, for God's sake Rose, you're in the hospital waiting area. Nobody laughed out loud there.

'And,' Olga grinned, 'when I said I had and that you'd refused they said I couldn't have done it right. I said I had done it right. They said my trouble was I went at things like a bull at a gate. They say I have to try again. I told them to go home and have a lie-down and a cup of tea.' Olga enjoyed mimicking her sisters' emphasis.

Rose decided to ignore this. Not the time or the place. 'Did you find Knock-Knock?'

'Of course.'

'You are being really irritating,' Rose hissed.

'Oh really?'

'All right, all right. I want to know about Knock-Knock first.'

'We found him,' Olga said, 'we found him.'

'Where? How?'

'I've got connections,' Olga said out the side of her mouth. She looked just like the little girl Rose first knew at Wai-iti Primary. Rose felt her eyes widen.

'Yes, well,' Olga said, 'only something I do if I'm really de-termined, but I thought if anyone knew where Knock-Knock was Matiu would.'

'Matiu?'

'One of my not-so-salubrious rellies,' Olga said. 'He likes to keep in with me, never knows when he might need me to put in a good word with the whānau. Used to be called Matiu, but since he joined the Bros he calls himself Spike. He made a few enquiries and eventually we found Knock-Knock. Boy was he thrilled to see us, I don't think. We must have looked like the three Furies when he opened the door. And then he saw Matiu standing behind us. Decided he'd better talk.'

'So what happened?'

'Hope I'm right Rose, I said you wouldn't be pressing charges, but on one condition, that he do some work for Safe and Secure. Kind of periodic detention without going through the courts. We need painting and gardening done and he needs to work. Matiu says Knock-Knock started a horticultural course at polytech but never finished it. However, he did enough to know not to pull out the roses and he's never been a prospect as far as the Bros are concerned for which we can all be thankful. The thing is we've got this house to rent, want to buy it actually, but that's for the future, we've got a cheap rent providing we do it up. It won't be used for accommodating the women long term, but it's a good central place to take them while we get their particulars and find them a safe place to stay. It's in a quiet street, and it's an ex-state house actually so it's not too daunting and not too obvious. We think it'll be perfect.'

'But will Knock-Knock? Be perfect?'

'Oh yes. If he steps out of line he'll have to answer to me. If that doesn't work I'll call in Matiu. Knock-Knock, whose real name is Miki, hails from further up the coast so we know his family. I think he might now have some glimmerings about personal responsibility.'

It was Rose's turn. 'Oh really?' she said.

'I know,' Olga said, 'but I felt a bit to blame too. I should have pointed out the possibility, no, probability, that he'd do it back only worse.'

'I wasn't in the mood to listen.'

'Are you now?' Olga asked and wouldn't you know it, the nurse chose that moment to beckon them into the clinic.

Immediately everything that has happened in the last three days, the row with Olga, the baby, Lizzie, Royston, Ada's tape, Jo, even Sib and Louise, all vanish as they follow the nurse into the clinic. There is now only one thing on Rose's mind. She is weighed, has lost a little bit, oh hell, and then it's into the room where the surgeon will see her. She removes her jersey and her bra and gives them to Olga to hold. Rose sits on the bed and Olga in one of the old chairs. Obviously the refurbishing hasn't extended to these rooms yet. The patient's chairs are still the same badly upholstered dingy clay colour and the table and chair where the surgeon sits look as though there'd be trouble giving them away.

They wait. They talk, but it's the kind of talk that goes on just to fill a space, not going anywhere. They both give it up and wait in silence, listening to the hum of voices from the next room, one of which is the surgeon's. Someone was receiving good or bad news. 'We're having dinner at the café tonight,' Olga said suddenly as if the silence is too much to bear.

'Are we?'

'You didn't think I was going to let you get away without celebrating your birthday did you? I've found a new chef. She'll be cooking. Puti and Marama will help her. Makere's hopeless in the kitchen but she can throw a few balloons around and keep her eye on the kids. That OK?'

Is it OK? What does that mean? The party seems to have grown and Rose doesn't really care. Why not, she thinks, why not. What does it matter? The surgeon hurries in followed by two medical students. He smiles at her, introduces the two students, she introduces Olga, he picks up her file, nods as he reads. It's a folk dance where they all know their moves off pat. 'Right,' he says. He asks her how she is and she says she's fine. He asks if she has any worries and she says she hasn't. A lie, but he hasn't got all day. She holds up her arms and he steps back to survey her breasts. The two students stand behind him and watch. While she's still sitting he pokes and prods underneath her arms, around her shoulders and neck. Then she lies down on the bed while he palpates and kneads her breasts. Time holds its breath. Occasionally he goes back to a place and those probing fingers go over it again. These seconds are the worst in her life and they never get any better. The world turns another hundred years before he says, 'No lumps or bumps where there shouldn't be. Good.'

She can't speak. She hears her breath come out in a rush as she sits up. Olga hands her the bra and jersey, he pulls the curtains around her and she puts her clothes back on. When she's dressed and has pushed the curtains aside he smiles happily at her. 'Everything looks great,' he says, 'and we'll see you again in three months. If you have any worries in the meantime ring me.' He smiles, the students smile, Rose and Olga smile, and he goes, the bringer of good and bad news off to deliver one or other to someone else. The two students scurry after him.

It's OK. It's OK. It's OK, Rose thinks as she sits at the end of the long table in Olga's Café, I've got another three months' grace. She smiles at Sibyl and Kitty. Sibyl looks happy. She's delighted with the trunk. Claude has cleaned and painted it and it looks like new. Kitty picked up Sibyl after school and carried it out to stow in the boot. Sibyl has begun collecting bits and pieces and, surprisingly, is really enjoying it. She had thought it might be a bit gruelling and perhaps it might be, who knows, but for the moment, she's rediscovered lots of things, especially songs she used to sing. 'So much of my younger life was tied up with dancing,' she says, 'I still know all the words too. Amazing.' She's brought her camera tonight because she wants a photograph of Rose's party to put in the trunk along with the other older mementos. Sibyl starts chemo on Wednesday, but tonight she's laughing, lively, joking with Olga and Puti, directing Makere with the balloons. Kitty watches her smiling. Poor Kitty.

On a small table beside Rose is the carrycot with Simmie asleep in it. Which is very considerate of him, Rose thinks. She's had more time away from him than she likes. Nearly all yesterday and practically all day today apart from lunchtime. He's very forgiving though and Bridget has been positively enthusiastic. 'He's so cute,' she says, then she sees Rose's expression and says, 'Yes all right Rose, I'd have looked after him anyway.'

It's amazing really how Bridget's settled into their lives. Who would have thought a relation of Peter's would fit in so well after the way his daughters behaved. 'You can choose your friends but not your relations,' Ada always said.

Elena and Claude are on their way. Marama and Puti are, as Olga said they would be, in the kitchen assisting the new chef.

Rose sees Olga teasing Makere about some of the balloons which are already hanging limply. 'We need a pump,' Makere says, 'we need more air.'

'You need some more hot air,' Olga says, 'ask those two in the kitchen. They got more than they need.'

'If you don't shut up I'll do just that,' Makere threatens.

Jo and Wesley have promised to come after they've visited Lizzie. Lizzie has to make some decisions. For the time being Royston will be at his parent's house, but that solution might not be the one Lizzie chooses. Neither she nor Jo sound quite sure they want to live together in the same house, even temporarily. They are like two soldiers from opposing armies who've declared a truce but who know war could break out at any time. The main thing is to do what's best for Simmie. Rose sees that Lizzie is genuinely fearful of what that other Lizzie might do. She might go out of control again. She is severely shaken by her own fallibility, panic-stricken and ashamed, partly because everyone will know, but mainly because she did what she did. She can't rely on herself and it's a shock. How will she face anyone when she can't even look at herself in the mirror? As for Royston, she knows they must meet, they must talk. Somehow they must meet and talk if for no other reason than that they are Simmie's parents. 'If it's any consolation,' Rose told her, 'he'll be feeling exactly the same. And you heard Alice say that any woman who's ever had a smidgeon of post-natal depression and anyone who's ever looked after small babies knows exactly what you were going through. They won't pass judgement, believe me.' Lizzie remains unconvinced. She will come out of hospital tomorrow and so far has not decided where she will go from there other than saying categorically she will not go back to the house where she and Royston lived.

'Don't end the tenancy,' Alice advised Malcolm who's all set to do just that, 'it's not the right time to be making those sort of moves. Believe me they'll both feel differently in six months. If their rent can be kept up I'd keep the place on at least for two months.' Wesley and Mr Hipp say of course, if that's what Alice thinks, they will contribute towards the rent in the meantime. Both Wesley and Ellie Hipp are clinging to Alice as though she's a lifeline, a guide along this uncharted path they both walk. In any case, until Lizzie and Royston decide what has to happen regarding the future they must all wait. 'That might take months,' Alice warned everyone. Later she says to Rose, 'What about Simmie?'

'He stays with me,' Rose says, 'he stays with me. That's what Lizzie wants.'

'Good,' Alice says, 'as long as "in the meantime" is OK with you. And Olga.'

'It has to be,' Rose says, 'it's all right Alice, I know it has to be. And,' Rose sighs, 'there'll be others no doubt. No sense wasting all this learning is there.'

'Oh,' Alice says, 'good. Good.'

'Just remember how lucky Lizzie and Royston are,' Alice says later.

'Lucky?'

'Plenty of people in their situation have no one. No one who wants to be involved anyway. Lizzie and Royston are two of the lucky ones.'

'OK?' asks Olga, sitting down beside her. She looks wonderful in a new purple shirt and white trousers. 'I'll probably spill something on this first time out,' she'd said, 'but I couldn't resist it.' Rose is wearing a top and trousers Elena loaned her. She's really grateful for the black pants and the bright peacock-blue shirt, but has made a vow that tomorrow she will definitely buy herself some new clothes. Other people's clothes are chosen for other people.

Olga gets up to hug Alice and her husband. Behind them there's an influx of people. Olga's sisters' husbands and children, followed by Carlos and Leo. They all just get seated when in walk Claude and Elena. Puti brings out the special chair she's borrowed for the evening, and Elena sits and is comfortable and everyone relaxes. All have observed Rose's command that there be no presents. 'Enough is enough,' she tells Olga.

There is a little hiatus as wine and water are poured by Puti and Marama, and the older children move from person to person with trays of delicious nibbles. The poor new chef, thinks Rose, this must be a bit of an ordeal.

'Everyone,' Olga calls, 'Puti, Marama, time to get this show on the road.'

'Need a hand?' Leo asks his mother.

There is a flurry at the door. It's Jo and Wesley. Jo is waving an envelope. 'Rose,' she says, 'Rose it's from the Stacy Committee.'

Rose starts to tremble. 'I can't open it,' she says to Olga.

'You?' Olga scoffs, 'you can do anything Rose.'

So Rose opens it. *The Skeleton Woman* has been awarded first in the novice class and second in Viewer's Choice. The judge's report is enclosed, but the decision was unanimous. Congratulations Miss Anthony.

There are shouts and hugs, cries of triumph and laughter and then someone says, 'What's your next project Rose?'

Rose smiles because she knows exactly what it is. 'A shield,' she says, 'a *Shield for the Children*. It will hang just opposite the door of the new house.'

'It will be the first thing the women and children see,' Olga says, '*He Hīra mō ngā Tamariki*.'

'*He Hīra mō ngā Tamariki*, cool,' one of the kids says and everyone raises their glass to toast the *Shield for the Children*.

Olga smiles at Rose enquiringly.

'Yes,' Rose smiles back, 'yes. Go for it.'

So Olga stands up and Rose stands up and everyone smiles and Olga says, 'Rose and I are going to live together.'

Rose says, 'We're going to buy Claude's place and he and Elena are going to buy the little house next door.'

'And everything,' Olga says with a big smile, 'is blissful.'

More toasts, more smiles, Claude says its great and hugs Elena who is weeping with joy. Puti, on behalf of her parents and her whānau says kei te pai, kei te pai – well, she says a lot more than that, but that's the gist of it. Sibyl and Kitty nod approvingly, Bridget smiles, Leo lifts his glass to Rose, Carlos raises an arm in a victor's salute, the children hand round more nibbles, Alice and her husband hold hands, even Jo and Wesley smile. For some reason Rose thinks of a small, stocky man who liked to stand in the rain in the dark green of the Catlins and of Ada smiling and she knows that somewhere out there beyond the wind and the stars the Skeleton Woman is dancing, tappitty tap, tappitty tap.

One day that girl will hear her, but in the meantime Rose has got some living to do.

Between Rose and Olga, Simmie, in his carrycot, immune to the excitement, dreams the dreams that all babies who are safe dream.

'I didn't want it,' the woman says, 'who would? Who'd want a love that separated me from one of my children? It was a cross of stars. Brilliant, once-in-a-lifetime, grab it and don't let go sort of thing, but at the same time a cross. I'm not religious, but that's how I felt about it. My love for him was a cross. A cross of stars.

From Peter Paul Pearl's unfinished novel, *The Cross of Stars*.